Death in the

A San Amaro Mystery

Marnie J Ross

Death in the Baja

A San Amaro Mystery

Marnie J Ross

MEERSCHAUM PRESS

Editor: Leighton Wingate
Cover: Bart Hopkins

This book is a work of fiction. Characters, names, businesses, places, and events are either the product of the author's imagination or are used fictitiously and any resemblance to actual persons, living or dead, businesses, companies, events, or locales is entirely coincidence.

ISBN 979-8-9860071-1-3 paperback

For Sharon, who made this possible

Contents

PART 1—Missing!

PART 2—What came before . . .

PART 3—Conclusion

Lead-Up to the Hike . . .

After the hike . . .

PART 1—Missing!

"She had the right idea, old man, don't you think—to disappear before it gets too late?"

Patrick Modiano, *Rue des Boutiques Obscures*

Chapter 1—March 8, 2018, San Amaro, Mexico

The sunrise over the Sea of Cortez washed the near-white desert sand a fire red. Through the bedroom window, Stella saw a shimmering line of pure silver where the sky met the sea. Above that line, a vivid orange and red sky announced dawn in the Baja. *A perfect start to the adventure ahead,* she thought. In the desert, both sunrises and sunsets are typically very colorful. Her excitement for the day ahead was tempered by a slight anxiety. That was not uncommon when taking an off-road trip through the wilds of the Baja desert.

But today felt different.

She had just finished tying the laces of her aging leather hiking boots when Simon called from the front door. The Jeep was ready with gas, water cans, and the myriad safety items wise desert adventurers pack. He also informed her Molly and Jaime were just driving up. She was glad for her well-broken-in boots, as she hoped they would protect and comfort the two black-and-blue toes of her left foot for the hike. Today, the group was going to see the petroglyphs and wall paintings in Cañon Del Demonio. At age seventy-four, today was her and Simon's first wedding anniversary, and they, with four friends, had been planning this hike for a couple of weeks as the start of the day's celebration.

She had layered her wiry five-foot-four frame in a zipper-fronted hoody; light, long-sleeved, white-and-red-striped shirt over a tank top; sports bra; and shorts. She knew even though it was a cool sixty degrees now, it would be in the low eighties by the time they got to the area from which their hike would begin. She'd lived in the Baja desert and sea town of San Amaro for nine years, which, because of its proximity to the US border, was a very popular vacation spot and retirement location for Americans wanting the Mexican experience with nearness to United States. She was well acquainted with the vagaries of the desert and this hike in particular. It was one she had done almost every one of those nine years.

Having taught science to young teens during most of her career, she had developed a love of natural science and anthropology. The petroglyphs, ancient rock and cave drawings of deer, antelope, and people still fascinated her. It set her imagination free to picture the Cochimi tribe a thousand years ago documenting their lives on the rocks and caves of the region. The arroyo in the canyon where the drawings were found had a very rugged desert kind of beauty that she had grown to first appreciate and later love the longer she lived in Mexico.

She'd moved to San Amaro when she retired at sixty-five from teaching in Helena, Montana. Although she'd been an avid hiker all her life and loved the east side of the Rockies, she'd had more than enough of snow and cold to last five lifetimes.

When she was sixty-two, years after she recovered from the pain of her husband's death from lung cancer when he was only fifty-six, Stella decided to change her life and move to Mexico.

She'd found San Amaro, a tiny town on the Baja California Peninsula that is nestled between the Sea of Cortez and the Sierra de San Pedro Mártir mountains, after a month of research. She thought it sounded idyllic. She'd gone for a visit on summer break before her last year of teaching. Summer was hotter than she'd expected, but she fell in love with the quaintness, the beach, the nearby mountains, and most of all, the people. San Amaro was nothing like Puerto Vallarta, where she had spent Christmas the year after her husband died, and that suited her fine. PV was just too big for her liking. In San Amaro, she'd felt an immediate sense of connection with the locals and met a few other gringos living in the area whom she liked greatly. Best of all for Stella, her best friend Molly, who had come along to make sure it was safe, also fell in love with the town and its people. They began making retirement plans at once to move together to this charming, beautiful, and out-of-the-way little town.

A double toot of the Jeep's horn brought her out of her reverie and told her that her good friend Rick and his new boyfriend, Rob, must have also arrived. This new man in Rick's life had previously been both a paramedic in the United States and an army combat medic in Afghanistan. Now that the Boys, as she called them, were here, they would be ready to head out.

Rob and Rick helped Simon carry the last of their supplies, packs, and walking sticks to Stella's Jeep. Stella looked out the window and saw Rob was admiring her homemade walking stick before he put it into the vehicle. She smiled. She'd made it herself from a fallen branch of an ash tree she had in her backyard in Montana. She'd had it for years, and it had assisted her on hikes there as well as here.

Stella whistled the three-note trill she used to signal Juba, her three-year-old border collie, that they were leaving. Juba dutifully trotted up with her halter and leash in her mouth, excited to be included in the day's activities. Simon, a relative newbie to Mexico and desert living, had taken his cue from Stella about how to dress and what to take, and that it was essential to include multiple vehicles in the plan to ensure safety. They hadn't discussed taking Juba, however, and he was surprised when he saw the dog sporting her neon-orange harness.

"You're taking the dog?" he asked, in a rather flat, but nonjudgmental, voice.

"Yes, she loves this hike, and she needs the exercise," Stella said, smiling at her handsome "younger" man. Well, ten years didn't matter much at their age, but they liked to kid about the age difference. Simon handed Stella her water bottle and smacked her on the bum teasingly as she and Juba walked past him and out the door to the waiting desert vehicles.

"Hang on a minute," Simon called to the group as he ran back toward the house. "I forgot sunscreen. I'll just be a sec."

"Okay!" Stella said when he climbed behind the wheel. "Let's get going. I can't wait for you to see the beauty of the desert with everything in bloom."

Chapter 2—March 8, 2018, San Amaro

Julia Garcia always tried to finish her morning run before it got too hot, and at this time of year, that meant starting out before six o'clock. Today, she'd cut short her favorite run. After heading down to the Malecon and running along the beachfront, she turned up Calle Guadalajara, the main road heading north to Highway 5, which eventually leads to the United States of America. Then, instead of going the extra kilometer out of town toward the gringo communities that lined the seaside north of San Amaro, she turned around and retraced her route home. She needed to be at work early today.

In an hour's time with the sun fully risen, the sky and the Sea of Cortez would be matching azure and the sand, almost white. At this hour, however, everything was bathed in red as the sun rose out of the sea. With sidewalks existing on only a handful of streets in San Amaro, Julia's morning runs were often obstacle courses of uneven terrain, littered not just with the detritus of Mexican daily life, but packs of three or four dogs running free and looking for food of any sort. They were rarely aggressive toward people, and Julia knew most of them by sight and had named them all. Today, she saw Gimpy, a brindle pit-bull mix with a bum back leg and Silly, likely Gimpy's sister. They looked very similar, though Silly's tongue seemed too long for her mouth. They were joined by a new recruit, likely a Lab mix, with short legs and an orange, shaggy coat, which she immediately dubbed Rudy. She kept a watchful eye on them during her runs. Feral dogs were just part of the landscape here. She was alert to any changes in their health or if a new litter of pups had been born. She was an active member of the San Amaro dog-rescue organization and did her part to help puppies get adopted and feral dogs get neutered or spayed and, if possible, find permanent homes.

There was a special all-hands meeting scheduled at the start of the morning shift today. She cut her usual seven-kilometer run down to five kilometers so she could get home, shower, and dress. That would put her at the station thirty minutes early. Being one of only three women in the San Amaro State Police Force, and the only one having reached sergeant's rank, she was always aware she had to be two steps ahead of the department's male officers just to be noticed by the brass. She had every intention of following in her grandfather's footsteps and becoming the station comandante one day. She was under no illusions that it would be an easy journey. She was also sure she was up to the task.

Her grandfather, her *papito*, Juan, was still frequently consulted on police matters by the current comandante. However, he had no insider information to share with her about today's early-morning meeting. Julia ran and let her mind wander, playing with potential topics. She'd finally decided it must be related to the upcoming *Semana Santa* festivities, the Holy Week, between Palm Sunday and Easter Sunday that was starting in ten days. In past years, upward of thirty-five thousand people descended on San Amaro for the week, an almost 200 percent increase from the normal population. Many of the visitors, almost all Mexicans, camped on the beach along the Malecon. The crowding and proximity to the Malecon's bars always provided a potentially volatile combination.

Julia arrived at the station at seven thirty, freshly showered with her still-damp ebony hair pulled into a tight bun at her nape and her statuesque five-foot-nine body clad in a clean and pressed uniform. She dropped her purse into the drawer behind her active files. The only thing differentiating her desk from all the others in the open-floor-plan office was the fact that her desk surface was neat and tidy, occupied only by her computer keyboard and monitor, a phone, and her in-box. The latter contained an internal office memo reminding her of the eight o'clock meeting but giving no indication of the meeting's purpose. *Typical,* she thought with a shake of her head.

Over the next fifteen minutes, she logged in and checked her email, which included an update on the robbery case she had been assigned the previous afternoon, and her work assignment for the day. She had desk-sergeant responsibilities starting at eleven o'clock for the remainder of her shift, leaving her only a couple of hours after the meeting to do what she considered her real work—investigating crime. *Oh well,* she thought. Being desk sergeant was an important rung on the ladder and brought her into contact with most of the incoming cases of the day.

The San Amaro State Police Station is located on the main north-south drag, Calle Guadalajara, about halfway between the Malecon and the north edge of town. It is a tan-colored, rectangular, two-story, concrete-covered cinder-block structure set back from the street. The fifteen-year-old building's color blended into the desert sand surrounding the fenced perimeter of the station's grounds. In many places, the building's stucco had been damaged by rain, heat, and neglect. Gray cinder blocks peeked out from beneath broken concrete coating, and blotches of still-unpainted stucco showed some of the more recent repairs.

The simple station housed the nineteen officers of the San Amaro detachment of the North Baja California State Police, a two-cell jail, and a small, inadequately equipped forensics lab. Inside, the shabbiness of the building's exterior continued with water-stained ceilings and grubby walls that at one time had been off-white. The main floor housed a reception area with a freestanding, brown-painted plywood reception desk, which was manned by the desk sergeant, the open area for officers' desks, two interview rooms, a meeting room that doubled as the coffee station, a lunchroom, and the jail area. Upstairs were the senior officers' rooms, another meeting room for the brass, the forensics lab, and a large record-storage area stuffed with aging and rusty gray, tan, and black four-drawer filing cabinets, which sat along one wall. Sagging plywood shelves containing moldering evidence boxes filled the remainder of the space.

Joining only three other officers in the room, Julia took a chair in the second row of the lunchroom/meeting room at ten to eight. No one ever sat in the front row at these meetings. A couple of minutes later, her friend, Sergeant Ricardo Hernandez, took the chair directly in front of her, his ubiquitous coffee in hand, and his height and broad shoulders completely blocking her view of the dais. A second later he swung around and gave her a wink, tossing a quick "¿*Qué pasa*, Lucy?" over his shoulder at Julia. What's up? Then he moved to the chair beside her. She smiled brightly at him, punching him none too lightly on the shoulder. "No mucho, Ricky! *¿Y tú ?*" she quipped back. Not much, and you?

Ricardo, while also a sergeant, was one level higher than she, a fact he liked to rub in whenever possible, as they had been in basic training together. They had developed a friendship while in training that had continued for the past seven years. Ricardo had tried to move it toward something more, but Julia had firmly maintained the friendship boundary. Julia was not concerned he had risen rank faster than she had. He was a man in this very man's-world profession in Mexico. She was proud of her rank and felt confident that she, too, would get level two in the next year if she could find an opportunity to shine for the brass.

Because of their fast friendship and jovial, though constant, competitive bickering, and the similarity in looks of Ricardo to Desi Arnaz, their fellow cadets had taken to calling them Lucy and Ricky after the *I Love Lucy* show. It was popular in reruns Saturday mornings when they were kids. The two still used the nicknames in their banter with each other.

The meeting started about ten minutes late, and the room was full of uniformed and plain clothed officers, on and off duty. As she'd guessed, the focus was indeed Semana Santa crowd control and safety. Four members of the Federalis, the other police presence in Mexico, were also in attendance and spoke to the joint planning between the two police forces working in San Amaro to ensure a safe week for the locals and visitors alike.

The plan was similar to last year's, in that there would be eight officers per shift, four state police, like Julia, and four federal police. They would patrol the

Malecon and do car checks at the traffic circle on the way into town. The car checks served the double purpose of allowing the police to give visitors a photocopied map showing locations for camping, eating, first aid stations, and restrooms, plus give the cops the chance to see if there were any known criminals coming into town. The Semana Santa plan meant no unscheduled time off and no sick leave for the week unless a person were dying. What was different this year was that the female officers would not be patrolling, but rather responsible for answering the phones, staffing the front desk, and participating in the car checks.

Last year, Constable Ana Maria Verde had been accosted on the overcrowded Malecon by a group of six drunken teenage boys who thought female cops were a big joke. They had tried, unsuccessfully, to get her gun from its holster. Her arm was broken in the scuffle, though two of the boys were handcuffed to a railing by the time the nearest federali officer showed up to help. Julia, Ana Maria, and Lucia, the three female officers in San Amaro, speculated that perhaps he took more time to arrive than necessary just to see if she could handle herself.

Sexism was officially against the police code of conduct, but still very much being practiced by nearly all the male officers in San Amaro. The three serving women knew the score going into training, but it didn’t make it any easier to live with. The comandante, though one of the good guys, still did very little to help the women out.

Julia believed this action of not having them on the front line was likely aimed at improving safety for everyone. If the all-male team of federal officers were going to test their female colleagues in volatile situations such as the one last year, bad things could escalate quickly, putting many people in possible jeopardy. Still, being sidelined like this was not the kind of help she or the other women wanted, and while she understood why the bosses had made that decision, she left the meeting frustrated and disappointed.

Chapter 3—March 8, 2018, Desert Southwest of San Amaro

Simon switched to low four-wheel drive as the track to the base of Cañon Del Demonio deteriorated from the more hard-packed desert sand they had been driving over for the last couple of hours into soft sand. The two-and-a-half-hour trip to the parking lot, a euphemism for the large shrub-covered sandy area where hikers left their vehicles, was dusty, bumpy, and beautiful as only a desert can be. Stella and Simon were bringing up the rear of the three vehicles.

Keeping safety in mind, Stella and her friends always went in a group of three or more vehicles when out in the desert off-roading, as they were today. The occupants of each vehicle had a responsibility for themselves and those in the other vehicles traveling together. There is no cell phone coverage back in the mountains where they were, and the desert is a vicious environment, not one to be taken lightly. Both Stella's Jeep and Rick's rig had radio systems allowing vehicle-to-vehicle communication. Jaime's Jeep did not, so Rick had lent them a walkie-talkie set to the same frequency as the in-rig systems the others used.

Rick and Rob, in Rick's RZR, an open desert vehicle that looked like a roll cage with wheels and spoken as the word *razor* (though spelled R-Z-R), took the lead and determined the best route to their destination. When off-road in the desert, any given track could be obscured by blowing sand within hours or days, so each trip required awareness of the destination relative to one's present location and careful observation of the shifting conditions. Rick's rig, in the lead, had a high-end GPS system onboard helping guide them. The occupants of the lead vehicle also needed to be sure to not lose sight of the vehicle directly behind them, Jaime and Molly's Jeep. They then had the responsibility to keep eyes on their rearview mirror, looking out for Stella and Simon's Jeep, all while not losing sight of the lead vehicle. The desert can be a dangerous environment for those not taking precautions. Each year people lose their lives by underestimating the beautiful but harsh Mexican deserts.

In addition to the safety preparation of the vehicles with extra gas, oil, antifreeze, transmission fluid, tow ropes, extra jacks, blocks of wood, first aid kits, tarps, and more, people making a desert run need to have their own safety in mind. They each had a bandanna, hat, sunglasses, sunscreen, lip balm, food, gloves, extra socks, small pack, Band-Aids, and a flashlight at a minimum. This group of travelers was prepared.

Twenty minutes later, all six of them disembarked their vehicles. Two northern-mockingbirds were trying to outsing each other in a creosote bush off to the left. A desert hare, the black-tailed jackrabbit, its outrageously long ears twitching at the hikers' arrival, loped casually away as Juba jumped from Stella's jeep. Even at top speed, the collie would have no chance of outrunning one of these large rabbits.

The six friends had organized their personal packs before leaving the vehicles. Rob, taking his role as medic seriously, made sure everyone's gear included a walking stick or two and all the safety requirements. His own pack contained a first aid kit, snake bite antivenom, and what appeared to be several bottles of a beverage in previously used plastic water bottles. He said he'd made electrolyte drinks for everyone to enjoy on the trip back. Rick noticed each bottle had a name on it in black felt pen and asked why they were specially labeled. Rob surprised everyone by explaining that a medical study done five or six years before determined that the proper electrolyte balance was different between men and women and that weight and age also affected the proper balance. Taking those factors into consideration, he had made different blends of coconut water, honey, orange juice, sea salt, and his own secret ingredients for each of them.

"I'll carry them to the rock paintings. No need for everyone to be weighed down," he said. Looking at his younger, superbly fit body, no one argued with him.

Finally organized, they headed up the trail toward the canyon's depths where the petroglyphs and drawings were located. The near-white sand was liberally strewn with a wide variety of scrubby bushes, small mesquite trees, and ocotillos. The latter, looked most often like ten-to-fifteen-foot-long dead, spiny sticks thrust into the sand in clumps by a juvenile giant. Because of the rain dumped by a recent hurricane, they were looking spectacular today with their covering of green, spiky leaves and crowns of orange-red, plumelike flower sprigs that resembled small pennants.

The canyon was wide at its mouth, with the mountain walls of the arroyo over a hundred feet apart. Its sandy floor was dotted here and there with subcompact-car-sized boulders, a wide variety of flowers, barrel cacti, and creosote bushes. The canyon began to narrow almost at once to the point that the main path through the rocks and flora became a trail capable of allowing only two people to walk abreast. The low mountains gave way to higher, more craggy ones. As the sun hit their deeply wrinkled faces at sharp angles, it created a play of light and shadows that Molly thought gave the hike a spooky feeling. She was sure it accounted for the name, Demon Canyon.

Stella was pleased that she was able to keep up with the others as they trekked, although her blackened toes were causing her some discomfort. How clumsy she had been dropping the frozen pot roast right on her bare toes last week. Nothing to be done with them other than taping them and waiting for them to heal. Her walking stick helped, and Juba trotted along at her heels offering moral support. By the time they got to the boulders lining the sides of the arroyo leading deeper into the canyon, however, her toes were screaming protest. She found herself putting more and more pressure on the wrist strap of her hiking stick. It finally tore away from the stick.

"Hey, guys, hold up a minute," Stella called ahead to her companions as she stuffed the ripped leather strap into her pocket. "I don't think I can make it much farther. My toes are giving me grief. Take some pictures for me. I want to see Simon's happy face below the cave drawings of the deer. I'll meet you back at the parking lot."

Simon, who had been walking with her, said, "I noticed you've been limping the last ten minutes or so. I'm going to stay with you. We can walk back together."

"No," she commanded adamantly. "I have Juba with me. She'll keep me company. I want you to get the chance to see the area when it's in bloom. I will be fine. I have lots of water, and there's more back at the Jeep. I know what I'm doing out here. Don't argue with me! I'll see you in a couple of hours," Stella said stubbornly. They all tried to argue, but they knew when Stella made her mind up about something, nothing would change it. Eventually, they acquiesced.

Before the rest of the group left their friend, Rob stepped up with a bottle of his electrolytes and one of his hiking sticks. "Here, you might want to drink this back at the vehicles. It will help you rebalance after the hike back. And I don't need two hiking sticks. I've shortened this one a bit for you. If it isn't a comfortable height, just twist here to make it higher or lower," he explained, showing her the process.

Molly started digging through her pack and came up with a baggie-wrapped sandwich. "Here," she said, handing it to Stella. "Take this, too. I made tuna salad with lots of sweet pickles. Your favorite!"

Simon took the bottle of electrolytes and the sandwich while Rob explained the workings of his hiking stick and placed the electrolytes in the bottle pocket on the side of her pack and the sandwich inside before settling it back on Stella's shoulders. She patted Simon's whiskery cheek, then turned and walked back down the path, calling behind her, "Have fun!"

With a bit more grumbling from Simon and Rick that she be careful and take it easy heading back to the vehicles, the group of five finally turned back up the arroyo and headed on toward the ancient drawings. Stella whistled to Juba and, using Rob's hiking pole and her own, now strapless walking stick for extra support, began slowly to head back to the parking lot.

Chapter 4—March 8, 2018, San Amaro

Back at her desk after the meeting, Julia carefully reread the file on the robbery she had been assigned. Being acutely aware her dyslexia could cause misinterpretation of written missives, she always read everything at least twice. With this precaution, it was rarely a handicap to her. She noted that the missing, reportedly stolen desert buggy had been last seen parked at Polly's Place. Polly's Place was a favorite watering hole of those Canadians and Americans who had retired to Mexico primarily because liquor was cheap. Fortunately, in her mind, that wasn't the draw for most gringos living in or near San Amaro. She dialed the bar's number.

She tended to get cases involving English speakers because of her fluency in English. Luis Flores, a handsome young corporal recently imported from Mexicali, had been assigned to assist her on this case. The previous evening they had pushed their desks together to facilitate more easily working together. Julia was just hanging up the phone as Luis returned from the meeting, having stayed to have a chat with Corporal Javier Bustamante, another ex-Mexicali officer who had joined the San Amaro State Police only a few months after Luis. They were friends.

"Luis, the bartender on duty the night that Polaris RZR went missing is just opening up Polly's. Let's go get that witness statement taken before the place gets too busy. Sign out a cruiser, and I'll meet you in the parking lot," Julia said before he could sit down at the desk. As a sergeant, she was his superior officer and, therefore, it was protocol that he would organize a vehicle and drive unless she expressly said otherwise.

There had been a handful of female officers in his station in Mexicali, but none of them with the rank of sergeant. While it rankled Luis to be getting orders from a woman, he'd heard that she was the old boss's granddaughter and that open hostility toward her wouldn't be tolerated by the station higher-ups.

"Okay, see you outside," he said without looking at her or without adding that he'd take his own sweet time signing out the car.

Julia noticed his eyes harden ever so slightly at her command and added in a firm but friendly tone, "I have desk-sergeant duty at eleven o'clock. If you can't get a car organized in the next five minutes, I'll have to head out without you in my own car," she said smiling, without a hint of rancor in her voice.

Her undergraduate degree in psychology that she earned in Mexicali had provided her with many insights that helped her when dealing with her male colleagues' macho approach to female officers and life in general. Head-on confrontation, she'd learned, was the worst possible option. She always tried to be clear, firm, and friendly when giving commands to junior officers, and mostly it worked fine. She hoped that Luis would respond to her as a senior officer and not as a woman. Otherwise, she would have to resort to firmer tactics.

After waiting in the parking lot for nearly five minutes, she was pleased to see him exit the station jangling a set of car keys and sauntering toward one of the late-model, white-and-blue Dodge Charger cruisers against the chain-link back fence of the station. "You driving or am I?" he asked civilly.

Good, she thought. "You do the honors," she said simply, sliding into the passenger seat.

Polly's Place featured lime-green walls and a palapa roof over the bar area. Outside tables also sported palapa-like umbrellas giving the entrance a Margaritaville feel. Once past the bar, the dining room was ringed with alternating sections of smoked mirror squares and fake wood panels. On the long back wall was a raised bare plywood stage fronted by a dance floor of black and white linoleum squares. The place looked quite sad at nine in the morning. The walls were chipped, gouged, and dirty. Julia knew that tonight and every night this place would be hopping, and the energy of the patrons and the band would transform it into a fun dine-and-dance retiree hot spot.

The bartender looked up as they walked in. He asked in a hesitant American southern drawl, looking back and forth between Luis and Julia, "How can I help San Amaro's finest today?" He showed only the slightest raise of an eyebrow when Julia took the lead explaining why they were there and establishing that he was the man they wished to talk with, one Billy Williamson.

"This is about a Polaris RZR reportedly stolen from in front of this establishment two nights ago," she explained in very good, only slightly accented English. After showing Billy a photo of the owner who was claiming it stolen, he looked amused. “Yes, ma’am, I was working the bar that night, and Ted was surely here in his RZR. But I don’t think it was stolen, ma’am. Ted is one of our regulars, so I know him and his desert buggy. He left at ‘San Amaro midnight,’ pretty much the same as he does every night, and I’m sure he left in his rig,” Billy explained.

Julia was familiar with the gringo reference to *midnight* as meaning nine o’clock at night. Many of the retired expats living in the area called it a night at ‘San Amaro midnight.’ “Was there anything unusual about Mr. Blair’s, Ted’s, evening? Did he sit with his usual crowd, or was there someone new that you noticed with him?” Julia asked while Luis made notes. Knowing his English was nowhere near fluent, she provided words and phrases in Spanish to Luis to include in his notes. These she said in a conversational tone without looking at him. Rather than feeling offended, Luis was appreciative of this assistance.

“Well, the whole place was full of different folks, ma’am. It being the evening after the Baja Two Fifty, like.” The Baja Two Fifty is an annual 250-mile off-road desert vehicle race that starts and ends near San Amaro. It has run for over thirty years and draws thousands of people to San Amaro each year. “We had several of the race teams here celebrating that night. Ted was chatting with anyone sitting at the bar, and a few of the racers were up here, closer to the tequila.” His slow manner of speaking was amusing to the rapid-fire Spanish speakers, but Luis was glad for his slow cadence as it allowed him to better keep up with at least parts of the conversation. Not being fluent in English, he had a harder time tracking the words and, therefore, spent more of his time reading body language. He believed the bartender, a man about his own age, was telling the truth.

As he took notes on all he understood of the interview and Julia's Spanish interjections, he watched her. While appearing open and friendly and keeping a neutral tone of voice, she astutely led Billy through the events of the evening, getting a full accounting of Ted's time at the pub. "And when you saw Mr. Blair's RZR leaving, you're sure he was driving?" she asked, appearing to begin winding up the interview.

"Yes, ma'am," Billy replied slowly, dropping his gaze. Julia had been waiting for a sign like this, now knowing there was more to the story than this gringo was telling her. She thought for a moment.

"Have you ever driven Ted's RZR, Billy?" Julia asked abruptly, startling both Luis and Billy with the unexpected question.

"Ah, well, ah, you see," Billy said hesitantly, looking at the bar for a few moments, struggling with how to respond. Finally, appearing to decide, he lifted his head and continued. "Sometimes Ted needs a hand getting home, like, if he has a few drinks too many. He just lives in Campo Cristal, here." Billy referred to the community on the beach less than a kilometer behind Polly's Place. "I take my evening break at nine o'clock, and I've driven him home before. Then I just walk back here to the pub."

"And the night Mr. Blair's RZR went missing, did you drive him home, Billy?" Julia asked, keeping her tone nonjudgmental and her eyes glued to his face.

"He was having trouble walking straight, ma'am. He could have hurt himself or someone else, even in a RZR," Billy mumbled.

"So, then he wasn't driving, was he, Billy? Why did you say he was?" Julia asked probing further.

"I didn't steal his buggy, ma'am. I didn't! I just drove him home. I left the buggy in his driveway and made sure he got in the door of his house. Then I walked back here. That RZR was in his driveway last time I saw it. I swear," Billy said in a rush. Luis thought it might have been the fastest he'd ever spoken. He was familiar with the language of denial; police heard it all the time. Still, he didn't get the impression this witness was lying to them.

Julia led Billy through the events of this new story twice more, verifying that there was no one lurking around Ted's house and that he hadn't seen anyone while walking back to the pub. They left the pub about ten minutes later. "Let's see what Mr. Ted Blair has to say about this, shall we?" Julia said to Luis when they climbed into the cruiser. "It's just after ten o'clock. He might even be out of bed by now," she said with a laugh.

Over the noise of a barking dog inside, Luis banged on the door again. "Police, Señor Blair, open up," he said in his best English, which was very accented and guttural. Finally, a pair of watery, red eyes and a spray of fuzzy white hair appeared at the window nearest the door. The dog quieted. "What the hell are you doing here at this ungodly hour?" asked a troll-like man as he opened the door.

Julia and Luis held up their identification while Julia explained they were there regarding his stolen-property case and needed to ask him some questions. The door opened wide abruptly and Ted Blair, wearing a sweat-stained, smelly tank top, boxers, and bare feet, called over his shoulder as he waddled down the hall adding to his troll-like image. "Better come in, then. That's Jake. He's friendly," he said, referring to a large golden retriever beside the door.

Sitting on stools in a simple kitchen littered with empty beer cans and pizza boxes and smelling of dirty dishes, dirty dog, and body odor, Julia got down to business. "Mr. Blair, the bartender at Polly's Place tells us he drove you and your RZR home from the pub Sunday night, the night you claim your RZR was stolen. Is that true?" she asked. Jake sauntered into the kitchen and sat beside Julia's stool. She idly stroked his fluffy yellow head.

"Hmm," he said, looking down at the floor as though the answer to that question was somehow hidden among the sand and dog hair. "I don't rightly remember if that was Sunday or some other night, but if Fred says he drove me home, then he likely did," mused the old man.

"I was referring to Billy Williamson, Mr. Blair, not Fred," Julia said evenly. "Do you remember if that was the case?"

"Oh, Billy. Yep. He's a good lad. Pours with a heavy hand," as if this were the epitome of virtue. "And makes sure I get home some nights. Yep. I do remember now. Was that the night my rig was stolen? You don't think Billy stole it, do you?" Ted asked as if finally coming out of the fog.

"I was hoping you might be able to answer those questions for me, Mr. Blair. Do you think Billy stole your RZR?" Julia asked, trying to keep her voice calm and friendly, though she was starting to get exasperated.

"Naw. Not that young fella. He's a good kid. He's driven my rig home plenty of times. Never seemed at all interested in it. I reckon he's more of a Jeep man, likes solid doors and windows. Me, I like the wind in my hair."

Julia's lips twitched at that image, but she continued. "Was there anyone at the bar that night who *did* seem interested in your RZR, Mr. Blair?" Julia asked in hopes of moving her inquiry along in the direction of a lead that might be useful.

"There were so many of them racer fellows at Polly's after the Two Fifty, but I don't remember anyone being interested in my little rig. It's fun in the desert and all, but it's not in the league of the things those guys race. Nope, I don't remember anyone even talking about it," Ted answered, tugging at the waistband of his boxers as though it were digging into his ample belly.

"Is there anything distinctive about your RZR that will make it stand out from the hundred or so other red RZR Nine Hundreds in this area? Dents, scratches, anything like that?" Julia asked. "Do you have any photos of your RZR? It might help us find it."

"Actually, yeah, there is, now you mention it," Ted answered with a surprised tone in his voice. "It has the shock and strut package, so the shocks and struts are the same color as the seat accents. Mine are orange. Well, all except the driver's front strut. I buggered it up going over a really big rock, and my mechanic, Ephraim, replaced it with a black one," he said, pointing to the strut on one of the photos he found for Julia. "It also has a Magellan off-road GPS system and an off-road radio and communication system with headsets for the driver and front seat passenger. It's a four-seater rig, see, but I mostly don't have passengers so didn't get more headsets, and Jake sure doesn't need one."

Julia asked if he had the serial numbers for the GPS and radio. Ted said he'd look for them, though she didn't hold out much hope. She asked a few more questions but got no new information and so, taking the photo of his rig, finally thanked Ted Blair for his assistance and left.

As she and Luis walked back to the cruiser, Julia said, “I've got to get back in time for desk duty, Luis. Would you please drop me at the station and then go back out to Polly's. The regulars will be settling in for the day soon. Maybe one of them will remember something useful. Then canvass Campo Cristal to see if anyone remembers seeing anything unusual the night it was stolen.”

She quickly wrote a few sentences in English on a notepad, reread it for spelling, and handed the torn-out page, along with the photo of Ted's RZR, to Luis. “If you have any trouble communicating with anyone, just have them read this. If anyone appears to have information, make an appointment with them for us to interview them over the next few days.” There was not a hint of superiority in her voice or expression at his lack of fluency, and Luis took the paper with a slight warming of the animosity he originally felt toward her. She seemed a thorough and talented interviewer and a decent partner. *There may well be a reason Julia was a sergeant, and it might not be just because of her grandfather,* he thought.

Chapter 5—March 8, 2018, Desert Southwest of San Amaro

The sun glinted off the boulders at the end of the canyon in the places where the overhangs more than thirty feet above did not block its intense rays. There were desert verbena and sand lupines everywhere creating a sweet-smelling carpet of purple contrast against the light beige sand and ocher boulders.

Any amount of water in the desert is transformative. Seeds lie dormant waiting for the loving touch of rain or a splash of water cascading from a natural spring farther up the mountain. The hurricane that came over these same mountains from the Pacific just a few weeks before dropped in ten hours more rain than usually fell in several years. The sleeping seeds awoke to bring vibrantly colored life to this normally monochrome environment.

When they arrived at the site of the drawings, Rob had handed out his personalized bottles of electrolytes, which had been consumed amid many questions about the contents and specializations he'd made for each of them. Jaime was busy snapping photos with his cell phone, and Rick was trying to find a way to climb up to the overhangs. Simon, Rob, and Molly sat on rocks; their necks crooked upward as they stared at the rock paintings on the underside of the overhanging rocks.

The drawings were white, black, and red figures of people, deer, lizards, and birds made using paints concocted from plants, charcoal, crushed rock, and ash, possibly as much as 7,000 years ago. How the ancient painters had been able to reach these rocks thirty feet from the arroyo floor seemed miraculous. Some archaeologists posited they had built scaffolds of cactus wood, while others believed the desert floor in this location had eroded as much as thirty feet in the passing millennia. Their reasons for choosing these potentially inaccessible sites, along with who these ancient indigenous peoples were, remain lost to history, though some scholars credit the Guachimi or the Cochimi people for this site. In all, the Baja peninsula is home to over 400 sites of cave and rock paintings and petroglyphs ranging in age from hundreds to many thousands of years.

Unable to get more than a few feet above the desert floor, Rick returned to where the others sat. He was the first to voice what they were all thinking. “We shouldn’t stay much longer, or Stella will be wondering what’s happened to us. It’s likely another ten degrees hotter back in the parking lot.” They all agreed and quickly gathered their removed outer layers of clothing, grabbed their packs, trash, and water bottles, and headed back down the path.

Just over an hour later, Rob, having jogged the last part of the way, was the first to reach the vehicles, calling out, “Hey, Stella, we’re back!” Not getting a response, he whistled and hollered for Juba. As the others neared their vehicles, they could hear his deep bellow as he called Stella’s and Juba’s names. Turning to the now fully assembled group, he asked with a furrowed brow, “Where would she have gone?”

Simon was the first to respond. "She's too desert savvy to have gone far. Let's just split up and keep calling her and Juba. She may be trying to find some shade where there is more of a breeze than here beside the vehicles."

Twenty minutes later, however, when no one had spotted any sign of either Stella or her dog, an atmosphere of concern descended on the five friends. Simon's worry was being expressed as anger. "She knows better than to wander off. What was she thinking? For Chrissake! Why didn't I just stay with her? This is my fucking fault!" He was not addressing anyone but himself, and the others gave him space while he blew off some of his anxiety. They were all feeling it.

As Simon started winding down his self-abuse, Jaime took command of the situation, asking, "Do any of you have flares or any other signaling devices in your rigs? I think we need to do a proper search of areas on both sides of the path toward the rock paintings, and the track coming into where we parked." Seeing only shaking heads at the flare question, he went on. "Okay, we'll go out in two teams, then. Since we don't have flares, let's meet back here in an hour. Rick and Molly, let us three go back up the path and see if she ended up waiting in the shade somewhere on her walk back to the rigs. Perhaps she was sleeping and didn't hear us. Rob and Simon, you head up the route we took to drive here and see if you can see any signs of her or Juba. The sand is very soft, so maybe you can see some tracks or something. Let's not lose sight of our team members and don't forget your water. We'll find her."

Chapter 6—March 8, 2018, San Amaro

It was getting close to quitting time. Julia's replacement on desk duty had not yet arrived for work when five gringos pushed through the front door of the police station. They looked upset, hot, and dusty as all five approached the desk together. One of the men, with longish silver hair, was the first to speak in halting Spanish, asking Julia if she spoke English.

"Yes, sir. How can I help you?" Julia responded in excellent English.

With obvious relief, Simon began, "We need to report a missing person. I'm Simon Wakefield, and my wife, Stella Monroe, is lost in the desert out by the rock paintings in Cañon Del Demonio." His words poured out like a gushing faucet, but before he could continue, Julia deftly and calmly stopped the flow of his story. "Before you proceed with your account of what happened to your wife, let me gather some details about you and her, so I can start the computer case file. That will speed things up. Then we'll all go into a quiet room, and you can tell me the whole situation."

Julia's first-rate command of English and her calm, strong demeanor seemed to cause the man before her and the group with him to visibly relax a degree or two. She led the husband through the demographic data gathering of his and his wife's names, their address in San Amaro, and the time and location where she was last seen. By this time, the evening desk sergeant had arrived to start his shift, and Julia moved the group into an interview room. They spent over an hour there going over all the details of the morning's hike, Stella's separation from the group, and all the actions they had taken in their search to find her when she wasn't in the parking lot as expected.

She videotaped the interview with their permission, because, as she explained to them, the detective assigned to the case might not be fluent in English. Being able to put Spanish subtitles on the video would help him more quickly get up to speed. They all signed the video waiver with no questions asked.

The five hikers provided Julia with a description of their trip to the location from which they began their hike up the canyon to the rock paintings. Each member of the group added details they thought were important. Julia asked probing questions when she was unclear and as the story emerged through the interview. A couple of the Americans showed her photos on their phones to better inform Julia of the story. She had several of the photos emailed from the hiker's phones to her work email.

Before she sent the five home, Julia let them know that, once assigned, the detective for their case would be contacting Simon. She reassured them it would be soon. Even though it was now nearly an hour and a half past the end of her shift, she settled at her desk to translate the statements the group had made into Spanish and add Spanish subtitles to the video. Translation software for written and spoken words made the process less tedious.

After two hours, she had read the translation through several times and was happy that both it and the subtitles were accurate and clear. She had also printed several photos from the hiker's phones. She took the file folder containing all the statements, photos, and a thumb drive containing the video to the evening desk sergeant who was responsible for contacting the brass to find out whom they wished to assign as lead on this new case.

With the formalities of statements completed, she headed home. Her thoughts shifted to the humanity of the situation. A woman, dressed and prepared for a morning hike in the desert, was most likely lost, disoriented from a day in the desert heat, hungry and afraid, trying to find a safe place to spend the night. Or perhaps she was lying hurt and unable to move in the boulders along the arroyo. Whatever her situation, Julia sent a quick prayer to San Cristo, Saint Christopher, that the missing woman and her dog be kept from harm through the night.

Julia lived in a small casita behind her *abuelos'*, grandparents', house. Their house was located on a large lot on the hillside west of the center of town. It had a view of the Bay of San Amaro, where open wooden or fiberglass fishing boats, called pangas, could still be seen on the beach along the Malecon. Julia's casita was a small self-contained cabin located on the same lot and originally built by Julia's parents shortly after they were married. After Julia was born, they had moved to another, larger house closer to the edge of town. She and her mother had moved back into the casita when Julia's much-loved father had been killed in a traffic accident in Mexicali when Julia was fourteen. It was a traumatic event in her young life made more so by Julia's cool relationship with her mother and the impressionability of a girl of her age. His death left scars on her psyche that remained. Julia's mother had remarried when Julia was finishing her master's degree in criminology in Arizona and had moved into her new husband's home. The casita was Julia's alone now.

The small house, the interior of which Julia had painted a cheery golden orange, consisted of a small bedroom with an armoire in place of a closet and dresser, a very modest bathroom with a sink, toilet, and small tiled shower area, and one other larger room comprising kitchen, dining, and living areas. It was less than 500 square feet in total. There were two stools against one side of the freestanding kitchen counter acting as the dining area. Opposite that against the wall were a two-burner stove, half-sized fridge, and a sink. The only other pieces of furniture were a shabby two-seater sofa over which Julia had thrown a brightly colored woven Mexican blanket to hide the tears in the cushions and a home-made wooden side table constructed by her father over thirty years before. It was one of the few things of her father's she had, and it was precious to her. The casita was as neat and tidy as it was small and humble.

She had just toweled off after a shower when her cell phone rang. Ten forty-five. It had to be work, though she didn't recognize the number. None of her friends would phone this late on a work night.

"*Bueno*," she answered, using the typical Spanish phone greeting.

"Sergeant Garcia, this is Hector Martinez Ortega." Julia's eyebrows shot up and she stood at attention, smiling inwardly at her reaction. Martinez was a well-respected detective inspector in San Amaro—"Hector the Inspector," people called him—and someone her grandfather spoke of with high regard.

"Yes, Inspector," she said with an aura of excitement tingling up her spine.

"I have been assigned the missing person case you took at the end of your shift today. I have reviewed the interview footage and transcripts you prepared. I appreciate that you spent the time to translate everything before leaving tonight. It helped me greatly." He paused briefly before speaking again. "You have been assigned to this case, to work with me as a liaison with the Americans. Sergeant Hernandez is also on the team, and I want the three of us out at the site where she disappeared at first light tomorrow. We will meet at the station at four thirty in the morning for a briefing, and then we'll head out. Be prepared for a day in the desert," Martinez admonished and then hung up.

Julia, excited but not completely surprised to be included, began gathering provisions for the day. She would need ample water, food, sturdy boots, warm jacket, short-sleeved uniform, and a good hat.

In the eyes of the male hierarchy in the San Amaro Police force, being fluent in English was one of Julia's main attributes. It brought her into important cases involving the English-speaking residents and visitors to San Amaro. She was incredibly grateful she had taken her graduate studies in the States instead of going to Mexico City, as her mother desired. She had studied English throughout public school, but it was her grandfather who had encouraged her to spend time studying in the US to be forced into fluency. That encouragement prompted her to explore scholarships to American universities, and her scholastic abilities had won her a full ride to Arizona State University. The fact that her father's brother and his family lived in Phoenix, and could provide her with a bedroom, was the final piece giving her the ability to spend two years at Arizona State completing her graduate-level criminology degree.

Julia went to sleep excited about the day ahead and saying another prayer to San Cristo for the missing woman and her dog.

Chapter 7—March 9, 2018, San Amaro

At seven thirty the following morning, near the entrance to Cañon Del Demonio, Inspector Martinez and his two sergeants pulled into the area where the Americans had reported leaving their desert rigs the previous day. This was the place they'd expected to find their friend Stella Monroe, wife of Simon Wakefield, awaiting their return. One of the friends, Rick Worton, a twelve-year resident of San Amaro, had emailed Julia a map from the software in his GPS system of the route they had taken through the desert and a photo of a hand drawing of their trek through the arroyo to the rock paintings. The inspector and his team each had a copy of Mr. Worton's maps, plus topographical maps of the region and the grid search plan developed during their early-morning briefing. The parking area was crisscrossed with tire treads and footprints. They were in the right spot.

When Martinez had contacted the husband of the missing woman the previous evening, he learned that he and several friends planned to meet at the same parking area at nine o'clock that morning, and the inspector wanted to precede them in case there might be some visual traces he and his team could find before the scene was trampled over by the group of well-meaning, but possibly unhelpful, gringos. He was glad of Sergeant Julia Garcia's presence to help communicate with the Americans when they arrived. He had managed to make himself understood by the husband over the phone the previous night, though it was a struggle with his less-than-fluent English. He knew, however, that he hadn't understood everything the husband had been trying to communicate to him. People tend to speak rapidly when upset or anxious, and Martinez's mental translation simply couldn't keep up with the speed of the husband's words.

Following their plan, the three police officers made as thorough a search of the parking area and several yards up the path taken by the hikers as possible before the gringos started to arrive. The inspector and Julia were waiting in the parking area by the time the gringos assembled, leaving Sergeant Hernandez to continue looking for signs of the missing woman on the trail.

Julia marveled at the efficiency of social media. By nine o'clock over twenty people had gathered in the parking area. Most said they found out about the missing woman and this morning's search on the local San Amaro Facebook page. In a town of fewer than 20,000 people, a certain kinship exists. People tend to look out for one another. It was one of the things Julia loved about her Mexican home.

"Buenos días. Good morning. I am Sergeant Garcia of the San Amaro State Police. This is Detective Inspector Martinez, the lead investigating officer looking for Stella Monroe. Sergeant Hernandez here," she said, motioning to Ricardo, who had just returned from his search and was now standing to her left, "is the other officer assigned to this search. I will be the communications liaison between Inspector Martinez and Sergeant Hernandez and your group of searchers. If you have questions, I am the person to ask. We all want the same thing, to find your friend and get her home safely."

"Inspector Martinez has some ground rules he would like you to understand and follow while you are here helping with the search. We have also developed a search plan to ensure we methodically cover the area in the most efficient way possible. Please listen carefully as I describe the plan and outline the role we ask you to fill." Julia then read from the plan Martinez had prepared, translating his further instructions and expectations, and answering questions from the group.

Before the groups dispersed, Simon stepped forward and thanked everyone for coming to help. "Stella has an irregular heartbeat. It's not bad enough for a pacemaker, but she takes pills. I don't think she brought any extras with her yesterday, so she likely hasn't had her dose for last night or this morning. She can get dizzy and possibly faint when she misses a few doses. I brought some with me, so as soon as we find her, I need to make sure she gets her pill. It also might mean, if she's fainted, that she won't hear us yelling."

The three police officers shared annoyed looks with one another. *Why hadn't he told them this before?* Inspector Martinez asked Julia to make a note to follow up with Simon when there weren't so many people around.

At ten after ten, the police and Stella's Facebook friends were splitting up in pairs, each pair going off to search their assigned area. Each group had been given a cheap plastic whistle and understood the signal to use if they found something that might be relevant. They also had a photo of Stella that Julia had obtained the previous evening from Jaime. It showed Stella and her dog, Juba, taken before the group left the parking area the preceding day. Julia noticed Rob and Rick talking earnestly for a few seconds before Rick walked up to her and spoke. "Don't you think it would be better if Rob and I search the path up the canyon? We know the exact route we took, and the couple you assigned to that search area won't have that knowledge."

It seemed a logical suggestion, so Julia spoke with the two assigned to the path area, and they switched search maps with Rob and Rick. The four went off in their newly assigned directions, and Julia went on with her own work. She was to stay in the parking area and act as the coordinator. Should additional people show up to help search, she would brief them and assign them a search area. She would set up the command tent, really just a canopy they brought with them to provide some shade, and she was tasked with doing a systematic, meter-by-meter search of the parking area, looking for any clues to the direction the missing woman may have taken if she had made it back to the vehicles before disappearing.

In the parking lot, in addition to the police 4x4 truck, were three Jeeps, another four-wheel-drive pickup truck, a couple of chopped VW bugs turned into desert rigs, four Polaris RZRs, and one Can-Am that looked just like the RZRs. Given the stolen RZR case Julia was still responsible for, she paid extra attention to those four vehicles although only one of them was red. One, she knew, belonged to Rick Worton, and she took a photo of his tire treads and measured his vehicle's width, tire to tire, just for a reference. On inspecting the other RZRs, she realized the tire treads and track widths did not match those of Rick Worton's and made a note to have Corporal Flores find out from Polaris and local race rig mechanics what tires and track widths were common to RZRs used in this area. Not that she thought it would help her RZR case, but it was a loose end she should follow up to be thorough. She took several photos on her cell phone before moving on.

All three vehicles driven by the hikers yesterday were available in the parking area. None of them was locked, and under Mexican law, therefore available for Julia to legally search. She found nothing unusual.

As her search took her to the far northwest edge of the open area used for parking, she noticed that the sand there was crusty and stippled, much like a popcorn ceiling. This happens when rained-upon-sand baked undisturbed under the intense sun. Her footfalls made a clear impression on the crusty sand surface. She slowed her pace, looking carefully to see if any other footprints or other traces could be seen.

It had been several weeks since the heavy rains of the hurricane, so tracks Julia might find could have been made any time since, but she knew older disruption of the stippled sand would be blown about. She was out of sight of the parked vehicles and just about to the last edge of the sand to the start of the boulders when she spotted vehicle tracks. She didn't see much loose sand around the tracks. They were recent. She pulled out her cell phone and began photographing the general area and then took several close-up photos of the tire-tread impressions and track width still visible in the sand crust. There were no indications people had gotten out of the vehicle. She was trying to determine the direction of the vehicle's path when she heard a whistle tweeting back at the path toward the arroyo.

Someone has found something. She rushed toward the sound.

A young desert iguana, about sixteen inches long, slim, and almost white, darted across her path and under a bush, rapidly bobbing its body up and down in a show of either aggression or fear. Julia hardly noticed as she headed up the arroyo through a landscape of boulders, wild buckwheat shrubs, and purple splashes of desert verbena. The desert was truly beautiful this year. A hundred-year bloom they were calling it because of excessive rain from the recent hurricane that hit the Pacific coast. Regardless of being intent on finding out the reason for the whistle alert, Julia was still aware of the beauty and the intoxicating smell of the verbena around her.

The whistle continued to sound about every thirty seconds, finally guiding Julia, Inspector Martinez, and Ricardo to a pair of gringos whom Julia recognized as the gay couple, Rick and Rob. Rick, the older of the two, was waving them all to a spot slightly off the main trail, behind a small grouping of reddish, round boulders. After clambering over the rocks, the police were able to join the two men.

"This is the leather thong from Stella's walking stick. It tore from her putting so much pressure on it to help support her walking with her bruised toes," Rick said, pointing to a three-quarter-inch-wide strip of soft, bluish leather with a turquoise bead threaded on one end. The other end looked partly frayed as though ripped from its previous home. Before Ricardo stepped up with an evidence bag and gloved hand to gather the thong, Julia snapped several photos of the location, both close up and then backing up a few meters to show the overall situation from back on the trail.

Inspector Martinez was a striking man, close to six feet tall. Owing to his being in the less than 10 percent of the Mexican population that can trace its heritage through generations to European land-grabbing settlers, his genetics, looks, and coloring leaned more strongly toward Caucasian than Hispanic. Instead of the typical black hair and dark chocolate-brown eyes of most Mexicans, Martinez sported a full head of brown hair and hazel eyes. It frequently found him sputtering, "My English is not so good," when working with the gringos, as they assumed from his looks and their proximity to the United States that he was American.

Standing with the two men who had discovered the leather thong, Inspector Martinez beckoned Julia over to assist him in gathering the details from them about how they found the thong. In rapid Spanish, the inspector told Julia what he wanted her to ask the men. "Tell us about the process you were using to search this area," Julia began.

"Well, we were kind of zigzagging back and forth across the main path. And crisscrossing each other, rather than working the same side of the path together. We thought it would give us the best coverage of the area," Rob explained. He was in his late thirties, Julia estimated. About six two, blond, bearded, and very well muscled. As he was wearing a tank top, Julia couldn't help noticing his strong shoulders and biceps. Most certainly, he lifted weights. His eyes flashed to Rick for an instant, but whether for corroboration or as a signal, Julia wasn't sure. Rick nodded his head in agreement but said nothing. Julia translated for the inspector, but she was fairly sure he got the gist of what was said.

"And which one of you actually found the thong?" Julia asked, noting an almost imperceptible nod from Martinez indicating that was the next question he would have asked.

"Rob did," Rick responded. In counterpoint to Rob's tall, muscular physique, Rick, a few inches shorter, was bald, with a belly stretching the bottom of his T-shirt. He was also at least twenty years older than Rob.

Rob took up the explanation: "At first glance, I thought it was a little snake or something. Then I saw that blue stone on it, and I figured it was the strap from Stella's hiking stick. I called Rick over and he agreed, so he started whistling, like you told us."

"Did you touch or move it in any way?" Julia continued asking questions when it appeared that Martinez was comfortable with her taking the lead.

"Yeah, I did. I didn't really pick it up, just gave one end of it a pull because it was slightly covered with sand, you know, and I wanted to see if there was more of it under the sand," Rob admitted, looking sheepishly at them.

"And was there? More of it under the sand?" Julia asked sternly. She then turned to her boss to translate in case he wasn't getting all the details.

"No. There was just a dusting of sand covering the frayed end."

It was clear that the inspector was unhappy about this. This morning he'd had Julia tell them all not to touch or move anything they might find. He thought to himself, *People never listen. Or these two are intentionally tampering with evidence.* He led Julia through a few more questions and he carefully watched the two men as Julia asked them for the additional information Martinez wanted. From the set of his shoulders and the cock of his head, Julia had the feeling the inspector was harboring, as was she, some suspicion about their story.

Rob mentioned having given Stella one of his own hiking sticks to provide her support for her return trip. "I'm almost certain that when it broke, Stella put this piece of the strap into the pocket of her shorts. And this isn't close to where the strap actually broke. That spot is at least several hundred yards farther up the trail," Rick interjected. "A few hundred meters, I should say." He corrected himself as he remembered that Mexico, like most of the rest of the world, used metric measurements.

In the end, the police had the two men show them where Stella's walking-stick strap had broken and from where she left the group. They then all returned to the spot where the strap fragment had been found, and the policemen let the two gringos continue searching the path. Ricardo and the inspector continued to explore the area surrounding the leather thong. The sand was so disturbed by Rick and Rob's footprints, it was hard to get any idea if there were any clues they might have obscured. In fact, it looked as if one or more people had tromped up and down making a new path in the sand on this side of the route the hikers had taken. Was someone intentionally trying to conceal something?

Julia returned to the base with the evidence bag. She logged the thong into evidence and placed it in their vehicle's lockbox. Once she made some additional notes in her notebook of the find and conversation with the two men, she finally returned to her post in the parking lot. Something niggled at her brain, but she couldn't bring it into a focused thought.

Chapter 8—March 9, 2018, Desert Southwest of San Amaro

With only a couple of hours of sunlight left, the gringo search teams straggled back into the parking lot and milled about the command tent asking Julia if anyone found anything. The five hikers from the previous day were standing off to one side. Rob and Simon were a few steps away from the others.

Julia, on instruction from the inspector, began updating the searchers on the results of the day. When Julia mentioned Rick and Rob's find, Stella's husband, Simon, demanded to see the leather thong. Julia took Simon to the locked evidence box in the police 4x4. Simon took the evidence bag into his hands. His initial excitement drained away as he looked at the strip of leather through the evidence bag, seemingly sucking the life out of him.

"This happened on our way up the canyon, and then she decided to head back to the rigs. As she started to have more trouble with her toes, she was leaning on her walking stick more and more. The wrist strap ripped off. I thought she put it in her pocket, but I guess she threw it off into the rocks. There was still a piece of leather left on the stick, but it didn't have any stones on it like this piece does. I'm sure this is the torn-away part of the strap," Simon said. When Julia mentioned that the thong was not found where the strap had broken, but closer to the parking area,

Simon's suggestion was that perhaps on her trek back, she went into her pocket for something, pulled out the torn thong, and tossed it away then. Julia thought this was plausible, but not provable. She wondered if it was relevant.

No one had seen any other traces of Stella or her dog, Juba, nor any tracks that might have been made by them. Back at the main tent, Julia shared this news with the people gathered there. It was a disheartened group that slowly got in their vehicles and headed back to San Amaro as the daylight started to leach from the sky. In the police vehicle, Inspector Martinez asked Ricardo first and then Julia for their thoughts on the day and the case so far.

Ricardo's thoughts were concise and expressed musings they had all had during the course of the day. They were all voiced as questions. "How do a woman and dog disappear with no trace? If she were hurt somewhere or dead, I would think the dog would be running around and barking. And why would a person who has lived in this area and hiked it extensively ever go off on her own in the first place? Do we have any evidence supporting the group's claim that she was ever actually with them? Is it possible that they have conspired to hide something, an accident, or a murder, maybe? Or could she have simply left her husband, and this is an elaborate ruse for him to save face? Also, do we believe the male couple that they did their best to not disturb the leather strap they found? The surrounding area seemed to have been trampled. That doesn't support their claim, does it?"

Julia's brow furrowed as she considered Ricardo's questions. She responded to the last one first. "They specifically asked to search that area. They had originally been assigned a quadrant south of the parking area, and they asked to swap quadrants with a couple from the Facebook brigade," she added. "And Stella was with them because we have the photo of her and Juba with Molly and Simon that Jaime took yesterday morning beside their vehicles."

Following on from Ricardo's skepticism, Julia raised her own questions. "Is it possible she planned this as a way to leave a marriage that turned out to be less than she'd hoped? Could she have an accomplice who picked her up from the parking lot?" she queried, then paused as her previous brain niggle finally coalesced into a clear memory. "I just remembered," she carried on in a rush, "I found something in my own search just before the men found the leather thong. At the northwest part of the parking area, edging where the boulders start, I saw a set of tire tracks in the crusty sand left over from the big rain. They were in an odd place, I thought, out of sight of the hikers' vehicles. Of course, they could have just been from one of the searchers driving in this morning, but I don't remember anyone coming that way. I have photos of the tracks in the sand."

Martinez perked up at this news. "Ricardo, you and I will search that area tomorrow morning first thing." He also considered each of the questions his team of two had posed for some time before speaking. "If she is hurt somewhere, it's possible her dog is suffering from dehydration or was attacked by a pack of coyotes and is also hurt or dead." He shifted to the side to better look at Julia from the passenger seat. "Julia, did you have any sense that the group was lying when you took their statements last night?"

"No, *Jefe*," she responded, using the Spanish word for boss. "They were agitated, for sure, and I did suspect there were more details they didn't share, but

I didn't get the sense they were telling a story they had all made up."

"No," Martinez said nodding. "That was my feeling, too, from watching the video. At this point, I think we proceed on the belief that they are telling us the truth and that there is every chance that a woman is missing in the desert. I know it's already been a long day, but I have some work for you to do when we get back to the station." The inspector outlined the information he wanted gathered and the analysis he wished completed before they headed back to the search site the following morning.

The three police officers spoke little the rest of the trip back to town, each wrapped in his or her own thoughts. Before Martinez left his two sergeants for the night, he reminded them, "We will meet here again tomorrow morning at four thirty for a short planning session and to get out to the site before others show up."

Chapter 9—March 9, 2018, San Amaro

Before she left the police station, Julia grabbed the report Corporal Lopez had left her regarding his interviews with patrons of Polly's Place and Ted Blair's neighbors in Campo Cristal. She shoved it into her backpack and headed home.

After a shower and two tortillas heated on a stove burner, Julia pulled Luis's report from her pack and read it through twice. He had learned nothing useful at the bar, but one of Mr. Blair's neighbors remembered something. According to Luis's notes, when the neighbor indicated she knew something about the night in question, he asked her to write it down for him. In her written explanation, she said she recalled hearing a guttural engine noise that could have been a RZR heading out of the community about four in the morning. It had caused her dogs to bark, thus waking her. She looked out her window and saw taillights driving up the road from the community to the highway, but she couldn't tell what kind of vehicle it was.

Julia sent Luis an email instructing him to check with the local truckers to see if any of them happened to see anything on the highway at that time of the morning on March 7. It was possible one of the early-morning grocery delivery drivers might have seen something. Next, she turned her attention to her assignment on the missing woman's case.

Julia, born into the millennial generation and a proficient social media user, was nevertheless amazed at the breadth and speed of Facebook as a communication medium. Part of her work for the evening was tracking the Facebook conversation about the missing woman.

She propped herself up on her bed and was using her personal laptop to catch up on the posts about the missing woman and her dog on the San Amaro group page. Though it was almost eight in the evening the temperatures were still in the high seventies outside and warmer still in her casita. After having spent the day in the sun in a hot, dark-blue uniform, she was still feeling overheated, even after a cool shower. Consequently, she was wearing only a cotton tank top and a pair of running shorts. To cool her neck, Julia twisted her thick, black, damp hair into a bun on top of her head. A few loose tendrils tickled the back of her neck.

Local gringos had set up a few Facebook groups they used to share information and sell such things as kayaks and desert buggies. The local businesses also posted on them from time to time when a band would be playing at their location or if they had specials on shrimp meals, one of San Amaro's major catches. Tonight, the posts were dominated with thoughts, questions, and information sharing—also known as gossip—about Stella and Juba. Julia began the challenging task of reading online. Words in electronic format had the nasty habit of jiggling as she read. Fortunately, her dyslexic brain, which caused the moving text, was still able to assimilate the information, though it was slightly slower for her than reading words on paper.

The first post she found was from last night and was made, somewhat surprisingly, she thought, by Molly. Julia had expected to see something from Simon first. Molly's post was emotional, edging toward panic. By the time stamp, she must have made the entry almost immediately upon getting home from the police station after the group made their missing person report. The post was accompanied by a photo taken of Stella on her and Simon's wedding day. Julia downloaded the photo and emailed it to the inspector and Ricardo. Julia noted that Molly had tagged the other four hikers on her post.

> *I have awful news. My friend, Stella Monroe, is missing in the desert, and I'm terrified for her. She got lost or hurt when she left our group on our hike to Cañon Del Demonio. I can't imagine being lost in the desert overnight. She has her dog, Juba with her, which is some small comfort. What if something happened to them? This is so horrible. Please help us look for her tomorrow. Come to my house at six thirty in the morning and we can caravan. Please, please pray for her.*

This post had over a hundred comments, many of them asking for more details, some reprimanding the other hikers for letting Stella leave the group on her own, some with just emojis of praying hands or a face with tears. Julia made note of everyone who had commented and placed an asterisk beside those doing the scolding. She had looked for, but not found, any comments that seemed to taunt or provoke, though one of the scolders skulked closely to it, berating the others for "being about as stupid as they come" to let Stella go off alone. That poster's name, Tony Ranelli, received two asterisks.

Simon's first post was made in the early hours of this morning; apparently and not surprisingly, he wasn't sleeping. His post, unlike Molly's, was just the facts, providing the who, what, where, and when of the situation and asking for anyone who wanted to help in the search to meet at the trail head to the canyon.

> *My wife, whom most of you will know as Stella Monroe, went missing in the morning of March 7th on a hike to the rock paintings in Cañon Del Demonio. She left the group early in the hike because her broken toes were bothering her and was supposed to be waiting for us where we left our vehicles. She wasn't there, and though we searched for her and called out for both her and her dog Juba for hours, we couldn't find either of them. We filled out a police report, but Stella is still out there. We couldn't find any trace of either of them. Please pray for her safety. I will be out there again tomorrow searching for them both. Join us if you can.*

He also provided GPS coordinates for the location where the search would begin. Julia jotted the latitude and longitude numbers in her notebook, checking twice that they were not transposed and pondered why he hadn't provided the GPS coordinates when he was making his report the previous evening.

This post had nearly eighty comments, many of which he had replied to providing more details and defending himself and his friends against the reprimands, saying such things as, "If you know Stella at all, you'll know how stubborn and independent she is." Again, Julia made notes of people responding to the posts. She also noted that both Rick and Rob commented on Simon's posts and replies, supporting him, and adding small details, some of which Julia knew hadn't been in their police report. She was surprised Rob had chimed in, as he was such a newcomer to the group. All of this went into her notes.

There were new posts today from Simon and Rob giving details of the day's search and that no trace of either Stella or Juba had been found. Most of the responses to these posts were emojis indicating support, though recriminations still showed up occasionally. Julia noted Tony Ranelli had also responded to Simon's post, and this time he was taunting in his reply. Another, bigger star went by his name. Interestingly, it was Rick who responded to this and other inflammatory comments. Simon judiciously ignored them. Molly had made only one post tonight, asking for anyone with search-and-rescue training or with scent dogs to please join in the search tomorrow. She also said she'd contacted the San Diego Tribune in hopes of getting more media focus that might lead professional search teams to join them. Apart from a few thumbs-ups, none of them indicated they had the requested additional skills or dogs.

By the time Julia had read all the posts, comments, and replies, she had several pages of notes to share with the team in the morning. She wanted to prepare a written recap, but decided she'd forgo her morning run and write it up in the morning . . . *only four hours away.*

A bleary-eyed Julia, coffee in hand, finished giving her report to Ricardo and Inspector Martinez. “So, of the seventy-five or so different people posting to the Facebook threads, I have flagged five people I think we should get more information on, one of whom will take priority because of the vitriol of his comments.”

“Good. Leave your list for Corporal Verde and ask her to do background checks on them today. Julia, you may need to take a day off from the search and do in-person interviews with any that Verde flags,” said the inspector. “Now Ricardo, what did you find out about the other five on the hike with Stella?”

“I managed to get Sergeant Gonzales to help me last night with some of the background, as he was on desk duty, and it wasn’t busy. He focused mostly on checking Immigration and Naturalization databases. That left me free to visit neighbors of the hikers. So, the information we gathered is a bit limited.

“As we already know, Simon and Stella have been married for a year. According to the Immigration office, the first record of Simon coming across the border into Mexico and getting a visa was only seventeen months ago, using the Los Algodones crossing. He was likely coming from Glendale, Arizona, where he had lived for eighteen years. So, they didn’t have a very long courtship, but I guess at their age, you don’t want to waste time. Simon is here on his third six-month tourist visa, and there’s no record of him starting the permanent-resident process. That seems odd but may just be because he’s a procrastinator. According to their neighbors, he’s a lawyer with a practice in Arizona, someplace called Surprise." Ricardo spoke without referring to his notes or the summary report he was in the process of typing when Julia got to the station at four fifteen that morning.

Ricardo carried on. "Rob Gurenburg, the young boyfriend of Rick Worton, whom I'll get to in a minute, was also an Arizona resident, from Phoenix, before coming to San Amaro. Unlike Simon, though, he's been coming into Mexico off and on for almost nineteen years. His recent visits started about twenty months ago." Ricardo then added as an aside before continuing with his report, "He's thirty-eight now, and his earlier visits coincide with the spring breaks of Arizona Western College, where he studied to become a paramedic, according to his Facebook profile. Also from his Facebook profile, I learned he was a combat medic in Afghanistan. And he told us during the missing person report that he is now a private investigator.

"According to Immigration, which of course has only spotty records, he stopped coming to Mexico for eleven years and then started again, as I said, about twenty months ago. He's here on a six-month visitor's visa only, which he got in late December.

"We need to get the US immigration records of his entries back into the States. I think he may still be doing some work in the US. I found a mention of a Rob Gurenburg, private investigator, on a Phoenix blog site. It is probably him. I've asked Luis to check into Phoenix business licenses for PIs. He is currently renting a casita in Campo Cristal."

Julia, though paying attention to Ricardo's report, perked up at the mention of Campo Cristal. It was interesting that her missing RZR case was also connected to Campo Cristal. It was one of the smaller gringo communities on the north side of town with about twenty or twenty-five homes. But then again, there were close to a dozen campos, or communities, in the five miles north of town and more south of San Amaro. There may not be any coincidence.

At this point, Ricardo stopped to refer to his notes and take a long gulp of coffee. "Rick Worton, the boyfriend, is fifty-eight and has been a resident of San Amaro for twelve years. He and Stella have been close friends for most of that time. He is a gas fitter and plumber and has a cash-only business here doing work for the gringos. He runs it from his home and doesn't pay Mexico any taxes beyond his property taxes. He lives in Campo Pelícano at the south end of town. I asked a friend in the Federalis to search everyone's names for arrest warrants, and he found a reference for a Rick Worton from the late nineteen seventies. It could be our guy, but I am not positive, as there are no pictures, and his US Social Security number wasn't recorded at the time." Ricardo went on to provide the details from the police file on Rick Worton.

Inspector Martinez stopped Ricardo after he finished his report on Rick Worton, tossing a set of truck keys to Julia and saying, "Let's finish this on the drive out to the Canyon. Julia, you're driving again today so Ricardo can finish his report."

Once on the road, Ricardo went on. "Molly and Jaime have been friends with Stella for a very long time. Molly and Stella knew each other in the United States before either of them moved to San Amaro, more than forty years, apparently. Jaime and Molly met and married in San Amaro, with Jaime being a local who moved to the States and then returned to open La Playa restaurant on the Malecon.

"Jaime also has a Phoenix connection, as he worked in a small Mexican restaurant there in his late twenties and early thirties, long before coming home to San Amaro. They married three years after Molly moved to San Amaro. Jaime's daughter now runs the restaurant. As you likely know, it is popular with gringos and locals alike," Ricardo said, finishing his report.

The desert sand was in the process of being washed with the scarlet-and-orange rays of the rising sun. As the sun's light reflected off the mountains, the colors crept across the sand like a brightly colored cloth being drawn over the landscape. All three seemed to take a break in their discussions to take in the beauty. Then, as if by mutual agreement, they picked up their conversation about the five people who had last seen Stella, given the information Ricardo had gathered and the Facebook posts made by some of them in the last two days.

Considering Molly and Stella's long-term relationship, Julia could now better understand the overly emotional tone of Molly's Facebook posts. Though Jaime had a Facebook account, he had not posted anything for months, and all his posts over the years were photo logs of trips he and Molly had taken.

"I'd like to ask the five of them for any pictures they may have taken the day of the hike. I did get photos from a couple of them when they were making the missing person report, but Jaime seems to be an avid photographer. Perhaps he or some of the others might have photos that can give us some added information," Julia mused.

Ricardo made a note to that effect as a task that could be assigned to one of the corporals and added it to the other information gathering and analysis they had noted. He was just finishing his notes, hoping he could read the scribbled words caused by writing in the bumpy 4X4, when Julia stopped the truck beside the command-post tent set up the previous day.

Before they disembarked the truck, the inspector turned in his seat so he could see both Julia and Ricardo and did a quick recap. “It sounds like this is what we have so far. Let me know if I miss anything.” He tapped the fingers of his right hand on the console, as though counting each point as he went through them.

- “Six friends went to the desert in the morning two days ago to hike to the rock paintings.
- “There were two married couples and one gay couple.
- “Two of the men have relatively recently moved to San Amaro from the Phoenix area, and a third man, a San Amaro native, also has ties to Phoenix.
- “One of the straight couples was celebrating their first anniversary.
- “On the hike, the anniversary-celebrating wife claimed her foot hurt and returned, alone, or at least with her dog, back down the trail toward the vehicles.
- “The others let her go, alone, supplying her with food, drink, and a hiking stick.
- “When the five hikers returned to the vehicles, neither the woman nor her dog was there.
- “The subsequent search by the five remaining hikers turned up nothing.
- “They reported their missing friend to us about five hours after they determined she was missing.

- “A search yesterday by the three of us and about twenty gringos turned up only two pieces of evidence, the torn leather strap, apparently from the missing woman’s walking stick, and tire tracks north of the parking area.
- “Forensics have the strap and will let us know if they find anything of note.
- “The missing woman’s husband and the gay couple accounted for the strap as having been torn from her walking stick on the first part of the hike when they were all still together.
- “The location where the piece of strap was found was not where it was originally torn.
- “We have several inflammatory Facebook posts about the negligence of the other hikers.
- “We have several as yet unsubstantiated speculations: this could be an abduction, a plot perpetrated by the missing woman to leave an unhappy marriage, or a conspiracy among the five remaining hikers to cover up something like a murder or suspicious death of the missing woman.
- “From previous experience with people missing in the desert, we know the chances of us finding this woman alive are decreasing very rapidly.”

The inspector finished by looking back and forth between the two sergeants. “Did I miss anything?”

Ricardo was the first to speak: “I don’t have anything to add to your list, but I have made a couple of notes of things we need to check. One, find out if there was any previous relationship among any of the three men with a Phoenix connection, Simon Wakefield, Rob Gurenburg, and Jaime Lopez. And two, as Julia mentioned on the drive here, to check each of their phones for pictures of the hike for any potential clues they might reveal."

Julia added, "I already have Corporal Verde looking into the Facebook respondents to the hikers' posts and, as I noted in my report earlier, Simon Wakefield posted the GPS coordinates where they left their vehicles on the day his wife went missing, yet he'd neglected to provide that information to us during the initial interview. I specifically parked here because this spot matches up with the coordinates he provided," she said, tapping the coordinates on the truck's GPS display. "I think we need to question him about that. And, I'm wondering, if we don't find the missing woman or any new clues in the next couple of days, should we bring each of the other five in for individual interviews? I think they may know more than they have told us."

Martinez was nodding his head. "Yes, we should start digging deeper with the remaining five hikers. We need to prepare for individual interviews with them soon."

With that, they climbed out of the truck and Julia walked the inspector and Ricardo a few hundred yards around a boulder hill, to the area where she had noticed the out-of-place tire tracks the previous day. After they had carefully walked the area that held the unexpected tracks, their interest was piqued. Along the tracks, it appeared that the vehicle had sat in one spot for some amount of time, as there were slightly deeper indentations in the track there and, behind the indentations, sand spray as though the vehicle had taken off quickly. From the direction of the sand spray, the vehicle had headed to where their base camp was currently set up in the parking area. Julia informed them that her measurement of the track width indicated that the vehicle was an off-road vehicle rather than a Jeep or a truck. The track width closely matched those of the two of the four RZRs she'd inspected the first search day.

The inspector asked Ricardo to take more photos, and when finished with that task, to take their police truck over to the location where the vehicle had stopped. He also requested Ricardo make note of the GPS coordinates and the distance from that spot to the one Julia had noted where Simon's GPS coordinates placed them this morning.

Chapter 10—March 10, 2018, San Amaro

Corporal Luis Flores had struck gold. He couldn't wait to tell Sergeant Garcia. He was sure she would be impressed. Today was Tuesday, the same day of the week Ted Blair's neighbor said she'd heard a vehicle that could have been the missing RZR being driven out of Campo Cristal at four in the morning.

After questioning all the local truck drivers he could find and learning nothing, Luis had gotten up at three thirty this morning. He had set up a police cruiser out on the highway to see what, if any, vehicles were going past the entrance to Campo Cristal around four. By four twenty when he hadn't seen a single vehicle on the road, he was beginning to think he was wasting his time. Then he saw headlights coming from town, heading north, toward the entrance to Campo Cristal. He was parked on the southbound side of the highway, as he'd expected a delivery truck to be coming from Mexicali. He quickly crossed the sandy verge separating the two sides of the roadway in time to put on his flashers and flag down the oncoming truck. It turned out to be someone he knew.

During the day, Moises Torrence delivered water to homes out in the campos, as each home had its own water cistern. City water from San Amaro didn't extend to these communities, so cisterns were the solution. He also had a contract to deliver water to the road-maintenance-machinery lot three miles north of where they were. The maintenance lot had several holding tanks their road crews used to fill the road watering trucks with which they wet the dirt roads before grading them. It was to this destination Moises was heading in the early-morning dark.

Luis was rewarded for his initiative when he learned, as he'd hoped, that Moises made this same run early every Tuesday. When asked about the previous Tuesday and whether Moises had seen any other vehicles on the road, Moises described seeing a desert rig driving in the ditch just south of Campo Cristal heading toward town. The ditches beside the highway all had well-used tracks for off-road vehicles. RZRs, ATVs, and the occasional souped-up golf cart could frequently be seen traveling on these tracks between the gringo campos and town.

Moises was not able to provide much of a description of the driver of the desert vehicle because it was still dark, but he did confirm it was a blond gringo in the open-air desert rig. He remembered his high beams catching the guy's curly yellow hair for a split second as they passed each other.

No other vehicles passed them on either side of the highway during the time Moises and Luis were talking. It reminded Luis to ask Moises if he saw other vehicles on the road on his early-morning Tuesday runs to the maintenance lot. He confirmed what Luis suspected. Normally, Moises had the road to himself. That was why the RZR in the ditch was such a surprise. "Only a crazy gringo would be out driving in the ditch in the dark at that time of the morning," Moises said.

Luis continued to ask Moises questions about what he had seen, and in the end, Moises said cautiously, "I can't be certain, because the road there has a slight dip in it, but it might have turned into the little road just across from the Pemex station about a mile south of here, into the Punto de Cono Ejido. I think I saw headlights swing to the left there, but then I didn't see them again. I was too far away and, like I said, there is a dip there. Anyway, that was the last time I saw it."

In Mexico, each town has one or more ejidos, an ancient form of land use providing the granting of access to government land to poor Mexicans for communal farming. In the late twentieth century, ejido land was made available to be privatized and, therefore, owned by individuals who wished to buy the ejido land they occupied. Punto de Cono and the other ejidos around San Amaro contain land of both sorts: lots that are privately owned, though only by Mexicans, and areas where individuals have built homes or hovels but have no ownership and who still share responsibility for any farming done on the communal land.

By the time Luis returned the cruiser to the station, Julia, Ricardo, and the inspector had already left for another day in the desert looking for the missing gringa. He typed up his report about Moises seeing a desert rig at the approximate time Ted Blair's may have been taken from Campo Cristal. As she had requested, he put a copy in Sergeant Garcia's in-box and emailed her a copy, as well.

He had traffic-patrol assignment today with Corporal Sanchez, so he kept his early-morning cruiser signed out for the remainder of his shift. Early Semana Santa visitors were already arriving in San Amaro to get the prime camping spots on the beach next to the Malecon.

Luis was feeling very proud of himself. Today was a good day to be a cop in San Amaro.

Chapter 11—March 11–14, 2018, Desert Southwest of San Amaro

Over the next four days, the police and local gringos were joined in their search by members of the military, marines, and a fellow from San Diego with two tracking dogs. He had come to San Amaro after reading an article in the San Diego Tribune about the missing woman. The military and marines had searched all three farms in the area surrounding the canyon, and the others had scoured acres of land surrounding the site where Stella Monroe was last seen by her friends.

No leads were found.

Inspector Martinez spoke with Ricardo and Julia to plan their next steps. "With this woman now missing for six days, we know from experience, the likelihood of finding her alive is very low. Also, with the missing dog added into the situation, I have a strong feeling there is something else going on, and it is possible that one or more of the other five hikers is directly or indirectly involved with it." As he was finishing his sentence, the satellite phone on his belt buzzed. He answered the call and listened for several seconds before he grunted, thanked the caller, and returned the phone to its holster on his belt.

"It seems we now have evidence that Stella Monroe may have been targeted in some way. Forensics has determined that while the end of the leather strap from her walking stick was partially torn and frayed, it had a series of equally spaced small round holes about the thickness of a sewing needle, weakening the leather at the place where it tore. They were all but obscured by the fraying of the remaining leather. We need to determine who had the opportunity to do this damage, how, and for what purpose. Later today, they will be treating the leather with ninhydrin to see if they can raise any prints on it. On the surface, it looks like someone didn't want her to complete the hike. But how could anyone have known she would leave the group and return alone when the strap failed? This is a very confusing situation, and this information seems to make it even more so," the inspector mused.

"We need to complete in-depth background checks on all of the six hikers. This needs to be a priority. I want to interview the five of them individually the day after tomorrow. Ricardo, you did a good job getting the quick version. I want you to oversee two officers on this and have them do a complete deep dive into the background of all these people to find out as much about them as we can. Julia, you will need to assist them with speaking to American officials on their background prior to their arrival here and to talk to their neighbors again. They may open up to you with your fluent English. We have less than forty-eight hours to finish some serious information gathering and analysis. Tomorrow, you two will stay at the station and find out everything you can. It will be a busy day.

"Finally, we need to make sure there are posters around town in English and Spanish asking for anyone who was in the desert the day Stella went missing to come forward to assist in finding her. Julia, please take care of that and be sure to post something to that effect on Facebook, too."

As he concluded, he instructed Julia and Ricardo to contact the station on the truck radio and making assignments for the tasks the three of them had outlined. With that done, they headed to the command tent to face the growing number of gringos and locals who had turned out to help in today's search.

It was another hot and frustrating day. By late afternoon, they still had nothing new in the way of clues.

A new tent had been added to the command post of the search area. It afforded some privacy from interested onlookers and was set far enough away from the main tent to keep conversations private. Julia and the inspector had used it to meet briefly with four of the five remaining hikers, in turn. Simon was next up and given similar instructions to the others.

"Mr. Wakefield, we would like to have you come into the station the day after tomorrow, in the afternoon, at three o'clock. We are setting appointments with each of you who were on the hike with Stella to go over everything that you can remember from that day again," Julia said in a neutral, matter-of-fact voice.

"I have told you everything I know about that day. I need to be out here looking for her, not in San Amaro talking to you. Does this mean you're calling off the search? Are you so inept that you are giving up already? I can't believe this!" His voice escalated with each sentence, ending with him red faced and almost shouting. A couple of the search teams getting water from the main tent glanced over at the interview tent with interest.

"No, Mr. Wakefield, the search is not being called off. And I understand you feel your efforts are better spent here. However, we need you to give us your time Thursday to aid the search. This is normal procedure in a case like this. We find that after a few days, memories can become clearer, details remembered. This will help better direct our efforts going forward." Julia's voice maintained its calm tone, while she shifted her words to be more commanding.

"How many of *these cases* have you actually had?" Simon asked emphatically, not yet placated.

"Many more than you likely realize, sir. People go missing in the desert more often than most people are aware. We do have a protocol for desert searches, and we are following it. Your additional input at this point is necessary. We can have up to a dozen missing persons each year in this region of the Baja. Most are found in a few hours, but when that isn't the case, we follow the protocol, as we are now.

"I have two more question for you this afternoon, sir. When you made the missing person report, you described the location from which your wife went missing, but later that evening, you provided the precise GPS coordinates for the location. Why didn't you give the police those coordinates, Mr. Wakefield?"

"I didn't know the coordinates when I made the report. Rick has a GPS system in his rig, and he or maybe Rob put the specific coordinates in a text to me sometime after I left the station," Simon answered in a huff.

"Okay," Julia responded. "Also, on the first day of the search, you told the searchers your wife has a heart problem for which she takes pills. You never mentioned that in your initial missing person report nor when the inspector spoke with you on the phone that evening. Why is that?"

"I didn't remember the pills until I was getting ready to go to bed. I opened the medicine cabinet and saw them. So, I mentioned it the next day. I'm not hiding things from you. You don't seem to realize I was in shock," he answered belligerently.

"I see. Thank you. We will see you Thursday afternoon in San Amaro." Julia stood while delivering that last sentence, hoping to cut off any further questions or bluster from Simon. "Gather any questions you might have for us, and we will address them the day after tomorrow. It's going to be getting dark before we get back to San Amaro, even if everyone leaves right now, and we don't want any more missing persons. We will see you Thursday." She finished firmly and moved forward as though to escort Simon out.

Simon looked as if he might have a bit more of a rant for Julia and the inspector. He opened his mouth, but then closed it again. Finally, with a look of frustration, he turned on his heels and left. Julia had the feeling that if there had been a hard door on the tent, he would have slammed it as he went.

As they drove back to San Amaro, Julia looked back toward the area of their search. The late-afternoon sun was slowly creeping behind the nearby mountains. The craggy faces of the mountainsides were losing their features, becoming gold-topped silhouettes. It would be pitch black in about an hour. Again, as it had so many times in the past week, her thoughts were of a woman in her seventies and her dog possibly being lost out there in the cold desert night that was beginning to fall.

Where was she? Where was her dog? What had happened to them? Julia's past experience with missing persons told her that finding the woman alive at this point would be a miracle. That they hadn't found any trace by now was also highly suspect. Yes, it was definitely time to reinterview Stella's hiking companions. Something wasn't right.

Chapter 12—March 15, 2018, San Amaro

Yesterday had been a challenging day in the investigation of the missing hiker, Stella Monroe. Julia, Ricardo, and Inspector Martinez had spent the day completing research and then reviewing all the information Ricardo's small task force had pulled together on the six hikers. Julia was aware of some of the background from the phone conversations she had initiated with several of the hikers' neighbors and organizations, including police departments in Phoenix, Surprise, Glendale, and El Centro, California.

What they were looking for, in addition to anything directly relevant to the missing woman, were angles they could use to rattle each of the remaining hikers, to get them out of their comfort zones and help create an environment in which they were more likely to share something about what might really have happened to Stella Monroe. The police no longer believed it was a simple case of a person missing in the desert, but they were still at a loss as to how else to label it.

They had taken over the upstairs meeting room. Whiteboards were covered with notes, pictures, pages from reports, topographical maps, diagrams, and timelines. They theorized several potential scenarios; some they had already brainstormed, and several new ones were based on the new information before them. By the end of the day, they were prepared for the interviews scheduled with the five hikers.

As it was going to be a long day with the interviews, Julia got into the station an hour earlier than her normal seven thirty. It actually seemed late, since she, Ricardo, and the inspector had been leaving the station for the desert by five each morning at the latest for the past week. She was hoping to meet up with Luis before her day got overtaken by the interviews of the five hikers. She had read with great interest, and more than a little pride in him, Luis's report about the trucker seeing an off-road vehicle driving in the ditch off the highway not far from Campo Cristal the night Ted Blair's rig had gone missing.

Today, there was an unpleasant odor in the officers' desk area. Unfortunately, that wasn't unusual. Julia suspected a forgotten lunch in the desk drawer of a fellow officer. It did smell a bit like rotting fish. Since half the men in San Amaro fished, it was a common filling for tacos and other lunch-bag meals. Julia tried not to breathe through her nose.

She had finished taking care of her email in-box by the time Luis sauntered up to his desk. He had said good morning to several of the male officers on his walk through the open area, so she was already aware of his arrival by the time he dropped into the chair opposite her. "*Buenos días*, Luis," she said in a friendly tone. "Excellent work in finding a trucker who was out in the early hours the morning Ted Blair's RZR went missing. What are you planning for the next steps in this investigation?" she asked, preferring to give him a chance to think about the next logical thing to do rather than just telling him what to do.

"I thought I'd go out to the place where Moises, the truck driver, thought he might have seen the headlights turn left at the dip a kilometer or so south of Campo Cristal. I know there are a few trailers and a couple of houses nestled in the ejido among the hills between the highway and the sea. Maybe someone there will have seen something," Luis answered, happy and surprised that she hadn't just commanded him to do what she thought the next steps should be.

"Perfect. You are doing a good job on this investigation, Luis. Thank you for stepping up while I'm so busy on the missing woman case," Julia said, looking directly into his face as she praised him. "Do you still have the English questions I wrote out for you in case you run into Americans who don't speak Spanish back there?" she asked. "I'm pretty sure all the places back there are locals, but there may be gringos camped out there, too."

"*Sí, Jefa*, I do. I will set appointments with anybody I find who has more information." Luis looked very pleased with himself. Again, the thought crossed his mind that Sergeant Julia Garcia was likely a better police officer than many of the men in the department gave her credit for. He knew she was giving him an opportunity that many other sergeants he'd worked with wouldn't give a young corporal.

The "yes, boss," *sí jefa*, comment wasn't lost on Julia. Her lips twitched just slightly as she resisted the urge to chuckle, instead giving Luis a nod and a small smile before turning back to her computer.

A new notification had popped up on her screen. Now that she had a chance to look at it, she saw that the first of the five friends of Stella Monroe had arrived. She gathered her notebook, pens, and a coffee and headed to the interview room she had booked for the day. She checked the recording equipment and then proceeded to the reception area.

Reception area might have been overstating it. The entry area of the station, the ten-by-ten-foot room between the main door and the desk sergeant's desk, had dirty walls with cork boards haphazardly hung to the left and right of the door. There were half a dozen chairs, no two the same, lined up against the left wall. Molly and Jaime Lopez occupied the two closest to the door. Julia wondered if that was a subconscious effort to be ready to flee if presented the option.

Mrs. Lopez, Molly, was scheduled for an eight thirty interview. Her husband's appointment was scheduled for nine thirty. "Good morning, Mr. and Mrs. Lopez. Thank you for coming in this morning. Mrs. Lopez, I will show you to an interview room in just a moment. Mr. Lopez, are you planning to stay here until your appointment time, or are you coming back?" Julia asked. "If you plan to stay, I will find a more comfortable place for you to wait."

"No, I was just waiting for Molly to go in for her appointment. I'll be back for my appointment," he said, standing and giving his wife a quick kiss on the cheek, whispering something to her as he did.

Chapter 13—March 15, 2018, San Amaro

Molly Lopez was about five foot four and at least fifty pounds overweight. Her gray, flyaway hair was cut in a pageboy bob, which didn't quite suit her. She was wearing a frilly turquoise blouse, which accentuated her size, and a cream-and-turquoise skirt. Her sandals appeared to have been home-blinged with turquoise-colored plastic flowers. Around her neck was a chunky necklace of what appeared to be real turquoise and silver. It was a beautiful necklace, Julia noticed, though it was almost lost amid the billowing frills of her unflattering blouse. Julia put her opinions away.

"Mrs. Lopez, please follow me," Julia said once Jaime was out the door. "We will begin by getting your fingerprints. Just standard procedure." Once that process was done using ink and a ten-card form, Julia provided her with an alcohol wipe to clean her hands and led Molly to the interview room. As Julia got Molly seated and arranged a coffee for her, Molly surveyed the room. It was not exactly what Molly had expected. Her sole source of knowledge of police interview rooms came from *Law & Order* and a British police show with a woman detective she had watched years ago, but at this moment could not name.

It was a simple rectangular box with a door, three plastic chairs, a table on which sat a tape recorder, and three plastic bottles of water. There was no large two-way mirror on one wall, as there was in every crime show she'd ever seen on TV. In fact, there wasn't anything else in the room nor on the walls she noticed, unless one considered the grimy marks adorning them and the hunks of missing plaster over the cinderblock walls.

Molly's appraisal of the room missed the small cameras in the top corners of the room, which were projecting onto a monitor on Sergeant Ricardo Hernandez's desk, where he sat with earbuds connected to the interview-room audio recorder. He was ready to watch the interview. He had a large thermos of strong black coffee to keep him alert. He smiled warmly to himself as he watched Julia get the frumpy woman settled.

In preparation for today, Ricardo had gotten some new software from the state police headquarters in Mexicali that would do an almost-live English-to-Spanish translation of the interview audio. He and Julia had played around with it the previous evening and found that it worked reasonably well, with a one- or two-second audio delay and mistranslating only a few words. It would allow him to watch the live video and hear the translated audio with just a slight lag. It was a vast improvement over the process Julia had used with the original meeting when the gringos made the missing person report.

Molly had just decided the grayish walls were originally either a pale green or cream colored when the inspector she'd seen each day at the search site entered the room. He greeted her by name and took a chair beside Julia and across from Molly herself. The tape recorder was turned on, and they said their names as the interview began.

Inspector Martinez took the lead, speaking slowly in less-than-perfect English. He informed Molly that Sergeant Garcia would be asking her a series of questions at his request and translating Molly's responses in case he wasn't clear on what she had said. Molly indicated she understood, and the inspector and the sergeant spoke briefly in rapid Spanish.

Julia began the formal questioning. "Mrs. Lopez, please tell us, in as much detail as possible, the events of the day Stella Monroe went missing."

Molly told them of her and Jaime's preparation for the drive to the rock paintings, the provisions they loaded into their vehicle, how they arrived at Stella and Simon's house at six thirty in the morning, and that Rick and his new boyfriend had arrived a few minutes later. She remembered that Simon seemed surprised that Stella was taking Juba, her dog, and that she had asked Stella if her foot was up for the walk. Stella had previously told her she'd likely broken her third and fourth toes when she had dropped a frozen beef roast on her bare left foot a few days before. Stella had replied that she thought she'd be fine. Molly also described the drive to the mountains, where they parked, and how they walked up the arroyo.

After each few sentences, Julia and Inspector Martinez spoke quickly in Spanish. There were nods and pondering looks between them before Julia would ask for clarification of a specific point or ask Molly to continue.

"Do you remember which of you was first back to the parking area on your return from your hike?" Julia asked, seeking to clarify a point of her description of events.

"Um, no, not really. Jaime and I were walking more slowly than the others. So, I don't know if they arrived together or if one of them got there before the others," Molly answered.

"Did you take any photographs on the day of your hike? If you did, we would like to review them," Julia asked when Molly was finished recounting her actions the day Stella went missing. Molly indicated she had not, and Julia moved on.

"Tell me about Stella and Simon's relationship. When and how did they meet? Are they happy?" Julia asked.

Molly paused before asking her own question. "What does that have to do with her going missing in the desert?"

"Please answer our questions, Mrs. Lopez. We need to understand everything we can about your friend in order to find her," Inspector Martinez said in his slow English.

Julia noted Molly's chin jutted forward just slightly before she answered. Mrs. Lopez was getting defensive, Julia realized. "It was their first anniversary. They are in love, and they are very happy together," Molly said, beginning. She told the officers about meeting Simon in the Crown and Anchor, and playing a trivia game there with Stella, and her husband in December of the previous year. She walked them through the brief courtship between Stella and Simon. She described their small wedding ceremony on the beach, which was attended by about twenty people, mostly friends of Stella's living in San Amaro.

"When did Mr. Gurenburg become part of your group of friends, Mrs. Lopez?" Julia asked almost conversationally.

"Hmm, not that long ago, really. I think he and Rick met five weeks ago, maybe six. They became fast friends. I'd seen him a couple of times before the hike when we all had dinner, once at Rick's place and once at La Playa, Jaime's restaurant. Well, actually his daughter's now," Molly answered after a moment's thought. "Rob seems to fit in well with the rest of us, even though he's a lot younger than we are. He seems nice. He even gave Stella one of his hiking sticks when she headed back to the vehicles, oh, and one of his special drinks—some electrolyte thing he makes."

"He gave her a special drink?" Julia asked.

"Yeah, he had one for each of us. He is into healthy stuff, and he made these drinks that are supposed to keep you from getting dehydrated or something like that. It tasted okay, a bit like weak Gatorade," Molly replied. "I also gave her a sandwich, in case she got hungry while she was waiting for us."

"That was nice of you," Julia acknowledged and then moved to a new line of questioning. "Did Mr. Wakefield, Simon, know Mr. Gurenburg prior to Mr. Gurenburg becoming friends with Mr. Worton?" Again, Julia spoke conversationally.

Molly paused, considering the question. "I don't know!" Molly said somewhat surprised by the questions. "No, I don't think so, but I never thought about it." She paused, thinking, her forehead creased, and her eyes blinked rhythmically. Julia thought it made the woman look a little like a turquoise frog. "Simon and Rob seem to get on well whenever we are together, but like I said, I really don't think they knew each other before."

Julia smiled and nodded to Molly, acknowledging her answer.

"Does Stella have any enemies here in San Amaro, or anyone who might wish her harm?" Julia continued the questions after another brief side conversation with Martinez.

This time Molly leaned forward, her face getting red. "What do you mean enemies? Why are you asking these kinds of questions? Do you really think someone has done her harm?"

Julia looked to her boss to see if she should address these questions. They were typical in interviews. Almost always, the interviewee got frightened or angry at the type of questions being asked. Normally, the police didn't even acknowledge those concerns, simply directed the person to answer the questions.

Occasionally, however, it could move things along more quickly by seeming to take the interviewee into their confidence by recognizing their questions and providing at least some answers. Julia and her boss had talked about the five people and thought Molly might be the best one to try this with. This was why she was their first interviewee. Martinez inclined his head slightly to Julia indicating his go-ahead. Molly was a regular poster on Facebook, and by the number of comments her posts received, she had a lot of "friends" online. She could, no doubt, be the police's unwitting accomplice in stirring up the community.

"Mrs. Lopez, is it possible that Stella might have been met back at the vehicles by someone?" Julia left it vague whether that someone was friend or foe. "And that she was never lost out there? It is important for us to consider all possibilities. Did she have any disgruntled old boyfriends? Or perhaps a new boyfriend on the side?" Julia watched the round, fleshy face of the woman in front of her and leaned back to see where this might lead them.

Molly appeared to consider these questions for a few moments before responding. Then she leaned forward in a conspiratorial posture, cocking her head slightly to the right and began. "Well, now that you mention it, she did date a guy not long before she met Simon. His name is Tony Ranelli. He is not a nice guy. He has a temper and wasn't shy about reacting physically when Stella did or said something he didn't like or agree with. He is not as bad when he's sober, but he isn't sober much and usually not at all after about one in the afternoon.

"They had a blowup one night at the Crown and Anchor, and Stella told him she never wanted to see him again. He got really pissed and said something like, 'You'd better hope I never see *you* again, bitch.' He'd grabbed her arm that night about something—I can't remember what it was—but it seemed really trivial at the time. He left bruises. That was the last time I ever saw them together, and Stella would have told me if they'd had another altercation." Molly finished and leaned back in her chair to catch her breath. Her eyes were wide and full of wonder as she considered this new angle in Stella's disappearance.

Julia remained silent. There was that name again. She realized she hadn't checked in with Ana Maria about speaking with Mr. Ranelli. Neither she nor the inspector moved, both hoping Molly would continue. And, after several moments, she did.

"You really think someone, like Tony, might have come out to the desert that day to accost her? How would they know she was there? Or that she would be separated from the rest of us?" Molly asked, perplexed.

Indeed, thought Julia, *how would anyone have known Stella would be separated from the group?* She, Ricardo, and the inspector had considered these very questions at length last night as they discussed the interviews of the five remaining hikers. They had some ideas, but nothing yet that fit together with the known facts. Julia remembered Tony Ranelli as one of the hecklers on Facebook who responded to both Molly's and Simon's initial posts with vivid criticisms of the other hikers who left Stella on her own. She couldn't wait to talk with Ana Maria about him.

The inspector instructed Julia how to reply to Mrs. Lopez's questions. It was important that Molly get just enough information to make her useful to them. They were almost certain she would at a minimum tell the other four and, they hoped, would post something about her interview on Facebook. They hoped to get people thinking beyond just a missing person and, if someone had done her harm, put the person on alert. That was when guilty people started making mistakes.

"If you could give us more details about Mr. Ranelli, and how we might find him, we'll speak with him," Julia requested and then took down the information Molly was able to provide about where he lived.

Julia now very carefully provided Mrs. Lopez with the information the inspector had decided he wanted to covertly start circulating. "Mrs. Lopez, we find it very odd that we haven't found a single trace of either Stella or her dog. It is causing us to consider alternatives as to what may have happened. If Stella were going to take someone into her confidence to help her disappear, who would she turn to?"

Molly's large blue-green eyes opened even wider as she absorbed this last question. "Oh my

God," she said almost to herself. Then louder, she went on, "Apart from Rick or me, I can't think of anyone here she'd confide in. Really. She knows lots of people, but most are more casual friends. Not really close like she is with me or Rick." She bit her lip and again took on her frog-like countenance as she gave the question more thought. "She doesn't have any family that I know of. She was adopted and an only child and wasn't really close to her adoptive parents. She didn't know anything about her birth parents. Hmmm . . . but I know she has a good friend from years ago in Wisconsin. That's where she grew up—Pippa something or other. I think she lives in Maine or someplace like that on the East Coast now, but I'm not sure. It's someplace cold. I can't think of anyone else, though. And besides, she didn't want to disappear! She and Simon are like lovebirds. Happy."

Julia got Molly to create a list of the people who were friends of Stella's in San Amaro. The list included people who had come to Stella and Simon's wedding and a couple who occasionally joined them for trivia night at the Crown and Anchor. Molly had a few phone numbers and a few email addresses to add to the list of names. Julia recognized a few of the names from her social media research as people who had commented on Molly's and/or Simon's posts about Stella's disappearance. Julia would have Corporal Verde see if she could locate these people so Julia could question them.

Julia terminated the interview a few minutes later, and escorted Molly to the door of the station. It was ten minutes before her husband was scheduled to come in for his interview—plenty of time for Molly to share her newfound knowledge with him.

Chapter 14—March 15, 2018, San Amaro

Jaime Lopez entered the station at precisely nine thirty. Julia was waiting in the reception area and was pleased to see that he and his wife had been sitting in their Jeep in the parking lot before his entering the building. Julia was sure Molly had shared the police's speculations with him.

Jaime was Hispanic, about five seven. Apart from a slight paunch, he was slim and wiry. Previous days in the desert, Julia had noticed he sported a red ball cap with a bulldog logo and the word Mack embroidered on it. Today, the ball cap was navy blue with Freightliner Run Smart emblazoned across the front. His thinning gray hair curled up around the sides where it was wet with sweat. Small, lively, penetrating black eyes, a prominent nose, and high cheekbones gave him a handsome face. Unfortunately, his weak, slightly receding chin detracted from that, leaving the impression leaning more to gentle uncle than matinee idol.

Once his fingerprints had been taken, Julia and Inspector Martinez followed the same protocol with Jaime they had used with his wife to start the interview. Julia started by asking if they could review all the photos he'd taken the day of the hike. With Jaime's approval, they had flagged eight they thought might be useful to the investigation and Julia emailed them to Ricardo, deleting the sent email from Jaime's phone when she was finished.

From there, the inspector took the lead, speaking in Spanish. After getting Jaime's version of the day Stella went missing, which matched closely with Molly's version, he moved on to the heart of the interview. "I think you are originally from San Amaro, Señor Lopez, yes?" Martinez wanted this man to know they had done their research and knew more about him than he had previously told them. They knew that he had come back to San Amaro twelve years ago. "And you started a popular restaurant here, which you ran until your daughter took over, when you *retired* eight years ago," he said, stressing the misleading phrase Jaime had used during a conversation with the inspector at the search site a few days before.

It had the desired effect. Jaime's lips tightened, and his eyes narrowed. "Yes," he said slowly, as though trying to understand why this would be relevant. Julia noticed a certain caginess in the man across the table from them. He was obviously not telling them something. She would have to pay close attention to his answers and his body language.

"And how did you first meet Stella Monroe?" asked the inspector.

"I met her through my wife. I met Molly on the annual *Caminata Contra El Cancer*." The annual cancer fundraising walk from the north edge of town down to the Malecon was an event in which both gringos and locals joined for a common cause. "My mother had just died of stomach cancer, so I did the walk that year. Molly volunteers at the Cancer Center to help with the walk every year, and I met her when I signed up to participate. At the end of the walk, Molly and I sat at the same table for the fiesta. You know, big tables, lots of people sitting together. Stella was there, and Molly introduced us. It was maybe four months after I retired from the restaurant, about eight years ago. Molly and Stella have been friends for a long time. Best friends. I like her, too."

"Did you notice anything different or odd with Stella the day of the hike? Or in the days leading up to it? Was she acting differently?" Inspector Martinez asked as he continued.

"No, I don't think so. She may have been a little quieter than usual in the morning while we were hiking. But that could have been because her foot was hurting," Jaime answered.

"Are you friends with Stella's husband, Simon?" This question came from Julia, and Jaime swiveled his head around to look directly at her, his black eyes slightly hooded. Julia was curious to see how he would react to being questioned by a woman.

Jaime answered with only a slight hesitation. "Sí. He's okay. We play golf sometimes. Mostly, I know him because Stella and Molly are such close friends."

Julia and the inspector waited to see if he would add anything else and were in luck as Jaime went on after a few seconds of silence. "At first, I thought *tenia el corazón de alcachofa*." Julia fought to keep her lips from twitching at the use of the outdated expression. Literally, Jaime had said he thought Simon had the heart of an artichoke. It was a term her *abuela,* grandmother, sometimes still used; *womanizer* was the meaning. "He came on to Stella right away, the first night we met him. But over time I realized he was an okay guy."

"I understand they got married shortly after they met. What did you think about that?" Julia asked.

"Stella was happy, so why not, eh? It doesn't matter to me." It seemed like a nonanswer to Julia, but the inspector seemed satisfied and carried on with other questions.

"Did Stella have any enemies that you were aware of?"

"No. People like her, mucho." Jaime's lack of surprise at this question confirmed to Julia that Molly had indeed told her husband that the police were starting to think this situation was not a simple missing person case. He also seemed to relax somewhat, which interested Julia.

"Did you know Simon Wakefield or Rob Gurenburg before they came to San Amaro?" Jaime moved his gaze to Martinez.

This question had startled Jaime. He frowned and scrunched up his eyes as though trying to see something obscure in the distance. "No. I met them both here," he stated emphatically, his head shaking to accentuate his answer. Julia believed him, but she'd be interested in the impression Ricardo and the inspector got from his overtly physical reaction to the question.

"Señor Lopez, what do you think happened to Stella the day of the hike?" The inspector paused for almost a minute between Jaime's last answer and this question. It had the effect of making this question stand alone from all the previous ones.

Sensing the question's gravitas, Jaime leaned back and appeared to be giving it some deep thought. His gaze shifted from the police officers to the wall behind them. Julia thought he was seeing events play out in his mind. After what seemed like a long time, he brought his gaze back to the table and his mind to the present moment. "Honestly, I don't know. I've thought about it, but nothing surrounding her disappearance makes sense. I was surprised when Stella left the group to return alone to the vehicles. It was not a wise thing to do in the desert, and Stella would know that. But she was adamant, absolutely adamant. That also surprised me. She is stubborn, but not stupid. Then when we got back and she and the dog were both gone, I had a foreboding feeling come over me. I don't know what happened, but I don't think she is missing out there." He sighed deeply, shaking his head. "I think something bad happened. How, why, what? I have no idea."

Yes, thought Julia, *that about summed it up.*

Chapter 15—March 15, 2018, San Amaro

The interview with Rick Worton began with the same routine as Molly's and Jaime's. With his fingerprints taken, Julia found only a few pictures on his phone. None seemed useful. She then walked him through his version of the events the day of the hike. She and the inspector heard much the same story the five had told when they filed the missing person report that first day. Rick's morning routine of preparing for the day's trip into the desert was similar to the one Molly told. He had a checklist of all the items he needed for a desert run, and he verified they were all onboard his RZR.

"Rob Gurenburg, a new friend of mine, came to the house to help me prep for the trip about an hour before we headed over to Stella and Simon's. He'd never been on a desert run before and was interested in all the things you need to take to be prepared for whatever the desert can throw at you. He also had a few extra medical supplies he wanted to take including some electrolyte drinks he makes himself. He was an EMT and a medic, and he still takes an active interest in people's well-being," Rick said.

Julia realized she had been paying less attention to his words and was more focused on his body and his body language. She had heard the term *bear* before in relation to gay men of a certain physical type. At a very hairy five foot ten, she wondered about the shaved head. His beard was thick and full, though neatly trimmed. Large amounts of black chest hair curled at the neck of his blindingly white T-shirt. Said T-shirt clung tightly to his protruding stomach, though he didn't look slovenly. It was an interesting look, and she could see a bearlike resemblance.

His body language was what really fascinated her, however. He seemed extremely relaxed, leaning back in his chair, his long legs carelessly sticking out in front of him, his shoulders down and loose. There didn't appear to be tension in the man anywhere. He seemed completely at ease, as if he were having a beer with friends. Very unusual. Most people when being questioned at a police station were naturally tense. It was an uncomfortable experience. This caused her to be very curious about this man, and she drew her attention back fully to what he was saying.

"Do you know why Mr. Gurenburg makes electrolytes? You can buy the premade and flavored ones anywhere in town," Julia questioned.

"He told me about this study he read from 2011 or 2012 about electrolyte balances in people being different. It varies by gender, weight, age, and physical fitness. So, he had formulated personalized drinks for each of us that were balanced to our specific needs. Mine was pretty tasty, and I really did feel more refreshed after I drank it," Rick answered easily.

"When and how did you meet Mr. Gurenburg?" she asked, getting a slight head nod from the inspector. He approved of this change in course for their questions.

"Six weeks ago, maybe you remember, there was a rally of motorcycle clubs from Baja, Sonora, and the southwest US here in San Amaro." Both Julia and the inspector acknowledged their familiarity with the event with a head nod, and Rick continued. "I really love motorcycles, so I was just walking along the Malecon admiring all the beautiful bikes.

"Back in the US and for a while once I moved here, I owned a Harley-Davidson, and I'd go annually to a place called Sturgis, in South Dakota, where thousands of bikers from all over North America get together for a few days. There was a guy from San Diego down here at the rally whom I'd met in Sturgis eight or nine years ago, and we got to talking. I recognized his bike more than him. It was painted with those fancy dressed Day of the Dead ladies. Katrinas, I think they're called. Beautiful artwork. Anyway, Rob stopped to look at this bike while I was standing there chatting. He asked the guy a couple of questions that showed he really knew motorcycles, and we all started talking. Then the three of us decided to go for a few beers, and Rob and I just hit it off. It was pretty obvious he's gay, too, and well, we just started hanging out," Rick said, finishing.

"On the hike, did you all get back to your vehicles together, Mr. Worton?" Julia asked, changing topic again.

"No, Rob and Simon were ahead of me for the last ten or fifteen minutes of the return hike. I guess they got back there together, but I couldn't see that far down the path," he said, rubbing his bald pate. "Oh no, wait, that's not right! I remember hearing Rob calling for Stella before Simon did. By a couple of minutes, maybe, possibly less. I was kind of lost in thought wondering what Jaime and Molly were discussing. They were fifty or sixty feet behind me.

Every once in a while, their voices got louder and carried to me."

"Could you hear what they were saying? Were they arguing?" Julia inquired.

Rick looked a little sheepish, as though he didn't want to squeal on his friends, but he answered. "Like I said, once in a while their voices carried to me, but most of the time I couldn't hear anything distinctly. Molly can be a bit emotional at times, and I got the impression she was angry about something Jaime was doing with or for someone in his extended family—one of his nephews is in and out of prison—and then later about something else. The only phrase that I heard clearly later was Molly saying, 'I see the way you look at her . . . ,' but I can't imagine Jaime cheating on Molly, so I don't know what that was about. And after that, Jaime said something that sounded like 'loco' or maybe 'poco.' But I didn't hear much more than that."

"Do you know the name of this family member who has been in jail?" the inspector asked.

Rick paused before answering, "No. I guess I don't. I only know he is Jaime's nephew. Jaime talks about his various family members here in San Amaro, but I don't think I've heard him mention names. I sometimes golf with Jaime, but we don't talk about much apart from the game. Other than that, I usually only see Jaime and Molly with Stella. He wouldn't talk about doing something with a criminal family member if Stella was around. She's a stickler for following rules and doesn't take kindly to lawbreakers."

Julia and the inspector exchanged a look at that answer. *Was Jaime on Stella's bad side?* Julia wondered and could see that Martinez's mind went to the same place. They wouldn't explore that with this witness, and so Julia moved on.

"Do you know if Mr. Gurenburg and Mr. Wakefield knew each other in the United States?" Julia asked.

"No. No, I don't think so. It didn't seem like they did, anyway. I was there when they met, at the golf course. It sure didn't seem like they knew each other," Rick answered, looking more curious than worried.

"How long have you known Stella Monroe?" Julia carried on with the more routine questions.

"I met her almost as soon as she moved here, so about nine years. At that time, she was renting a casita behind a house that belonged to an old boyfriend of mine from twenty years ago. He and I had stayed friends, and we used to get together a lot back then. I met Stella there. I met Molly then, too, because they have been friends forever, Stella and Molly, that is, and they moved down here at the same time. We became friends, and we just started hanging out. We've become really close in the last few years," Rick said, continuing in his laid-back manner.

Throughout the interview, Julia and Inspector Martinez shared ideas back and forth in Spanish. There were very few fluent Spanish-speaking gringos in San Amaro. Many Americans and Canadians made an effort to learn the language and could communicate at restaurants and grocery stores, but unless a Spanish speaker spoke very slowly to them and in only the present tense, gringos usually couldn't keep up with the conversation. It was obvious Rick did not understand Spanish, so Julia and the inspector were able to speak without worry of being understood. At prompting from Martinez, Julia moved on to a new topic.

"When Simon came here, how did things change with Stella?" Julia asked.

"Hmmm . . ." Rick put his hands behind his head and appeared to be thinking. "Well, beyond the obvious, that she fell in love with him and is really happy, I guess the biggest change is that I don't see her as much as I used to. I mean, I see the two of them fairly frequently, but I don't see just Stella anymore. The same thing happens when I have a boyfriend and a couple of times when she was dating other guys. It's natural, right? You get infatuated, you want to spend a lot of time with that person. Friends aren't quite as important for a while." Rick stopped, scratched his bald pate, and then asked, "Is that what you meant? It's kind of a weird question."

Martinez answered, "What you answer is good." He dipped his head toward Julia to continue.

She moved to the next question on their list. "Do you have a theory about what has happened to your friend, Mr. Worton?"

"What do you mean? She got lost in the desert. Do you know something else that you haven't told us?" Rick brought his arms down from behind his head and sat forward, finally looking more like an interviewee at a police station and less like a guy in the bar with friends. Julia's senses when on high alert. He looked alarmed.

Julia ignored his question and simply tipped her head to one side, indicating she was waiting for an answer.

"I have to keep believing we'll find her. She's my friend. I'd be devastated otherwise," he said quietly.

For such a big, burly man, he became, for that moment, almost soft and small. For the briefest second, the image of a different kind of bear flashed through Julia's mind, a cuddly teddy bear. She shifted the questioning again.

"Are you retired, Mr. Worton?" Julia asked, maintaining the friendly tone she had used throughout the interview to this point.

Rick looked tentative for the first time. "Not completely retired, no. I was a plumber and gas fitter in the States, and I still do a few jobs for folks down here." Rick spoke more cautiously now, his words more clipped. He was not sure if working in that field was licensed here in Mexico or if not paying income taxes was a problem.

"Mr. Worton, are you still making sex movies?" Julia's question punctured the air.

For a moment, the complete unexpectedness of the question stunned Rick into a stupor. Then slowly, he remembered. Of course, he should have known they'd dig this up. The woman police officer was asking another question before he had a chance to formulate a response. "Did Stella Monroe find out and threaten to unmask you, so to speak?"

When he was nineteen and on spring break in Puerto Peñasco, he'd been filmed for a few scenes of a gay porno a college friend of his was making. He'd had sex with a hot-looking Mexican guy about his age. At the time, he thought it was just a fun fling. He was so high he hardly noticed the movie camera, let alone anything else. It was only later that he found out the Mexican guy was, what was the politically correct term? Mentally challenged. They hadn't exactly had a conversation. How was he supposed to know? Apparently, in Mexican law, mentally challenged people are considered children with regard to sex. He believed he'd narrowly escaped being taken to Mexican jail as a child molester. Fortunately, he'd gotten back to the US before the Federalis caught up with him, if they had even been after him. He hadn't crossed the border from the US after that until he started thinking about retiring somewhere warm, many years later. By then, the statute of limitations had run out on his supposed crime.

"Stella? What? That was decades ago. Of course, she doesn't know anything about it. And no, I haven't done anything like that since I was nineteen. Besides, the other man was just that, a man. He was my age, and he seemed perfectly normal to me. No one was forcing him to do anything. He was a willing participant." Rick looked back and forth between the two police officers. *The statute of limitations* had *run out, hadn't it?*

Chapter 16—March 15, 2018, Four Miles North of San Amaro

The road Luis drove down was no more than a rutted track through the sand. Many roads in the gringo campos were sand, but they were maintained with watering and grading that gave them a smooth, hard-packed surface, until it rained. The awful condition of this road led Luis to believe there wouldn't be many, if any, gringos living back here in the hills where the Punto de Cono Ejido was located. He had taken the next turn off the highway from Campo Cristal, the one in the dip of the highway across from the Pemex gas station that the truck driver, Moises, had told him about.

After bumping along the sandy track for half a mile, first over an arroyo, then up into low, rolling, rocky hills, he came to a ridge and stopped to view the dwellings of the little community below. Ahead of him in a small valley were a handful of ancient, rusting travel trailers and as many hovels built from scrap wood, tin, and in one case, cardboard fridge boxes, cobbled together. Surprisingly, there was a power line that ran behind the encampment. Many illegal wires ran from a junction box on one power pole. These people had electricity, but they were stealing it from the power company.

Several dogs ranging from tiny to huge were roaming among the dwellings. They all were matted, dirty, skinny, and hungry. One with sagging teats had pups nearby. They were likely looking for garbage they could scavenge. These kinds of dogs were so common throughout Mexico that Luis hardly noticed them. His focus was fixed on a building behind one of the trailers. It looked like a large shed and was constructed from the siding of several RVs, judging by the logos showing on a couple of wall pieces. *There must be a solid framework holding the building up,* Luis thought. As he drove closer, it appeared more solid than any of the shacks.

By the time Luis parked and got out of his police cruiser, an old man stood in the doorway of a tiny trailer on wooden blocks, off to the right. Instead of a door, there was a filthy piece of canvas, perhaps from an old tent, hanging in shreds over the trailer's entrance. It was from this ragged canvas flap that the old fellow had emerged. His trousers were filthy and holey, but they were in much better shape than his undershirt. What material was left in the shirt was gray with grease spots, and it had more holes than material. Luis could smell him from ten meters away.

"*Buenos días, señor. Como esta usted*?" Good morning, sir. How are you? Luis greeted the old fellow formally, showing respect rather than using the informal *como estas tu*. "*Yo soy*, Corporal Flores."

He waited for the old man to introduce himself. They discussed the weather, that the shrimp this spring were especially good, and their hopes for a good Corvina catch soon. In Mexico, there is never a rush between people. It is more important to connect than to transact. Once Luis thought the connection had been made, he got around to asking the old man if he had seen a RZR driving through his community in the last couple of weeks. "Maybe in the middle of the night?" he said, encouraging him.

The man scratched an armpit and ran his tongue over the few teeth he still possessed. “You mean one of them fancy desert bugs that looks like a giant spider on wheels? Who here would be driving a RZR? Are you crazy, policeman? Nobody with money for something like that would be coming here,” he said, shaking his head, his voice raised for the last two sentences.

Luis realized the man hadn’t really answered his question and wondered why. Maybe he was covering for someone, or maybe was afraid of someone nearby. *That could account for the raised voice,* Luis thought. Concerned he wouldn’t get anything useful from him, Luis decided to change his approach. “Okay, then. Thanks. I’ll just look around a bit and then be on my way. *Buen día, amigo*,” he said, good day, friend, and began walking away from the old man and toward the shed.

The old man cleared his throat as if he were going to say something else, but instead spat into the sand and stepped back into his trailer, leaving Luis to carry on with his investigation. As he walked toward the shed, he wondered how many ears had been listening to his conversation with the old man. He had a sense that there were many, and the hairs on the back of his neck told him to be alert.

Possibly not all those ears were friendly.

Though the sheets of siding used in the construction of the building were old and faded, Luis realized the shed before him was of solid construction. Good-quality decking screws with washers had been used to secure the siding to the building’s frame. It was possible that it was a garage, Luis decided when he’d walked around its perimeter. There were two large doors on the far end of it that when opened would be big enough to admit a vehicle.

They were chained and padlocked. The building had no windows.

Luis tried to look between pieces of the metal siding, but there were no spaces that would allow him to get a glimpse of what lay inside. His neck hairs were very active through his circumnavigation of the shed. Locking doors of any sort was an uncommon practice in San Amaro among the locals. Whatever was inside, someone wanted it to remain hidden from view.

Luis walked back to the old man's trailer and stood outside calling to the fellow within. "Grandpa, whose shed is that over there? What's inside it?"

"Go away. Don't ask me these questions. I don't know anything. Whatever you're looking for, it isn't here. Just go away," the old man yelled out at Luis without coming to his doorway.

Luis took a couple of steps closer to the trailer and again the old man yelled at him. "Go away! I can't help you. Go away!" This time, his voice sounded as if he were leading. Luis realized he was getting a warning from the old man. Someone nearby, someone listening could do him harm if he said anything more to the police. Luis took the hint. "Okay, grandpa, adios."

He left, but he knew he'd be back.

Chapter 17—March 15, 2018, San Amaro

The three police officers on the Stella Monroe case had taken their lunch in the officers' meeting room upstairs once their first three interviews had concluded. They had turned it into their war room over the past few days for this case. They had a couple of hours before Rob Gurenburg would be coming in, and they added the information they had gleaned from the morning to their previous day's planning to better prepare for Rob, and then Simon's, interviews.

Ricardo had made some interesting observations about body language and physical responses that the camera angles had provided as he watched the interviews on his computer. Yet another layer of information added to their planning. By the time the meeting-room phone rang, and the desk sergeant informed them Rob Gurenburg was in the waiting area, they were ready for the two remaining interviews.

Rob Gurenburg was the youngest of the five hikers. Julia knew from the files they had created on each of the five that he was thirty-eight years old. He was six foot two, with a strong, lean body and very muscular shoulders and arms. Each day at the search site, he had worn skimpy tank tops that accentuated his physique. Today, however, he wore a patterned, short-sleeved shirt, primarily red, green, and a shade of blue that exactly matched his eyes and over knee-length khaki shorts with hiking sandals. His blond hair was very short on the sides but longer and curly on top. Julia thought he likely spent more on a haircut than she did on a week's groceries. Oddly, this gave her a bothersome feeling she couldn't put her finger on.

An officer with the fingerprint kit met them in the interview room and took Rob's prints. As he was leaving, the inspector spoke to him in rapid Spanish before dismissing him. The inspector then began the interview, turning on the recorder, having them say their names and then turning the questioning over to Julia. She walked Rob through his version of the events of the day Stella went missing, and his statement was very similar to the one Rick Worton had given them. He added some personal insights about the search the five had done upon returning to the vehicles and not finding Stella. Nothing was vastly different from all the other accounts, except that he didn't mention the electrolyte drinks he made for everyone.

Julia started the specific questioning there. "Mr. Gurenburg, other members of your hiking group mentioned you had brought special drinks for everyone. Can you please tell us about that?"

"Well, it's pretty simple, really. I am always looking for healthier alternatives to store-bought stuff. I like to work out a lot, and I was always buying Gatorade to help restore my electrolytes after workouts. I normally try to stay away from processed sugar and Gatorade is full of it, so I started looking for a better alternative. I came across a study done by a group of Swedish scientists on electrolyte balancing, and they determined that electrolyte balance was different for men and women, for young versus older people, and that body weight and a few other factors also came into play. So, I got interested in making the ideal post-workout drink for myself. A few people at my gym saw my homemade brew and were interested, so I tried making drinks for them that matched their specific needs. It really isn't that hard. It's something I do now on a regular basis for myself and, since we were going on this hike, I thought it would be nice to make one for each member of the group," he answered confidently.

Almost too confidently. Julia thought it sounded like a sales spiel. But, after a quick look at the inspector, who appeared uninterested in this aspect of the inquiry, she moved on to other questions.

"Did you all return to the parking area together when you finished your hike?" Julia asked the question the interview team had determined might be important to this mystery.

"No. Jaime and Molly were walking more slowly than the rest of us. I think Simon and I got there about the same time. Rick started lagging behind us at some point shortly before we got back to the vehicles. So, yeah, I think Simon and I were there about the same time. I was the first to call Stella's name, but when I didn't get a response, both of us started yelling our heads off." Rob's response was smoothly given. Julia was aware he was exceedingly slick with his responses.

"How did you come to be in San Amaro, Mr. Gurenburg?" Julia said, continuing.

"I came here a couple of times in my college years and liked it. I thought I'd check it out again." Rob's answer was concise but mostly a nonanswer.

"When did you arrive?" Julia asked.

"A few weeks ago, I guess." Another nonanswer.

After getting a nod from the inspector, she moved into a more direct approach. "You crossed the border at Los Algodones, December 29, last year, Mr. Gurenburg. Would you please tell us what you've been doing for the past thirteen weeks?"

At this, Rob sat up in his chair a bit taller and looked directly at Julia, and then at the inspector as he answered, almost casually . . . though Julia noted a slight tightness in his voice. "Wow, has it been that long? Time flies. First, I drove down to Puerto Peñasco on the mainland. It was not at all how I remembered it from when I was in college. So, I didn't stick around there for more than a few days. Then I checked out Mexicali and Ensenada for a week or maybe more. So, I must have arrived here in mid-January." His gaze had remained on the inspector for the duration of this answer. Now he shifted his eyes back to Julia, as if to say, "Next question!"

Julia made a note to check his credit card and bank statements reviewed for corroboration. Then she led him through questions about meeting Rick and the rest of the hiking group. His answers matched up with those given by the others, so, with a nod from the inspector, she moved on.

She referred to the list of questions the team had developed. When she looked up from her notebook, Rob's eyes were still on her. "Have you retired, Mr. Gurenburg? It's just that you are much younger than the average American who comes to Mexico for several months."

"I guess you could say I'm semiretired," Rob said, giving Julia the slightest of smiles.

"And from what career are you semiretired?" As usual, Julia's tone of voice and manner of speaking were neutral and calm.

"I'm a private investigator, licensed in Arizona and California. I do mostly domestic-relationship stuff," Rob answered easily.

"And what specifically does that entail?" she asked.

"I get hired by one spouse to catch the other spouse doing something they aren't supposed to be doing. I watch people's houses. I follow them, and I take pictures that depict transgressions." Rob's answer was glib.

Julia needed to rattle this man. He was far too comfortable. "Did you know anyone in the group before coming to San Amaro?"

"How could I have known any of them? They were here, and I was in the US. These questions aren't of any value in finding Stella. What are you getting at?" Rob was no longer leaning back against the chair.

Now he looked frustrated, and Julia feared he might shut down. She shifted to a different question. "Mr. Wakefield mentioned that you provided him with the specific GPS coordinates of where you had parked your vehicles before starting the hike. How did you know the coordinates?"

Rob made a point of looking at Inspector Martinez for several seconds as if to question the sanity of Julia and her questions before turning to Julia and saying with a shake of his head, "I don't know what you're talking about. I have no idea what the GPS coordinates for that place are. If Simon got them from anyone, it might have been Rick or maybe Jaime, but it certainly wasn't me. And all these questions are pointless. If you don't have any valid questions, I'm leaving," he blustered and stood up.

Inspector Martinez was on his feet in a flash. "Sit, Mr. Gurenburg. We tell you when we are finished. Not the other way."

In fact, there were very few questions left to ask this hiker and Julia made her way through them calmly, at a steady pace. For his part, Rob sat down and answered them with terse replies.

"What do you think has happened to Stella Monroe?" It was Julia's final planned question. All three police officers waited for his reply.

"How the hell would I know? I hardly know these people. I've met them all within the last six weeks," he said evenly. Then his demeanor relaxed, and he mused, "Maybe she got lost like Simon thinks, or maybe the sore toes were just an act, and she took off somewhere. Maybe she arranged with someone to meet her, and she's disappeared because she wanted to. I really have no idea." This time, instead of being on the offensive or slick in his response, the man seemed to be honestly trying to problem solve the mystery of Stella's disappearance. It was a surprising shift and it caught Julia off guard, sending warning bells ringing in her mind.

"Interesting theories, Mr. Gurenburg. Do you have any others?" Julia asked.

"Sorry, no. Isn't that your job?" Rob asked snidely, all traces of the previous thoughtfulness gone. It made Julia wonder if the previous ideas he'd shared were a smoke screen.

There was a knock on the interview room door. Inspector Martinez invited the knocker to enter. The same officer with whom he'd spoken at the beginning of the interview beckoned the inspector to the door, spoke briefly with him, and then left. The inspector returned to the table, said a couple of sentences to Julia, and leaned back in his chair.

"Mr. Gurenburg, our forensics analyst found your prints all over the strap from Stella's walking stick. Please tells us how that occurred," Julia said.

"Yeah, all right. I should have been honest with you when I found it," Rob said with a hangdog expression of a reprimanded child. "I picked it up out of the sand and held it up for Rick to see. Then I remembered what you'd said that morning, to not touch or move anything we found, so I put it back as close to where I found it before Rick whistled for you to come. Sorry."

Julia heard his words and observed his guilty expression. Still, she had the distinct feeling that it was an act. She didn't believe he was sorry. There was, however, no way to know if he had planted the strap or found it as he and Rick had said. She had no further questions in her notebook. So, she asked quickly in Spanish if the inspector had any additional questions. He gave a single shake of his head. Julia ended the interview with the final time for the tape recording and escorted Rob from the building.

Why had this man suddenly become helpful and then just as suddenly become spiteful again? Was deceit lurking behind his helpfulness, his admission of handling the strap? Julia wasn't sure what she had hoped the interview with this witness would produce, but she felt as if a game had just concluded, and she was not the winner. It was a frustrating feeling. She believed this man knew more than he was saying, but she had no idea what it might be.

Chapter 18—March 15, 2018, San Amaro

As Rob was being escorted to the door, Simon Wakefield was sitting in the other interview room at the San Amaro State Police Station. He had been taken there as soon as he arrived for his interview at three o'clock. The interview with Rob Gurenburg had intentionally run long, finishing at ten past three, to ensure that Rob and Simon didn't have an opportunity to talk before Simon's interview. The inspector had a niggling feeling there was some kind of relationship between the two men. Several of the pictures from the day of the hike showed the two men standing together, a few feet from the others. It made him wonder.

With Rob safely out of the building, Julia ushered Simon through the fingerprint process and then into the interview room, where the inspector waited. Ricardo was still sitting at his desk, ready to listen and watch as their most important interview of the day started. He had poured a fresh cup of coffee in anticipation.

"Good afternoon, Mr. Wakefield. Thank you for coming in today." Inspector Martinez began the interview as he had most of the others this day. After the preliminary formalities for the recording were completed, he again handed the interview over to Julia. They had developed a handful of specific questions for him, but Julia began with the mundane ones, getting him talking by providing his version of the day during which his wife had gone missing. As expected, he continued to tell the same story he provided during the missing-person-report interview with Julia a week ago.

To the questions about meeting Stella, the Lopezes, and Rick Worton, his responses matched up with those from the day's previous interviews. Simon had maintained a cool demeanor through the questions thus far, making sarcastic remarks about the waste of time this day was when his wife was out in the desert needing their help. Julia maintained her usual approach, not rising to the bait of his criticisms.

Simon's six-foot, lean frame was clothed in neatly pressed khaki slacks and a silver-gray-and-olive short-sleeved shirt. He had just turned sixty-five years old, according to the information amassed on him. His longish hair matched closely the silver-gray color of his shirt. His green eyes flashed darkly when his mood blackened, as it had a few times already in the interview.

With the initial questions out of the way, Julia began the specific ones for Simon. Her tone of voice did not change. "Sir, I understand you are a lawyer and that your practice is estates and wills, is that correct?"

"Yes." Simon would not give them anything more than they asked for.

"So, you and Stella each have wills with the other as the beneficiary?" Julia asked.

"Yes," Simon said again.

"Do you also have life insurance on your wife, Mr. Wakefield?" asked Julia.

"No." Another one-word answer.

"Please elaborate, Mr. Wakefield," Julia said, pressing.

"Life insurance is for situations where the death of a spouse would create a financial hardship for the remaining spouse. That isn't the case for either Stella or me. Though neither of us is wealthy, we each have enough money without the other's financial assistance. Therefore, no life insurance." Simon's confidence was back, his voice strong.

"I understand that you are a frequent client at the casino downtown. Do you enjoy gambling?" Julia queried.

"Oh, for the love of God, what does that have to do with anything?" Simon ranted, and then knowing the policewoman would simply direct him to answer the question, he relented, glaring at Julia. "Yeah, I do. It's fun," he replied flatly.

"Why did you and Stella get married, Mr. Wakefield?" Julia caught him by surprise.

"That's a damned impertinent question. Why does anyone get married? Because we wanted to!" Simon huffed.

"It has been my experience with Americans here that people of a certain age seem rarely to feel the need for marriage. So, I am curious why *you two* chose to marry," Julia said, persisting.

"If you must know, I'd been a bachelor all my life. I'd had a lot of girlfriends. I wanted to show myself, Stella, and the world that this relationship was different. It is important to me because I love Stella like I've never loved another woman before." Simon's voice had raised significantly, and his face was red when he finished speaking.

"Mr. Wakefield, what made you pick San Amaro as your new home?"

He seemed to hesitate for just a moment before answering, but when he did, the timbre of his voice had not changed from his previous answers. "A friend in Phoenix sold me on the place. He told me how much he loved it here and what a great community of expats lived in the area. I thought it sounded perfect, so I came to check it out and just stayed. Unfortunately, my friend had passed before I moved."

Convenient that there was no one to corroborate his assertion, Julia thought. "You didn't have a home in Phoenix to deal with, no loose ends in the States? You just moved here?" Though she tried to keep the disbelief out of her voice, there was a slight edge of doubt in her voice.

Simon didn't miss that tone, and again he took a moment before he responded. During his career as a lawyer, he had enough experience of dealing with police. Heirs could be frighteningly malicious when the terms of their inheritance didn't match their expectations. Unfortunately, there had been instances when Simon had needed to involve the police. He never felt completely comfortable when dealing with them, but in the US, he knew the rules of the game. Here, the police were an unknown quantity. He had heard of police corruption and wondered if it was the same in this tiny backwater. He'd expected them to be relatively incompetent and possibly open to bribery, if needed. Not that he expected that would be necessary in this situation. Now after almost a week of seeing them every day, his estimation of their competence was higher than he'd anticipated.

"I have a friend living in my house. He was looking for a place to rent at the time I was heading down here, so I let him live there. Originally it was just for a few weeks while he looked for a permanent situation, but when I decided to stay here, we made it a formal rental arrangement," Simon answered, feeling confident they wouldn't have the capability of or need to verify his claim.

"How convenient for you both," Julia commented and briefly updated the inspector on this information. "Tell us about your relationship with your wife."

"What? For Crissakes! What does that or any of this have to do with finding her in the desert?" Simon finally exploded. "I've had enough. I don't have to stay here for this!" Simon's face was red, and he was breathing like a bull about to charge.

"Sir, your rights here are not the same as in the States," Julia informed him. "We have the right to detain you if you try to leave this interview. Please answer our questions. It is the best chance we have of figuring out what's happened with your wife." She spoke firmly but calmly, trying to placate the angry man across the table while ensuring he completed his interview.

Inspector Martinez turned in his chair slightly away from the table to face Julia and spoke quietly to her in rapid Spanish. Julia looked surprised but nodded agreement.

She took a calming breath before she spoke. "Mr. Wakefield, please listen to what I have to say before responding. It is important that you seriously consider what I'm going to tell you." Simon was startled by the change in the tenor of the interview. He leaned back in his chair looking intently from Julia to the inspector and back, arms crossed tightly over his chest.

"We have strong doubts that your wife is still in the desert. With all the searching that has taken place, it is highly unlikely we wouldn't have found some trace of your wife or her dog in the vicinity of the hiking trail, the parking spot, the surrounding area, or nearby farms. At this point, we have to expand our consideration of what is going on here. We must contemplate other possibilities and think of what might have made Stella want to disappear. Please be honest with yourself, you must have wondered why she would not allow you to return with her to the vehicles. So, I'll ask you again to tell us about your relationship with your wife."

Simon's face was a mask, a poker face. It looked frozen, unmoving, but not unmoved. Simon's eyes bored into her, blazing, but not with anger, Julia thought. It was something else she couldn't put her finger on. She held his gaze. For a moment she thought he was going to crumple. Then, slowly, he leaned forward and placed his palms on the table in front of him and shifted his eyes from Julia to his hands.

Several seconds passed, then his hands turned to fists, and he banged them on the table. "Yes, of course I've played that situation over and over in my mind. I should never have let her go alone. But, no, I don't think she had some disappearing act planned. We have been happy. She had no reason to want to leave. Especially not like this. If she didn't want to be with me, all she had to do was say so. I'm not the kind of person who would force her to stay or make it difficult to leave. So, what exactly are you saying? Do you think she met someone back at the Jeep and just took off? Why would she do that? She could have just taken off in the Jeep."

"We are exploring several possibilities. We must consider all the options. So, if you have any ideas that might be helpful, now is your chance to share them with us," Julia said, spreading her hands in invitation. Simon shifted his gaze back to his hands, slowly shaking his head.

"Do you know of anyone who would want to harm your wife, sir?" Julia changed course slightly.

"Goddamn it. My wife went missing in the desert on a hike that no one else knew we were taking. She decided to go back to the vehicles alone. Who could have anticipated that? How could something nefarious have happened to her?" Simon stood rapidly, his chair falling over in the process. Julia thought he looked in shock, at the very least, dazed. Inspector Martinez had also gotten quickly to his feet. He interjected, "Please sit back down, Mr. Wakefield. And answer the question!"

Simon took a ragged breath and tried to calm himself. He righted his chair and retook his seat. He wiped his right hand over his face and sighed. "Ah, no, I don't think so. Who would want to hurt Stella? Hmmm. Well, she was seeing a guy named Tony before we met. He got physical with her, apparently. Maybe him. But I don't know why. It's well over fifteen months since she stopped seeing him. I can't think of anyone else. Really."

"Did you want to hurt your wife, Simon?" Julia slipped in his first name, making the question more personal. She expected him to bluster against this one. Instead, the man seemed to collapse in front of them. His head tipped forward, and his shoulders slumped. He appeared to begin to cry, though neither Julia nor Martinez could see his face.

"No. I just want her back. I would never hurt her." Simon's voice was soft. His breath shuddered. It took almost a minute for Simon to sit back in his chair. His face was ashen, though there was no sign he had been crying.

"Very well, Mr. Wakefield. That's it for today." Julia terminated the recording and walked Simon out to the main door. Before he left the building, he turned to Julia and asked, "What are the chances Stella is still alive?"

"We will keep looking, Mr. Wakefield. We want to find your wife, too. But we must be prepared for all possibilities." Simon nodded solemnly, a look of deep sadness settling upon his face. Then, just for a moment, Julia thought she saw something else flicker across his features. It was gone almost immediately, but it caused Julia to lay her hand on Simon's arm and say in a gentle voice, "If you have any idea what may have happened, you must tell us. We will explore all the leads we get." For a moment, Simon looked as if he were going to speak. Then he started to turn from Julia to leave. "Here's my number," she said, handing him a small slip of paper. "Please call me if anything else occurs to you."

Chapter 19—March 15, 2018, San Amaro

"What do you make of these five people now that we've concluded our interviews, Sergeant Garcia?" the inspector asked Julia as they headed upstairs to the senior officers' meeting room.

"Well, I think Mrs. Lopez will be ideal to spread the word that we aren't convinced Stella is missing in the desert and something more obscure is going on. I'll be watching Facebook tonight to see what the chatter is. Her husband seems very easily jangled. I don't think he would be able to hide his guilt if he had something to do with Stella Monroe's disappearance. However, if Stella is as law abiding as Rick Worton implied, and she was threatening Jaime because he was doing something illegal with some family member, he may have a motive. For that matter, if she learned about Rick's porn movie with a minor under our law, perhaps he could have a motive, too. I can't see any reason for Rob Gurenburg to want her out of the way. He hardly knows anyone except his boyfriend, but I still have a sense that he knows more than he's saying. I was at a loss to think of any questions to ask him, though, beyond the ones we developed for him."

They climbed the last few steps to the second floor in silence. As the inspector opened the door to their war room, Julia continued, "I was most surprised by Simon Wakefield, sir. I know he's holding something back, but I don't get the feeling he was actually lying to us about not knowing where his wife is. As he was leaving the building, though, I had the feeling that something occurred to him that he hadn't thought of before. At the door, I admonished him to tell us everything he knew or suspected, but he said nothing. I'm curious, though. While he doesn't seem to know what has happened to his wife, I think he has some ideas," Julia said.

Ricardo was waiting for them in the war room, his umpteenth coffee sitting on the table in front of him. His fingers tapped a rapid beat. The inspector put the same question to him. "Since I heard only Julia's last sentence, I don't know what all you've already talked about, but I completely agree that there is something going on with the missing woman's husband. Also, what is it about that private investigator? He hardly knows these people, yet he makes special drinks for each of them." His voice carried deep skepticism. "He doesn't strike me as someone who feels the need to suck up to people to make a good impression. So, what was that all about?"

Ricardo carried on: "I was surprised you didn't press Jaime Lopez with the suspicion we have about his nephew transporting illegal totoaba bladders down to Loreto for the cartel. Jaime was obviously a truck driver at some point in his life. Otherwise, why would all his hats be major truck manufacturers' swag? Maybe he's also involved helping his nephew and was afraid Stella knew something that could get him or his nephew in trouble," Ricardo said, speaking rapidly. Julia wondered how many cups of coffee he'd had. As he flipped open his notebook, Julia noticed coffee stains on the page from which he began to scan for something specific. "I also wondered if you'd picked up on Simon's lack of surprise when you started talking about other possibilities being considered. Does he know what happened or has he just been thinking, as we have, that something else might be going on?"

"Yes, Julia and I had the same thoughts about that, Ricardo, but it's possible Molly has spoken with him already," Martinez interjected. "But did you get the impression that Wakefield knows what's happened with his wife?"

Ricardo thought for a few seconds before tilting his head to the left and saying, "Not really. But I still don't trust him."

The three of them spent the next two hours debating that and other points from the interviews and planning next steps. By the time they called it a day, they believed they had some solid ideas of how to proceed. All in all, they thought it had been a productive day.

As Julia was gathering her purse and the files from the in-box on her desk, Corporal Luis Flores approached her with a very intense look on his face. "Have you had a chance to read my report from yesterday? About my visit to the place where the missing RZR may have potentially been taken?"

"No, Corporal, I haven't. It's right here. I plan to read it tonight. Is there something critical I need to know before tomorrow?" she asked, hoping desperately he would say no but knowing instinctively from his expression the answer would be yes.

"I think I may have found where the missing RZR is stashed." He rushed on telling her about the locked garage, and the old man and his veiled warning. "I think there was someone within earshot that the old man was afraid of. I think we need to go back out there with backup and see what's in that garage."

"Well, we won't be going out there at night, Corporal. Let me read your report, and we can talk tomorrow morning and make an appropriate plan. Thank you for your initiative of going out there and your good instincts to not try to push the situation alone." Julia gave him a tired smile and headed home.

Between her desk and her car, however, Julia had an idea and pulled out her cell phone.

Her grandparents had not had supper yet and welcomed her suggestion of her bringing home food for them to share. It was not quite dusk as she drove down Calle Guadalajara. The blue of the sky was deepening to twilight, and the few streetlights that flickered on cast halos on the people walking on the broken sidewalks. Food stalls and taco-laden handcarts grew more prevalent as she neared the Malecon. Julia was delighted to see her favorite food stall was still open. She parked her fifteen-year-old brown Honda Civic—La Chica, she called it—and crossed the street toward the stall.

The smell of charcoal and cooking chicken reached halfway across the street, making her mouth water. She placed her order with the woman inside a closet-sized storefront, and the woman yelled Julia's order to the man working the barbecue grill outside in the sidewalk stall. In only minutes, he pulled two half chickens from the flames onto his cutting board. With deft strokes of his cleaver, he reduced the large pieces into a dozen small hunks of perfectly cooked meat, bone in, which he slid into a Styrofoam container. He handed it to Julia with a nod.

The woman emerged from her closet with a bag containing warm tortillas and containers of refried beans, potato salad, coleslaw, and a giant-sized bottle of orange soda. With her feast in hand, Julia headed home to share a meal with her *abuelos*, her grandparents, Juan and Elda Pérez.

Their house was a simple two-bedroom, two-bath home with a kitchen and a combined living/dining area. It was built hacienda style with a large door entering an enclosed courtyard with a fountain. On either side of the fountain was a bedroom and bathroom, and along the back of the house, with a view of the sea and downtown San Amaro, were the kitchen and the living and dining areas.

The house and Julia's casita were surrounded by a cinder-block wall, which also contained a hard-packed earth parking area and a variety of desert trees—mesquite, elephant trees, and paloverde, which were currently sporting beautiful tiny yellow flowers over the perfectly raked sand yard. The trees provided shade for the casita and house and homes for a range of birds.

Both the house and casita had the flat roof style typical of most houses in Baja. With an annual rainfall of less than two and a half inches, sloped roofs are unnecessary. Also, a flat roof provides additional living space, and many homes had chairs, tables, and occasionally a bed or two on their roofs. It was a beautiful home by San Amaro standards. It was a fit casa for the ex-police comandante.

April is notoriously bad for flies, so Julia and her grandparents had eaten their dinner at the table inside the house. Now, however, Julia and her papita, Juan, were seated on the roof enjoying the last sunset colors tingeing the lapping waves. "Something is on your mind, Julia. Out with it," Juan said, sensing a certain restlessness in his granddaughter.

"I'm working on a missing RZR case, and the corporal I've been assigned thinks he's found where it might be." She had pulled out Luis's report and went on giving her grandfather the overview. "There is a locked building in one of the small encampments of locals north of town, Punto de Cono Ejido. When he found it, an older man living in a broken old camper trailer in the campo warned him off as though it would be dangerous for him to investigate the building. Fortunately, the corporal heeded the warning, as he was alone. I really want to get a look inside that garage or whatever it is, but it's padlocked, and I don't think I have enough evidence to get a warrant," Julia said. She further outlined the details from his report of how Luis had ended up in that campo in the first place.

Juan sipped his orange soda and considered the situation. "Well, the Mexican Supreme Court ruled a couple of years ago that the search of a private vehicle was legal under our constitution, but the only cases in which I've seen this applied are vehicles out in the open, not in an enclosed or locked building. Is there any way you can have the owner open the building for you? Do you know who owns it? It's not likely, if it's as well built as your corporal describes, that it's built on communal land. The owner may not be the person whose possessions are locked inside. He may be willing to open it or allow you to break the lock."

The two continued to consider alternatives until the deep-purple color was gone from the heavens and the stars were bright jewels in the new moon sky. For a while, they sat in companionable silence. Then, realizing she still had files and Facebook to read and email to answer before she could call it a night, Julia kissed Juan and Elda goodnight and walked to her little casita, seventy-five feet away.

Chapter 20—March 16, 2018, San Amaro

Julia decided to interview Stella's old boyfriend, Tony Ranelli, first thing in the morning, given Molly's assertion that he was always drunk after noon. She headed to his home, which she found was in San Amaro's only mobile-home park, at the south end of town on the bay. It was a small park containing about twenty-five mobile homes ranging from the ancient and decrepit to the newer and attractive. Mr. Ranelli's trailer fell in the middle, leaning toward the former end of the spectrum. It was single wide, about eighteen years old, and in need of maintenance.

She expected her early-morning arrival would awaken the man and was somewhat surprised when the door opened just as she was about to knock. A fully dressed man of medium height and ample girth with thinning brown hair peppered with gray yanked open the door, saying, "What do you want?" as he took in her uniform and the police car parked at his curb.

Julia showed her credentials and introduced herself. "Mr. Ranelli, I would like to ask you a few questions about Stella Monroe. May I come in?"

"Yeah, okay," said the man, stepping back to allow her entry and then closing the door behind her. He pointed to the living-room sofa and chairs. Julia chose a chair close to the window. She would be a silhouette to him, but she could see him clearly as he took the sofa opposite her. As he was getting settled, he began speaking unbidden. “They were all completely stupid. Her for leaving the group and the others for letting her. Being in the desert alone is idiotic.”

Julia noted his comments were very similar to those he posted on Facebook at the time of Stella’s disappearance. She didn’t rise to his bait, however, and began with her questions in the order she wished the interview to proceed. “Mr. Ranelli, I understand that you dated Stella Monroe up until about fifteen months ago. Can you please tell me about your relationship and how and why it ended?”

“She really wasn’t very smart, and I like smart people. Yet she was always acting like she was smarter than me.” Julia tried very hard to not let her lips twitch as his incorrect grammar somewhat belied the assertion of his own intelligence. The man went on. “We were never very serious, you know, because she wasn’t smart, but we went out for a couple of months. And then we just drifted apart.”

“I have heard from a firsthand witness that you were physically abusive to her. That she said she never wanted to see you again after one of your physical altercations, and that you threatened her life,” Julia said, pulling off the gloves.

“That’s just bullshit!” he stated with vehemence. “I’ll bet you heard that from her turquoise toad of a friend. Talk about not very smart!” he said, shaking his head. “You shouldn’t trust everything people tell you. Stella needed a firm hand to keep her on the rails, if you even know what that means,” he said dismissively.

“I know what that means, Mr. Ranelli,” Julia replied, trying to keep her dislike of the man from showing in her body language or tone. “You were heard saying that Stella ‘better hope you never saw her again.’ That sounds like a threat to me. Also, your posts on Facebook about Stella’s disappearance were incendiary.” She wanted to add *if you even know what that means* but didn’t.

When she asked where he was at the time and for the days leading up to when Stella went missing, she learned he was in Kentucky for a week for his cousin’s funeral. Julia could see through his bluster and, since he wasn’t in the area at the time leading up to and including the hike, she ended the interview. She also reminded him to check in with the police should he plan to leave San Amaro for any length of time.

Back at the station, Julia and Luis were discussing some of the options Julia and her grandfather had come up with the previous night when the desk sergeant of the shift walked up to Julia’s desk. There was an urgency in his step and a look of excitement on his face. Julia looked up, sensing the frisson in his approach.

“Sergeant Garcia, there are two English-speaking men out front who say they may have information about the missing woman. Inspector Martinez is out at the search site, as you know. They said they would speak to you. Shall I put them into an interview room for you?” Sergeant Escamilla was not a fan of female officers in the police force, and Julia could tell it pained him that this potentially important information might have to go to Julia rather than directly to Martinez or Ricardo. Ricardo was in the office, but his English was not strong enough to lead an interview with English speakers.

She nodded curtly to Escamilla and said, "Yes, thank you, Sergeant, Interview Room Two, please. I will be there directly." She turned to Luis, saying, "Find out who owns that building if you can. I doubt there will be any record of it on the books, but perhaps you can befriend the old man and encourage him to tell you. We can reconnect later today and figure out what to do next. Be sure to take another officer with you if you go back to the site of the shed."

After debriefing the interviews of the five hikers the previous day, Inspector Martinez had decided going forward that he would man the tent at the search site with another sergeant, leaving Ricardo and Julia to dig into the details they needed to move ahead with their new plan.

When Julia entered Interview Room Two, she was greeted by two young men, likely early twenties, with deeply sunburned faces above scruffy beards. Both were wearing wide-brimmed hats over longish blond hair. As she came into the room, both pulled off their hats. The fellow on the right set his on the table in front of him; the other placed his in his lap. Both faces looked at her earnestly, eyes alert. Julia surmised they could be twins.

"Good morning, gentlemen, I am Sergeant Julia Garcia. I understand you have information you think might pertain to our investigation of the missing woman, Stella Monroe." At hearing her excellent, if slightly accented English, the two men relaxed somewhat.

The one with his hat in his lap was the first to speak in a slightly accented, lilting, and sibilant English. "Hello, I am Günter Amundsen, and this is my brother, Anton." At this, Anton dipped his head in greeting. "We have been camping in various places in Baja for the last three weeks and just got to San Amaro last night. Anton noticed a poster in our hotel lobby asking anyone who had been in the desert between here and the petroglyphs on March 7 to assist you with an investigation into a missing woman. We were camping about forty minutes north of the arroyo leading to the rock paintings the previous night and most of the day of which the poster spoke."

Julia felt a crackle of excitement. When she spoke, however, her voice was calm and even as usual. "Thanks for coming in, Anton, Günter. I would like to ask you some questions about that day and anything you may have seen or heard. I would like you to suspend your judgment about what might or might not be important and just tell me everything you can remember about that day. This may take some time. Can I offer you coffee or water before we start?"

After grabbing Ricardo to sit in on the interviews and getting two bottles of water for the Amundsen brothers, she got their approval to record their conversation. The interview began.

"Today is March 16, 2018, and the time is ten twenty-three a.m. This is an interview with Anton and Günter Amundsen, who have come forward with potential information regarding the Stella Monroe missing person case." Julia spoke for the recording and had each of the others say his name. Julia led them through some preliminary demographic information about the men, learning they were both engineers, Anton recently graduated, and visiting from Europe. She then moved on to where they had been camping. She was delighted when Günter was able to provide GPS coordinates of their campsite.

"Please tell me anything you might have seen or heard on March 8 of this year," she requested, looking from Günter to Anton and back to Günter.

It was Anton who spoke first. Julia could see that Anton was younger now that she had spent a few minutes with the men. From their birth dates, she realized only eighteen months younger. "The first thing I noticed was dust from vehicles rising up on our horizon. I gauged them to be only about four miles from us. They were heading south and west toward the mountains. I didn't see the vehicles, and it took a bit of time for the muffled sound of their engines to reach us. I could tell there were two or more of them. Which we have been told by almost everyone we've met on this trip is the only smart way to travel into the desert here. I guess we have been lucky. Nothing went wrong for us." He said this last a bit sheepishly.

"And what time would that have been?" Julia asked the question looking at Anton, but this time it was Günter who responded. He consulted a small notebook he'd pulled from his pocket. "Nine ten a.m.," he said in the same precise, slightly lilting English used by his brother. Both were clearly fluent in English but spoke with an accent Julia now knew was Danish.

The two brothers then spent a few minutes talking about their morning actions—taking down their tents, having breakfast, and other minutiae. Julia did not interrupt them. She wanted them to be as detailed as possible when they got to something relevant. Stopping the flow now might restrict the flow later.

"The next time we saw dust on the horizon was at ten thirty," Günter said after glancing again at his notebook. Julia's neck tingled slightly. "It was going the same direction as the previous ones. It sounded like a lone vehicle, but it must have been pretty loud, because we heard it. That's actually what caused me to look for the dust, not the other way around."

"Did you see the vehicle at all?" Julia asked, trying to keep the pleading tone she was feeling out of her voice.

"Yes. I used my binoculars to look. I was up a hill from Anton, birdwatching. When I heard the engine, I was curious. It wasn't as far away as the previous vehicles had been. It looked like one of those things they race in the Baja Two Fifty and those other races you have here. A bit like a rhinoceros on wheels. I could tell it was a four-seater just because of its length. It might have been blue or black, maybe red," he said and shook his head. "I really couldn't see the color very well because of the sun. I thought I could see two people in it, though," Günter said.

Julia was excited by the preciseness of these men's observations. She was going to ask a follow-up question, but Günter continued unprompted.

"We saw it again a little less than an hour later, at a quarter after eleven, going back the way it came. By this time, I was quite far up a large hill, where there is a small grove of mesquite trees and several nests. I was getting some great photos of verdans, mockingbirds, and butcher birds. I could tell it was the same vehicle, but this time I could see there was also someone in the back seat. They were in my field of view for less than a minute, then they turned east and headed directly away from us, toward the sea. They must have driven into an arroyo or something, because after that, all I saw was their dust."

This information was the break the police had been needing, and Julia and Ricardo were visibly excited. Günter, picking up on their energy, went on: "I can give you an estimate of the GPS coordinates of where I think it was when it went past us, where they turned west, if that would help."

Julia looked fully into Günter's face with a quizzical expression on her face. "How can you do that?" she asked, probing.

"Well," Günter began, his voice becoming that of a teacher. "You know that GPS coordinates are a notation of latitude and longitude. Latitude is measured as the distance north or south of the equator, and longitude is measured as the distance east or west of Greenwich, England. The measurement is done in degrees, minutes, and seconds. It's not important to this purpose that you understand the specifics, but just know that a 'second' is just over thirty meters in latitude and about twenty-four meters in longitude. I know the GPS location of where I was standing, because I track that in my birding logbook. The vehicle I saw was less than a kilometer, probably three quarters of a kilometer due west of my position."

He pulled out his cell phone and did some calculations after referring to the small black notebook he'd retrieved from the side leg pocket of his cargo shorts. He jotted down a couple of numbers on the back page of his notebook and then did two more calculations and announced the latitude and longitude in two numbers, each with six decimal places.

Julia wrote the numbers in her own notebook and then looked a bit confused. "Where are the degrees, minutes, and seconds?" she queried.

"Oh, yeah!" Günter spoke with a slight laugh in his voice. "The common way to express coordinates these days is as a decimal value. It's what allows computers to process the information. The degrees are the numbers before the decimal point, and the minutes and seconds are calculated using a formula to give the decimal portion."

"Thank you for explaining it to me. Could you show me the formula, please? This is very interesting to me," Julia, a bit of a math nerd herself, said with enthusiasm. She handed Günter her notebook, and he wrote out the formulas and a couple of notes in explanation. Julia reviewed it to make sure she understood the process and thanked him again. After a quick conversation with Ricardo to be sure he didn't have any more questions, she intended to bring the interview to a close.

Julia was about ask the men if there was anything else they remembered, when Anton picked up the narrative. "It was just before one in the afternoon when the plane went over. It was one of those things—I'm not sure what they are called—that have wings made from material like parachutes, an engine, and the pilot hangs below in a small cage with a chair in it."

"An ultralight?" Ricardo jumped in, not sure Julia would know the name of this type of plane.

"I've never seen one before, except in photos. I was surprised it was out in the desert that far. I don't know how far they can fly on a tank of fuel. I guess by air we were not that far to San Amaro, maybe sixty miles."

Ricardo was visibly excited now. "*Sí*, they go very far."

Julia asked the next question. "Which way was the plane traveling when you saw it?"

"It was heading north and east, toward San Amaro," Anton said.

"And how many people were in the plane?" To Julia's knowledge there was only one ultralight plane in the San Amaro area, and it was a two-seater.

Because the pilot and passenger basically hung suspended open to the elements below the wings, it should be easy to see if there were two people in it.

"Only one" was Anton's reply.

"Had you seen or heard the ultralight earlier in the day?" Julia asked hopefully.

"Yes, I think so," Anton replied, "but we were still in our tent and only heard. It was early that morning."

Ricardo and Julia conferred for a moment, and Julia asked a few follow-up questions to review the men's stories. Ricardo stepped out and grabbed a photo book of off-road vehicles, which he brought back for Anton and Günter to look through. They flagged a couple of photos they said looked like what they'd seen driving to and from the area where the hikers had left their vehicles. One was a four-seater Can-Am and the other a four-seater RZR.

Not only had another desert rig been seen going to and from the general location from which Stella Monroe had gone missing, but an ultralight plane had been in the area, too! Neither could be a coincidence. Julia and Ricardo talked excitedly about this new information. "Martín Robles is the only person around here who has an ultralight. We need to get him in for an interview as soon as we can. This afternoon, if possible," Ricardo was saying as he picked up the conference-room phone. He called downstairs to the desk sergeant and asked him to track down Martín and to get him in to the station. Julia and Ricardo could hardly wait to bring the inspector up to speed with these new developments. At last, they were getting somewhere.

PART 2—What came before . . .

Chapter 1—August 21, 2016, Pleasant Valley, Arizona

"I've found your daughter, Mrs. Cutler," said Simon Wakefield as he carefully watched his client. He wore his very best suit and had splurged on a Shibumi Firenze tie for this meeting. Simon Wakefield had a niche law practice. He was well known in every retirement home, nursing home, and assisted-living facility in and around Phoenix. All he did was wills and probate. Today, he was meeting Mrs. Cutler in the finest retirement home in Paradise Valley, the richest city in Arizona. The Villas was home to fifty-six of Arizona's wealthiest elderly, most of them widows.

This meeting was taking place in a stunningly appointed private lounge, which Mrs. Cutler had booked for their discussion. From the butter-soft leather wing chair Simon had chosen, he admired the gleaming dark hardwood floors and the giant antique Kashmiri carpet on which the two nut-brown leather wing chairs and two tastefully floral-fabriced settees created a sanctuary. The only other furniture in the room, a Queen Anne sideboard, an armoire, and end tables, perfectly complemented the elegance of the room itself. The floor-length drapes shared the lime and peach highlights of the settees. An expertly arranged bouquet of lilies on the sideboard perfumed the air. The late-afternoon sun shining through the floor-to-ceiling west-facing windows added warm, yellow hues, enriching the natural colors of the room. The room had a decidedly feminine feel. Simon wondered if there were another equally palatial lounge catering to the much smaller number of male residents, perhaps furnished like an Edwardian English men's club.

Mrs. Cutler's steely-blue eyes were set in what was surely once a formidable face, though now the crepe and crow's-feet of her still-rosy skin softened her appearance as only age can. At ninety-three, Althea Cutler, née Reinhold, was a grande dame. To Simon's news, she gave only the slightest lift of her chin in response. Whatever emotions she was feeling at the news of a daughter seventy-three years lost from her life and now found, she gave no visible indication. Mrs. Cutler's thinning hair was styled in a beautiful chignon and was certainly the product of a visit earlier in the day to the on-site salon. Its length drew the eye to the single strand of glistening creamy pearls at her neck and naturally complemented her perfectly tailored silk dress with a subtle pattern in pale gray and sage green on a background of pure white. Simple and elegant dove-gray flats and small matching handbag finished her ensemble. She wore only a little, expertly applied makeup. Simon wondered if it also was the result of the salon visit or if Althea Cutler's own hands had applied it. Unlike so many of his aged female clients who chose rosewater or lilac scents, surrounding Mrs. Cutler was only a tasteful waft of Chanel No 5.

Simon had employed a private inspector to find her daughter, Mrs. Cutler's only surviving kin, who was adopted at birth. It had taken eight weeks and a considerable number of financial incentives, given to the right people in records offices to track down her daughter. Mrs. Cutler had been of little help beyond providing the date and private hospital where the child was born. “Her name is Stella Monroe, and she is living in Mexico in a small town called San Amaro, on the Baja peninsula. She retired there after her career in teaching middle school in . . .” Simon stopped speaking as Mrs. Cutler held up a diamond-glittering hand, palm out. The universal stop sign.

“I told you, Mr. Wakefield, I don’t wish to know about her or her circumstances, though I am grateful you have located her. I will now modify my will to accommodate her receiving the bulk of my estate, as we previously discussed.” At last reckoning, said estate was worth just over $18 million in investments and properties. “When you have drawn up the changes, let me know and we can finalize my estate. You may submit your final statement then.” Her voice was firm and clear, as, it appeared, was her mind. It was obvious, Simon thought, that she was accustomed to giving orders and having them fulfilled. However, he realized, not accustomed to showing the help, as he reckoned he was in her mind, any emotion. He had done as she asked, and now was expected to complete the legal work for which she had originally hired him and nothing more. Grief, joy, curiosity, or shame, whatever she was feeling would be experienced in the privacy of her own mind and heart. She did not want his empathy, compassion, or judgment.

With no further conversation, Mrs. Cutler dismissed him, neither rising from her chair nor offering to walk him through the marble foyer to the glass atrium that formed the entrance. She had been seated, much like a monarch on her throne, on one of the settees in the lounge when Simon was shown in by the reception attendant. Idly, he wondered if she perhaps used a wheelchair that vanity impelled her to have removed from the room before she met with him.

As he drove down the winding, bougainvillea-lined drive with its sweet smell, to the stately iron gates, Simon pondered the will he was to complete for this client. Althea Cutler was a very wealthy woman and ninety-three years old. She appeared to be in excellent health. *I wonder when Stella Monroe of San Amaro, Baja, will get the surprise of her life and become a very wealthy woman herself? Surely it can't be more than a few years at most. I'd love to see the look on her face,* he thought.

Leaving Paradise Valley, Wakefield headed west toward Interstate 17. The late-afternoon, mid-August weather was a relatively cool ninety degrees. Much cooler than normal for summer. He pulled over to the curb and put the top down in his BMW Series 4 convertible. It was several years old, but still looked great. That's what mattered. Like most of Wakefield's possessions, it was selected to project the image of a successful lawyer with a flourishing practice. He did have a flourishing, if not financially lucrative, practice, but the majority of his clients lived not in places like The Villas, but nursing homes for those of modest means. His bread and butter came from the thousand bucks he charged to set up a simple will for people with a small retirement nest egg and a handful of grandkids they wished to help through college with whatever remained on their passing.

The black Bimmer had been bought cheaply at a city auction. It had been rolled and was in awful shape when he bought it. Simon had traded some legal services with an ex-con autobody magician named Rudy. Rudy restored the body to almost new. He had less success with the slightly bent frame, though, and the car always pulled slightly to the right. The tire wear was anything but even.

Before pulling back into the street, Simon carefully took off his $200 tie and placed it in the glove box and laid his suit jacket, lining out, in the trunk. Feeling the wind in his hair and on his face as he drove off again, Simon had a sense things were turning around for him. This felt like a lucky day. And God knew he could use some luck!

According to his business card, the law offices of Wakefield & Dunn were on the tenth floor of the prestigious Newcombe Building in the downtown core of Surprise, Arizona. There was no name on the door of the tenth-floor office in the Newcombe Building, however, and anyone entering and asking for Simon Wakefield would be informed, "Mr. Wakefield is not in the office today but will contact you to make an appointment to meet you at your home, at your convenience." The story was similar for the thirty-seven other businesses using this front for their business address. In reality, Simon worked out of his tiny bungalow in Glendale, Arizona. His partner, Dunn, did not exist. The name Wakefield & Dunn was selected to project the air of a larger firm. Since Simon worked nursing homes and care facilities, no client had ever tried to go to his office. Clients considered it a benefit that he came to them. The receptionist at 1001 in the Newcombe Building answered calls to Simon's business number and transferred them to his cell phone or forwarded calls to the business voice mailbox provided with the phone-answering service. When Althea Cutler had called him from the promotional brochure he had left for each patron of The Villas, it had seemed like a miracle. In moments of self-honesty, though, Simon recognized she had not wanted to open herself and her unwanted, out-of-wedlock pregnancy when she was nineteen to the awareness of any of the lawyers in law firms she might use for other business. He fitted her needs.

Leaving the interstate, Wakefield drove to his humble home in the run-down Ocotillo district. Only ten miles from Phoenix and fifteen miles from Paradise Valley, Glendale couldn't have been more different from either of these adjacent metro areas. The Caucasian population in Paradise Valley was 97 percent and in Phoenix about 70 percent, while Glendale was predominantly Hispanic. House prices were considerably lower in Glendale and, though crime was slightly higher, the town worked for him.

Simon noted that the single palm tree in his front yard had dropped more fronds since this morning, bringing the number covering his hardscape front yard, code for gravel, to about a dozen, more than remained on the tree. At least they covered the prolific weeds that grew through the gravel. One of his neighbors was a palapero, a maker of palm-frond thatched roofs called palapas. Simon would see if he could come collect the fronds, though he didn't know whether the guy's trendy palapa-thatched patio umbrellas were made from green or long-dead fronds.

Ocotillo Lane, one block long, on which Simon's house sat in the middle, was one of the nicer streets in the community. Glendale was home to more apartments than single-family homes, but Ocotillo Lane was a mix of duplexes and small bungalows. Most of Simon's neighbors were couples with kids and first-generation Mexican immigrants. They were modest homes, but most were lovingly maintained. He liked that he could get his car washed and his shirts laundered and pressed without going more than a couple of doors down his street.

Simon parked at the curb in front of his house. His garage was overwhelmed with legal file storage boxes. He was met with the odor of stale beer as he unlocked his mud-gray, peeling front door. *Time to clean up the empties strewn over the coffee table and kitchen counter,* he thought. After changing into golf shorts, a polo T, and Keens, Simon checked his voice mail and returned some calls. He updated Althea Cutler's estate plan and will, again thinking of the amazing surprise awaiting Stella Monroe sometime in the next few years. At ten that night, he decided the bag of chips he'd called dinner needed some backup. He headed to the local bar for a real meal and a beer.

El Tapatio Restaurant and Bar was owned and operated by Stan and Maritsa Cole. Maritsa inherited it when her Mexican parents decided to move back across the border for their retirement. She made the best burritos Simon had ever eaten. Behind the bar, Stan poured libations and made book on sports games, mostly basketball and soccer. For Simon, it was the perfect retreat. It met all his needs, well maybe not for sex, but sometimes even willing partners were met there.

At a hair under six feet and a trim 165 pounds, sixty-four-year-old Simon Wakefield caught the eye of women from thirty to one hundred. He was fortunate to possess a full head of wavy, slightly too-long silver hair. He was striking looking, though rarely described as handsome. His nose was too long and hooked, his eyes, a piercing gray green, were set slightly too far apart, and he had overly large, almost feminine lips. Still, he cut a very dashing figure.

Taking a seat at the bar from which he could see four games in progress on the various TV screens spread through the place, he ordered his usual— two beef-and-cheese burritos with rice, and refried beans, and a Dos Equis lager. By the time his dinner arrived, Simon had put down $250 on the Celtics and the same on the Bulls for their games the next day. "I'm feeling lucky today, Stan," he told the bartender as he passed over the five crumpled hundreds.

The next day, Simon was still feeling lucky. His good mood prompted him to take the next step on an idea that had been floating around his head for a few weeks. He pulled out his laptop and brought up his master list of care facilities, nursing homes, and assisted-living residences and started making calls. His idea was to offer a free, short seminar on wills and estate planning to people living in these places as a way to drum up some new business.

After calling over half the places on his list and not receiving a single taker, his optimism was beginning to wane. Still, he'd managed to snag the Cutler dame. The moniker made him smile at the thought of it. She acted like an aristocrat, so calling her a dame was sort of fitting. *Why not keep trying?* Even one facility taking him up on the idea could be worthwhile for him.

By late afternoon, however, having called every place on his list and not getting one opportunity to present his as yet nonexistent seminar, he decided to pack it in and abandon the idea. *Who was he kidding, anyway? That wasn't his strength.* It was just as well he hadn't wasted the time to actually develop a PowerPoint presentation with talking points. He'd do the usual and go door-to-door and try to find new residents who hadn't yet heard his spiel. Maybe tomorrow. Tonight, he still had a couple of games on which he could make some good money if his teams came through.

Stan would have the games playing. That was all the enticement he needed. He closed his laptop and headed to El Tapatio. The Celtics game started at six o'clock in Arizona. With a Dos Equis in his right hand and a dish of tortilla chips and salsa next to his left, Simon settled in to watch the Celtics beat the Bucks. When the game concluded at about eight thirty, the Bucks were the victors, and Simon's mood continued to blacken. The Bulls were behind by eighteen. Not insurmountable, but in the end, the Bulls, too, lost their game. Goodbye, $500.

On his fourth beer, and with his good mood a distant memory, Simon decided he needed to take a new tack all together. Althea Cutler and her millions and the look on Stella Monroe's face when she inherited them had been a regularly recurring thought since he'd left Cutler yesterday. He'd almost convinced himself he deserved to have a windfall like that. Well, maybe more than almost. He picked up his cell phone.

Chapter 2—August 23, 2016, Glendale, Arizona

The call was answered before the second ring in a hoarse whisper. "What?" asked Rob. It was a quarter to eleven at night, and Rob was hunched down behind the wheel of a silver Dodge Neon. It was as nondescript a car as he could rent on short notice for this stakeout. He held a Nikon digital SLR camera with a very long telephoto lens to his eye with one hand and juggled the cell phone with the other. "I'm working. Can this wait?" Simon Wakefield's name had displayed when the phone vibrated on the passenger seat. Though their relationship was mostly business, Simon and Rob considered themselves friends, so the call could be an invitation for a beer or a job. Just then, the door to the town house upon which Rob had his camera focused opened, and he started shooting one-handed pictures.

"Never mind. Gotta go. I'll call ya," Rob whispered and dropped the phone to better capture the photos he hoped would show his client's husband for the cheating jerk his wife believed him to be. After the husband had driven away, Rob reviewed his shots. They were just what he needed. From his research, Rob knew the girlfriend, the woman in the photos, had a husband away in Vegas on a conference, who was returning tonight. In his photos, the girlfriend was wearing thigh-high leather boots and a smile as she and his mark lingered over their goodbyes at the partially open door. His timing was perfect. These photos were gold. Maybe he could get extra cash by playing both sides of the cheating pair. He'd try sending Mrs. Thigh High Leather Boots a photo or two and see if she'd pay as an incentive for Rob not to share them with her husband.

It had been only twenty minutes since Simon's call and not much past eleven. Rob decided to return the call on his drive home rather than wait for the morning. Simon would certainly still be up. "Hey, man, what's up?"

"Meet me for a drink at El Tapatio?" Simon asked without a greeting.

"Sure. Be there in ten" was the equally brief reply from Rob.

Simon had moved from the bar to a table near the back of the restaurant. He already had Rob's preferred rum and Coke on the table awaiting his arrival. Though smoking hadn't been allowed in restaurants in Glendale for decades, their table sported several cigarette-burn holes in its Arborite.

Rob was twenty-six years Simon's junior and a couple of inches taller, placing him at six foot two. He worked out and his lean frame was strong, with muscular shoulders and arms. He had a full head of blond hair, very fashionably cut, and styled. His brilliantly white T-shirt traced every muscle in his arms and chest. To anyone paying attention, it was obvious he was either gay, a model, or both.

Simon had been given Rob's name by another lawyer several years before when he needed to track down heirs of a client. Rob was a professional private investigator, good at his job, and had done several similar jobs for Simon over the years. Rob knew Simon was straight, but that had never stopped him from flirting with Simon. Simon good-naturedly flirted back, though both men knew it would never lead anywhere.

"Hey, buddy, thanks for coming. I wondered if the file you gave me on Stella Monroe, the gal in the Baja, was everything you'd gathered on her, or if you had any more background, photos, or anything like that," Simon said, beginning without any preamble.

"Hello to you, too, and yes, thanks, I'm doing fine. My job tonight was a success. Thanks for asking and oh my, what a handsome devil you are." Rob grinned at Simon, knowing he would get a rise out of him. All Simon did was smile and shake his head, finally raising one eyebrow and cocking his head while he waited for Rob's answer. "Yeah, I do have some more pictures of her, her house, dog, car, her favorite haunts, friends, you know the stuff I do when I'm surveilling someone. I also have a map of San Amaro, names of a couple of places where I ate while there. Why, was the file I gave you not enough for your client?" Rob asked at last.

"No, it was all I needed for my client, but I have a personal interest in this now. You said Stella was a widow and that she lived alone, right? Any sign of a boyfriend?" Simon asked.

"What do you mean, a personal interest? I mean, she's not a dog or a slob or anything, but she's not your usual forty-something-skirt-in-heels. Or me," Rob with a wink. "What's up?" He leaned forward, obviously curious, putting his elbows on the table and cupping his highball between his beefy, but manicured hands.

"Ah, it's just a fantasy I'm having. She will be inheriting a lot of money in the next two to three years would be my guess, but she doesn't know that. It got me interested is all. I can't get the idea out of my mind of being there when she finally gets the news. I keep imagining seeing the look on her face when she becomes a millionairess. What a trip! Like I said, just a fantasy. Never mind about the other details in the file. It's just beer brain talking."

Changing the subject, Simon said, "So, tell me all about tonight's escapade. Did you catch the wayward spouse in action?"

Chapter 3—September 6, 2016, Tempe, Arizona

Rob's upcoming job didn't start until that evening. He had been hired to tail a woman from Sky Harbor airport and report to her husband where she went. According to what she had told her hubby, she was attending a conference in Scottsdale at a Hilton resort there, but her husband was suspicious. Whether or not she went to the Hilton, Rob was pretty sure the husband would want photographic evidence of what she was doing and with whom. That left his day free until his mark's seven forty-eight flight arrival tonight. He decided to tackle his to-do list.

In the morning, he'd moved Tristin, his bearded dragon, into the bathtub and given his terrarium its monthly deep clean. While he worked, he could hear a high-pitch scratching sound as Tristin tried unsuccessfully to escape his white porcelain prison. Rob vacuumed and scrubbed the entire six-foot-long tank and cleaned everything in it. He then placed fresh shredded newspaper in as flooring, using his office shredder and yesterday's Phoenix Republic for the lizard's gigantic home. He then replaced all the cleaned contents. On one side was a large sunning rock with a heat lamp set to ninety degrees and on the other, a commercially made rock-and-twig den with full-spectrum light set to seventy-five degrees. There was also a tree branch spanning the length of the enclosure. In addition to the temperature controls, the tank was designed to maintain the proper humidity, ensuring the perfect environment for his much-loved pet.

Once Tristin received his sponge bath, Rob returned him to his home and prepared his morning meal of lettuce, mango, and live crickets, which had been in a container with a handful of fish food—creating the bearded-dragon equivalent of a fatted calf. All Tristin's food was dusted with calcium powder to ensure his diet was as nutritious as possible. Rob watched Tristin hunt and devour five of the crickets before turning his attention to the next task on his list.

When his phone rang just before lunch, he was busily preparing some tracking devices for another job he was starting in a couple of days. It was his mother. *Thank God she lived in Miami and not Phoenix,* Rob thought as he picked up the phone. Otherwise, she'd likely have been ringing his doorbell, not his cell phone. While he listened to her recite everything she and her new husband had been doing in the two weeks since her last call, Rob continued with his current job.

He'd discovered dog tag tracking devices a couple of years before when dating a guy who raised retrievers for duck hunters, and he quickly saw an application for their use in his own line of work. Now he bought them in cases of twenty-four. For the upcoming job, he had three dog trackers set out, each about the size of a stack of four quarters, three magnetic car key hiders, his glue gun, and a disposable cell phone he'd bought from the 7-Eleven a couple of blocks away.

The first steps were to download the app from the dog tag tracker company to the phone and then sync each tracking device to the app. He liked to use a separate phone for each job. It was just cleaner. When the job was done, he'd destroy the lot with a hammer and toss it in a dumpster someplace. Next, he glued a tracker tag into each of the car key hiders, as he found this provided a more stable result in the app. These he would hide on each of his mark's vehicles so he could easily follow him or her without having to be right on the car's bumper. It also covered his ass for situations in which a mark got through an amber light, leaving Rob stopped at the red. He could check the phone app and see the mark's car on the app's map, making it easy to catch up and continue tailing it.

His mom was still reciting her litany of mundanity, and for his part, Rob was making appropriate responses. So far that consisted of "Oh?" "Uh-huh!" "Really?" and "Hmmm." He could tell she was winding down and now was his "opportunity" to share the tedium of his life with her. This was something he avoided at all costs.

"Great to hear from you, Mom. I do have to go now, though, as I have a couple of work things I need to get done. Have fun at your square-dancing thing tonight. Love you. Bye!" He managed to disconnect before she could start pumping him for details of his life, or worse, deriding, again, his decision to quit his degree in chemical engineering to become an EMT, then to sign up and go to war. At least he'd avoided that conversation today. He sighed. He'd never be able to explain his addiction to the adrenaline hits he got from the work choices he'd made, nor did he want to. His mother knew him well enough that she might see the darkness within him that led him to take chances and to be thrilled by the carnage of life's traumas.

With his three trackers ready for installation, he verified everything was working by tossing one into his bedroom, placing one on his kitchen counter, and taking one with him as he headed out for a walk. He stuck this third tracker under the engine casing of his Triumph Tiger. He then walked a few hundred yards away. At the end of his block, he pulled out the burner phone and brought up the tracker app. He could clearly see all three tracker devices on the map as small, red dots. He walked back to his condo building, watching the phone's screen.

When he got a few dozen yards from his motorcycle, one tracker's dot on the map turned from red to yellow and then to green, indicating he was within sixteen feet of it. After retrieving that key holder, he returned to his apartment and verified the remaining two devices' dots also turned green as he approached their locations. Rob was satisfied with his handiwork.

In his fastidious way, Rob chipped the excess, dried glue from the tip of the gun, returned the glue gun to its home with his other small tools in a toolbox in his front closet, tidied up the bits and pieces on his dining-room table, removed the drop cloth he had down to protect the tabletop, and returned that to one of the drawers under his bed. With his home back to normal, he had another task to cross off the to-do list. He decided it was time to head to the gym for his daily workout.

Rob didn't have a huge income from his investigation business, but with it he was able to comfortably cover all his living expenses. He had received a decent-sized inheritance from his maternal grandfather when he passed almost three years ago. He'd used almost all of it to buy a condo apartment in an older building in the popular Mill Ave area of

Tempe. It was within a five-minute walk of the Salt River, about the same to the Arizona State University campus, and just two blocks from Mill Avenue with its trendy eateries, art galleries, and high-end clothing stores.

He'd spent the remainder of the inheritance on good-quality furniture that reflected his taste, and that taste ran to the expensive and the beautiful. His color palette consisted of grays, muted dark blue, and moss green with sunflower yellow for accents. Tristin's terrarium was artfully used as a room separator, creating a dining area separate from the living room. As with many older buildings in upper-end neighborhoods, there were large windows, deep baseboards, door headers in dark wood, crown moldings, and high ceilings.

While he loved the Mill Avenue area, it was sometimes difficult to be that close to so many beautiful things and be unable to partake to the level he felt entitled. However, if his mom didn't spend everything from his dad's estate, he could expect another modest windfall at some point.

As he still had four hours until he needed to get to the airport to start tonight's job, he decided to forgo riding his motorcycle to the gym and instead walked the ten minutes there, heading first to the river walk, taking that to the fitness center he frequented almost daily. It had state-of-the-art machines, a full free-weight area among other great facilities, and it was a popular workout spot for lots of thirty- and fortysomething fit and handsome gay men. That was something Rob appreciated.

By seven thirty that evening, Rob was showered, fed, and clad in jeans, rugged suede desert boots, a plain green T-shirt, a logo-less ball cap, and sunglasses. A battered large briefcase rested on the floor at his side. He'd positioned himself against a pillar near the baggage carousel for the arriving flight his mark was on. He'd bought the latest issue of *American Iron*, a motorcycle enthusiast's magazine, and was casually flipping through the pages as he waited. The airline website had shown the flight was arriving a few minutes early and, sure enough, at about seven forty-five, passengers started coming down the corridor from the gates from the flight he was awaiting.

He placed the picture the husband had sent him into the open magazine as he tried to recognize his mark. He was not disappointed as he caught sight of her mincing along amid the sea of fellow travelers from her flight. She appeared to have left work and gone straight to the airport in Salt Lake City, as her slightly rumpled baby-blue business suit and tightly clutched briefcase attested. At her side was a fiftyish handsome fellow, possibly her boss, and quite likely her lover, Rob gauged. He was shepherding "Baby Blue" with a hand on the curve of her back, rather lower down the curve than would be considered platonic.

Rob had his cell phone in hand and began surreptitiously snapping pictures. His Nikon was in the hard-sided luggage on the Triumph. He wouldn't need that until later. The motorcycle allowed him to tail marks more easily when they took taxis than he could in a rental car. Sky Harbor had a motorcycle parking area right off the curb of the arrival level. Since the taxi ranks were just a bit before that parking spot, Rob knew from experience that he could be on his bike and ready to tail his mark well before they got into a cab.

When he saw the pair gather their luggage, he headed to his bike and was able to pull in right behind their taxi as they left the airport.

Chapter 4—October 3–November 29, 2016, Phoenix Area

After his lack of success betting on basketball, Simon eschewed sports, deciding instead the casino was where his luck was hiding. Chandler, Arizona, was just over a half-hour drive from his house. Just south of Chandler was the relocated home of the Pima and Maricopa tribes and their lovely casino, the Iguana Resort. Hoping to build on his success with Althea Cutler, Simon had headed there to recoup his losses from the Bulls and Celtics games, which had not provided the happy and lucrative outcomes for which he'd hoped.

He'd arrived at ten thirty that morning, heading first to the ATM located inside the casino proper, just across from the slots. He'd decided a grand would be all he needed to regain his recent losses and get on a winning streak. He checked his bank balance. It was just under $1,300. He withdrew $1,000. The curving neon orange and purple lights on the ceiling were matched by a patterned carpet containing the same colors, though more muted than the lights. The walls were a dusty-beige color and contained contours of mountains, mesas, and saguaro cacti in bas-relief. Against them, the neon colors cast light and shadows like an Arizonan sunset, giving patrons the feeling of perpetually dusk.

Simon sat himself at a Casino Hold-em poker table with two midsixties-aged women and a young male croupier and stacked his chips on the felt in front of him. The table had fifteen- and thirty-dollar limits on bets. Simon calculated that with two other players plus the dealer, he could be sitting pretty in a couple of hours or less and have some fun in the process. The current game was in the turn round, and the pot was sitting at $120. He watched with interest as the river round commenced to see how these women bet. The woman to his near right raised thirty dollars, and the women to his far right saw that bet and raised another thirty dollars. The dealer stayed in. The final board showed a pair of twos (clubs and hearts), a seven of clubs, a ten of diamonds and a king of spades. The final pot of $360 went to the house with a full house of twos and kings.

Simon anted into the next round. He won his first game. The house won the second, while the woman on his far right took the third. Simon again won in the fifth game, but by the end of the eighth game, he was down to seventy dollars in chips, so he stepped away to get the remaining $280 out of his account. When he returned, he won the next round and then the one following. He believed his luck was back. By three thirty that afternoon, however, he was down almost $5,000, having taken most of the money from his savings account. He had also written an IOU for $1,000 to a bouncer he knew, from previous visits to the Iguana Resort, who lent money on the side.

Emotional darkness had now descended completely on Simon. He'd done nothing productive the past two days. He didn't have any clients who needed anything and no new ones in the hopper. Things felt bleak for him. Rather than hitting the streets and trying to get some new clients, he'd moped around his house in his boxers. Beer bottles, Chinese food takeout containers, and pizza boxes were starting to pile up.

This is all that Cutler bitch's fault, he'd convinced himself. She was taunting him with her riches. He couldn't keep his mind on anything else for any length of time. All he could think of was her giving her millions away to someone she hadn't even met, someone whom she'd thrown away decades ago. When he thought of Althea now, she tended to have horns and a tail. In his better moments, he laughed at that image. At his worst, he cursed her and threatened to steal her millions and build for himself the life he deserved. Only problem with that was he could think of only one way to make that happen, and he had to work pretty hard not to let himself feel ashamed of his mind for going there.

Simon needed something in his life to just be easy. He decided to try something that had worked in the past. He called the receptionist at his business office, Lilliana. She was a second-generation Mexican American who had worked at the business center as the main receptionist and primary employee for almost five years. She was smart, reasonably attractive, about five foot five, and only slightly overweight. In those five years, she and Simon had hooked up a few times for a drink or two and casual, pretty athletic sex. Simon hadn't talked with her for anything other than work for almost a year, so he wasn't sure if she would still be amenable, but after a brief chat, Simon was delighted to have a date for the evening.

He set about tidying up the house and managed to get the detritus of his slovenly living of the past few days dumped in the trash and his flung-about clothes confined to the clothes hamper. He even ran a damp cloth over the surfaces in the living room and made the bed. By six, he had shaved, showered, and dressed in khakis and a Hawaiian shirt. Before he left the house, he made sure he had condoms in his bedside table, in the box with the TV remotes on his coffee table, and in his wallet. *Never hurts to be prepared for any eventuality,* he thought.

By quarter after seven, he was sitting in one of the nicer booths at El Tapatio. He'd ordered a bottle of red wine that Lilliana liked and had it open to breathe. True to form, she arrived a few minutes early for their seven thirty date. Simon stood up and gave her a hug and a light kiss on the cheek before they both sat. Initially, their conversation was a bit awkward, but by the time Simon poured their second glass of wine, they were easily chatting about sports. Lilliana, having grown up with five brothers, had begun her love affair with all things soccer at a young age. Her knowledge of the teams and their players' stats and probabilities of success in the current season was prodigious and both entertained Simon and gave him some tips for future games to bet on.

After a light meal of chile rellenos for Lilliana and two carne asada tostadas for Simon, Liliana drove them the two blocks to Simon's house. Simon had another bottle of wine and two glasses already on the coffee table, and once they each had clinked glasses and had a few sips of their wine, Simon leaned in to initiate a real kiss. Lillianna met him halfway, and their evening of sexual aerobics began. Simon had some Viagra in his medicine cabinet, just in case, but it turned out to be unnecessary. At two in the morning, when Lillianna rose from the bed to leave, they were both spent after several bouts of very satisfying sex.

Simon awoke late the next morning and was pleased his home no longer looked like a frat house. He picked up his khakis from behind the couch, washed and put away the wine glasses, and was still feeling pretty up when he went to the mailbox by the curb in front of his house. Thoughts of Althea Cutler, with or without horns and tail, had been swept from his mind by a night of sexual release. However, when he grabbed his mail, he found a manila folder from Rob containing the additional information he had gathered on Stella Monroe, her friends, and haunts in San Amaro. Attached was a note saying simply, "I don't need this, so do with it what you choose." He looked it over and, in the end, decided fate was telling him that taking a simple step in that direction wasn't the same as making a commitment. It was just a way to explore options. Back in the house, he pulled out his laptop and typed "moving to Mexico" into Google.

It took him almost two months to work out his plan for moving to Baja. Maritsa from the bar knew a fellow looking for a house to rent in Glendale. Simon and he agreed on a deal starting in December. Since Simon would still need to make money, he'd devised a plan to continue his current business.

The drive from Phoenix to San Amaro is about six hours on good roads, and so he had decided he could continue to work his existing clients by setting appointments for every other week when face-to-face meetings were necessary. He could drive up one night and stay in a motel, visit his clients on the next day, and either drive back that night or the following morning. As he needed new clients, his new hunting grounds would be Yuma. It was teeming with retirement homes and was only three hours from San Amaro.

He had taken a day and dropped by every assisted-living home, retirement complex, and nursing home listed with the Yuma Chamber of Commerce, leaving flyers and business cards at each one. This business plan had served him well in Phoenix, and he had no doubt that would continue, providing him sufficient funds to live in Mexico. He had already had a couple of calls and had picked up one new client in Yuma. His business front in Surprise would continue to take his calls and now added booking his appointments to their services. Until new clients started to pay the bills, he'd live on his line of credit. It wouldn't be the first time.

Simon and Rob had met for libations at El Tapatio a couple of times in the ensuing weeks after the latter left Simon his file on Stella Monroe. At first, Simon was cagey about his decision to go to San Amaro to see how things played out, but Rob quickly saw through his evasive answers. The second time they met for drinks, Rob came out and asked directly what Simon was going to do. This time he didn't let Simon get away with nonanswers. Simon admitted he was planning to go there, figure out a way to meet Stella, and then see where things went. If everything went perfectly, and he believed he could live with himself for doing it, he'd marry her. In the end, Rob broached the subject of his going down with Simon to act as his wingman. "No," Simon had said. He wanted to test the waters on his own. If he thought Rob's help were needed, he'd let him know.

It was a cool day at the end of November when Simon drove through Andrade, California, a hamlet in the Fort Yuma Indian Reservation, and crossed the border into Los Algodones, Mexico. He chose this crossing as it was the smallest of the three most convenient border crossings between Phoenix and San Amaro. He was rewarded for this decision. The automated border lane lowered a barrier arm, photographed his car license, and lifted the arm, providing his entry into Mexico. He drove straight through the border without even seeing a border guard, though he did stop at the immigration desk to get his six-month visitor's visa for thirty dollars. From the border he took the Highway 2 toll road into Mexicali and then went south on Highway 5 into San Amaro.

Chapter 5—December 7, 2016, San Amaro

San Amaro is a fishing and desert sport town of under 20,000 people. It sits on a strip of sand bounded on the east by the Sea of Cortez and on the west by the Sierra de San Pedro Mártir mountains. The sea is a unique aquatic biosphere. The famous underwater explorer Jacques Cousteau called it the world's aquarium. It is home to vast and unique aquatic species.

That area of Baja is a land of buff-colored sand, silvery desert shrubs, and olive-green mesquite trees. It is also home to coyotes, road runners, long-eared rabbits, myriad lizards, and mouse-sized, ground-dwelling, chipmunk-like rodents called juanitos by the gringos.

And now it was home to Simon Wakefield.

The nearby bare-granite-and-lava mountains range in color from deep rust to light sand to black and are characterized by vertical crevasses that resemble the deep wrinkles in the faces of the oldest of the indigenous peoples in any hot, sunny climate. They jut from the sand like misshapen wrinkled chains of pyramids.

Simon had been in San Amaro eight days and was becoming acquainted with his new little town. He had managed to find a cute little one-bedroom house on the beach to rent. It was in a small community just past the south end of the main downtown area. He could easily walk into town on the beach, following the natural curve of the bay on which San Amaro was nestled.

This early Wednesday evening, with the sun still caressing the tops of the mountains to the west, Simon had decided to drive rather than walk. The weather was hotter than normal for early December, and he didn't want to be sweaty when he reached the Crown and Anchor. This little English-style pub and restaurant sat half a block from the Malecon. Outside, it looked like a replica of Anne Hathaway's cottage, though most of the features were really a painted mural rather than built in. The mock roof, which extended out over the main entrance, was of palapa construction trying to pass as a cottage thatched roof. The effect was a cross between quaint and quirky.

Inside, however, the illusion of a British pub was more convincing. The wood of the ceiling beams was dark and matched the wainscoting around the walls and the bar. One could even get some international beers including Guinness, which Simon enjoyed occasionally, though only Mexican beers were on tap. Horse irons, three dart boards, and paintings of fox hunts covered the deep-green walls. It had air-conditioning, which was surprisingly rare in a restaurant in San Amaro. Simon surmised that fact alone might account for the pub's popularity.

Tonight, based on Rob's reconnaissance information indicating this was a favorite haunt of Stella's, Simon entered this obviously gringo bar, stopping for a moment inside the door to let his eyes adjust to the dark interior. He noticed Stella immediately. She was sitting at a table to the right of the bar, under one of the bar's TVs, with two other people, an American woman and a Mexican man.

Again, based on Rob's research, Simon recognized them as Molly and Jaime Lopez, good friends of Stella's. Simon took a seat halfway down the bar. It gave him a view of the TV and allowed him to casually watch his quarry while appearing to be watching the televised soccer game. In fact, he had some money riding on this game, so the game vied with Stella for his attention.

Stella was wearing a white scoop-neck top with some kind of bling stitched into the neckline, with white capris and white sandals. A red chunky necklace and matching bracelet provided a nice contrast to the white. She was not a beautiful woman—*too thin,* Simon thought—but her features were artistically enhanced by her choice of attire and makeup. Her hair was her least attractive feature. It was dyed jet black and cut in what may have been intended as a shag, but her listless and thin hair couldn't pull off that style. Instead, it looked more like a drunken barber had attacked her hair with a dull razor.

She had a great laugh, though. It was infectious and Simon found himself smiling several times as something funny caught her fancy, and she let loose five or six belly-shaking "ha has" complete with head tipped back and eyes scrunched shut. Simon liked people with a good sense of humor. She appeared to love to laugh. Perhaps he could use his dry wit as a way in.

Molly Lopez was roly-poly and entirely clad in turquoise. Jaime was wearing a Hawaiian shirt of deep blues and greens over khaki slacks. He had a slight gut on a skinny body and was only about five feet seven in his cowboy boots.

Simon was on his second beer when a sixtysomething stout, bald man of medium height and wearing a green vest over a “No Bad Days in San Amaro” T-shirt, purple surf shorts, and flip-flops walked into the middle of the room, microphone in hand. The TVs were muted, and he announced that the Wednesday night trivia game would begin in thirty minutes. He outlined the rules and reminded the patrons that competing teams must consist of two to four people only. Teams could register with him for the next fifteen minutes. Simon was wondering whether he should ask Stella and her friends if they wanted a fourth player when a man who had been sitting down the bar a way and drinking heavily for the past twenty-five minutes went to their table and, without any interaction with the three friends, sat himself down in the fourth chair. The man, who had receding thin gray-and-brown hair, a good-sized potbelly stretching his tie-dyed tank top and blue jean cutoff shorts, put his hand over Stella’s. The gesture appeared to be more an indication of possession than one of endearment. Stella left her hand where it was for several long moments and then subtly withdrew it ostensibly to reach for her wineglass.

Simon hadn’t counted on competition. He sat back against his barstool watching the muted soccer game and watching the four as the evening progressed. The trivia game was amusing. It consisted of three rounds of ten questions. Participating teams could be seen debating the merits of conflicting answers within their team, heads together, so as not to be heard by their competition. Most groups were clearly having fun as laughter erupted from several tables as they developed consensus for their final answers. Stella’s potbellied beau was not one of the lighthearted players. He appeared to be becoming more belligerent as the evening went on, and he continued to consume two drinks for every one his tablemates enjoyed.

In the final round, as teams deliberated on the eighth question—Which of your body parts continues to grow through your life?—anger erupted at Stella's table. It appeared to Simon that they were simply trying to answer the trivia question when Potbelly slammed his hand down hard on the table, upsetting Stella's half-full red wine in the process, causing wine to slosh over their answer sheet and onto Stella's top and white capris. She jumped up in hopes of minimizing the damage to her outfit, and Simon watched as Potbelly roughly grasped her arm, pulling her away from the table. There was no subtlety this time as Stella yanked her arm out of his grasp. Aware of the tension between Stella and the jerk, Jaime stood up and stepped beside Stella, effectively blocking Potbelly's access to her. Simon was watching with interest, and something in the speed with which Jaime had moved and the physical barrier he provided made Simon think this wasn't the first time he had intervened to keep Stella out of harm's way from this man.

Only a few people had noticed the altercation. The trivia game master was reading the final question in the final round by the time Stella and Jaime sat back down at the table. Stella had said something to the drunk. It caused him to grab his drink and slosh it down his throat. Before he lurched from the room, banging the door loudly on his way out, he spoke loudly to Stella. "You better hope *I* don't see *you* again!" When Simon looked back to their table, Molly was comforting Stella and Jaime was paying their bill. They ended up waiting to hear the answers to the final round's questions before heading out.

Simon decided to leave, too, but it took several minutes for him to pay his tab. By the time he exited the pub, the three friends were nowhere to be seen. The moon was almost full and was reflecting beautifully on the sea. Simon wandered out onto the beach, kicked off his shoes, and sat watching the moonlight shimmer in the movement of the water. The night air was cool and smelled sweet. If nothing came of his pursuit of Stella, at least he'd found a piece of heaven here in this small town in Mexico.

Chapter 6—December 21, 2016, San Amaro

It was less than a week before Christmas and another Wednesday evening when Simon saw Stella for the second time. He had gone to the Crown and Anchor last Wednesday, but neither Stella nor her friends were there for the trivia games. Tonight, however, they arrived shortly after Simon. Again, Simon was seated at the bar with a beer. The trio of Stella, Jaime, and Molly sat at a table close to the middle of the room, making it more difficult for Simon to surveil them under the pretense of watching TV.

Simon noted that again tonight, Molly was dressed entirely in turquoise. This time, it was a flowing tunic over below-the-knee leggings and sandals with ugly plastic flowers on them. Stella's outfit was almost the exact reverse of what she wore the previous time he'd seen her. She had on a sleeveless red blouse with red capris accented with a white belt and jewelry. *The red clothes made her look more robust, less skinny, more attractive,* he thought.

At seven o'clock, the same bald emcee came out with his microphone to announce the trivia-game rules and timing of team formation. He was wearing the same tatty green vest, swim shorts, and flip-flops, but his T-shirt tonight announced he was a 49ers fan. Simon had a plan, and since Stella and her two friends were still the only ones at their table, he decided to move forward with it, approaching them.

"Are you folks looking for a fourth player for the game?" he asked in a friendly tone, looking at each person in turn around the table. "I'm new here and wondered if I could join you. I was here a couple of weeks ago and watched. It looks like fun. I'm Simon." He held his hand out to Jaime and then Molly and Stella.

He was welcomed to the table, and introductions were made all around. "Does anyone want another drink before the game begins? I'm going to get another beer," Simon said, smiling at the group before sitting down.

"Rosita will be by in a minute. Let her bring us a round. Otherwise, you might end up standing at the bar for fifteen minutes," Jaime advised.

"Great," said Simon, sitting in the vacant chair. "Do you folks live here, or are you here on holiday?"

"Oh, we all live here," Molly answered for the group. "What about you?"

"I just moved here. I guess you could say I'm semiretired now. I'm a lawyer in Arizona and I still have some clients up there I do work for, but I'm planning on making this my home now. I can do a lot of my work from here on the phone and internet. I plan to go up to Phoenix once or twice a month for face-to-face meetings and the like, if need be." Simon spoke easily, a casual, relaxed air about him. "I love the easygoing pace of life here. And you can't argue the natural beauty." This last remark he seemed to address to Stella. He held her eyes for just a second and smiled.

She smiled back and agreed. The game master was back on the microphone with the first question of the evening, so further conversation was halted as the four of them put their heads together to come up with an answer to “How many stars are on the Australian flag?”

In an hour, the four of them were laughing together over their poor showing in the first two rounds of the evening’s game. “How on earth did we let you convince us that a hippo is the second-fastest land animal in Africa?” Molly asked Simon with a laugh, shaking her head. “You must be a good lawyer. If I’m ever caught in some crime, I want you in my corner. You could probably convince the judge it was a hippo that was guilty and not me.” Stella started to laugh at this and nearly spilled her wine.

“Yes, but I was right that it was Charlie Chaplin, not Johnny Carson, who was known as the ‘King of Comedy,’” Simon countered. “And I let you and Jaime convince me I was wrong.” They all laughed.

Fifteen minutes before the end of the second round of trivia, Simon noticed the potbellied guy who had been the fourth with Stella, Jaime, and Molly the previous time they had played. He entered the bar, looking around. After a minute, he spied them at their table. Again, he looked as if he had already had too much to drink. Molly was the only other person at their table with a view of the door and the bar, but if she’d noticed him come in, she hadn’t given any indication. Simon watched with growing concern as the guy made no effort to hide watching the foursome. Tonight, he was drinking neat scotch and was already ordering his second glass since coming into the pub less than ten minutes before.

As the trivia master walked back to his preferred spot with his microphone to start the final round, Simon watched as Potbelly tossed back a third drink and stood up, none too steadily. Simon was frantically trying to think what to do if the guy came over to cause trouble. He was filled with a deep sense of relief when the man shuffled to the door and left. Simon thought he caught him looking back at their table as the door swung shut behind him, but with the glare from the outside light, he couldn't be sure.

The third round was a winning round for the foursome. They managed to get nine of the ten questions answered correctly while still making one another laugh with off-the-wall answers thrown out to the team for that express purpose. Simon had made them all laugh heartily with a couple of his more bizarre answers. Once he learned that Stella had been a middle school science teacher, he proposed several ridiculous sciencey answers specifically to make her snicker. It worked.

As they finished their drinks at the end of the evening, Simon said to the group, "Thanks for letting me join you. I haven't had this much fun in a very long time." He was surprised to realize he meant it. He really had enjoyed himself in their company. "Is there a place you'd recommend for breakfast?" he asked. "I'm getting tired of toast and peanut butter at home."

After some discussion among the three friends, they suggested he check out La Azteca north of town near the gringo communities and near where Jaime and Molly lived. As they tried to explain how to get there, Simon asked, "Stella, would you care to join me? Maybe I could follow you there, since you said you live here in town, too. Do you two want to meet us there?" he asked Jaime and Molly. And as easily as that, his plan began to unfold.

Chapter 7—December 31, 2016, San Amaro

The Crown and Anchor provided a roast beef dinner for New Year's Eve. They even made Yorkshire pudding. After dinner, a band whose members were all retired expats in their seventies got most people up dancing with music from the 1960s through to the '80s. Stella, Molly, and Jaime already had their tickets in hand by mid-December, but Stella invited Simon to join them, and he was able to get one of the last tickets. He was delighted that Stella asked him to join her in the New Year's Eve fun.

Their breakfast with Jaime and Molly had been a success, the rapport among them becoming more comfortable and Stella opening up more to Simon. In the nine days since breakfast, Simon and Stella had also met for a walk on the beach, where they hunted for unicorn horn shells for Stella's craft project. They managed to find enough to finish her project two times over, she'd said. Then, they walked the beach, hand in hand, getting to know each other.

To his delight, Simon found Stella pleasant company, and she seemed to be glowing with his attention. He found it was pretty easy to keep to the truth when describing his life to her. He was grateful for that, as every lie required remembering and opened the way to difficulties in the future if misremembered or worse, forgotten. For her part,

Stella shared her life's story freely. She spoke openly about her happy marriage and her heartbreak when her husband, Don's, terminal-cancer diagnosis put a full stop in the middle of the chapter that was to have been their golden years. She became animated again as she spoke of moving to San Amaro and her love affair with Mexico and its wonderful people.

As she told him about her teaching career, Simon imagined her as one of those teachers students remembered fondly. She obviously had loved teaching science, and "her kids," as she referred to them. They laughed together as she recounted stories of a couple of failed experiments, one including an exploding, rather than erupting, volcano that left her with covered with cola. The kids loved it. A great teaching moment. From then on, however, she eschewed Coke and Mentos for plain old baking soda and vinegar volcanoes. She showed no embarrassment in telling of her teaching foibles, and Simon admired her passion for opening the minds of the young to science.

At the end of their afternoon on the beach, Simon had simply leaned down and kissed her lightly on the lips. It was his intention to leave it at that, but Stella embraced him and held the kiss for several moments. "Well, that was lovely!" he said, smiling, as they resumed their walk back to his car.

"Yes, it was!" was all Stella said in reply.

She had asked him to come in when he pulled up outside her house, but he had declined, saying, "I don't want you to get tired of me quite yet. Can I please get a rain check?" They kissed again before she left him. This time he traced her mouth with an index finger before gently drawing her face to his. That kiss told him everything he needed to know. He could see his plan was working.

The Crown and Anchor was hopping for its year-end celebration. Each table, in addition to a bottle of bubbly included in the ticket price, had a quintessentially British component—the Christmas cracker. Designed to be pulled apart by two people, one on each end of the tube-shaped novelty, the crackers contained within a paper party crown, a small plastic toy, and a joke. At their table, Molly, Jaime, Stella, and Simon had each donned their paper hats. This was guaranteed to loosen up any participant, as it's virtually impossible to look anything but ridiculous while wearing one. After they had all laughed at one another's funny hat-topped countenance, they proceeded to try out their jokes on one another.

"What are a shark's favorite two words?" Jaime asked, holding the slip of paper with the joke on it from his cracker. They all were shaking their heads. "Man overboard!" he finished. A wry chuckle was the best result he achieved. Still, they all decided it was a better joke than some of the others.

Dinner arrived shortly after they had finished with their jokes. The roast beef was cooked to perfection, but the Yorkshire pudding was a bit too doughy. The champagne helped, and no one was complaining about the food. At their table, Simon and his new friends were very merry. By the time the band started, they were happily tipsy, and Simon invited Stella to join him on the dance floor.

While not his favorite pastime, Simon had a good sense of rhythm and moved with a loose sexiness that gave Stella a slight thrill. They had danced to a couple of disco favorites when the band shifted to an old Barry White love song. Simon held his hand out and Stella took it, allowing herself to be pulled into Simon's close embrace. For a few moments, her body was tense, then she began to relax, and by the end of the song, they were glued to each other. "You're a lovely dancer," he said into her hair, and he meant it.

That was the first night Stella asked him to stay with her and the start of their spending almost all their time together. They were what they were, a couple in the thrall of new love. For her part, Stella felt like a girl again. Her heart fluttered when she saw him, whether after a night on her own or his return to a room after a few moments' absence. It had been decades since she felt the full thrill of romance. It took her completely by surprise.

"So, Mr. Wakefield, how is it that you have waltzed into my life and swept me off my feet? What's your magic, sir?" she asked one afternoon as they walked up the beach north of town. She had packed a small picnic lunch of salami, bread, and cheese, and a bottle of white wine. They were looking for a place to spread their blanket on the sand.

Simon's step faltered slightly as he scanned her face before answering. Seeing no malice, he replied, "And here I was thinking you were the one with the magic pixie dust. I guess we're just lucky to have found someone who makes us happy, at least speaking for myself."

"All I know is that I'm having fun. I am glad you decided to check out San Amaro." She smiled at him and then pointing, said, "I think this spot looks lovely for our picnic, don't you?"

Chapter 8—January 16, 2017, Tempe

The holiday time from late November through December was historically a very slow time for Rob's business, as it seemed it was going to be again this year. He wasn't sure whether the Thanksgiving spirit started a period when domestic angst was set aside, if only temporarily, to accord happier family holidays. It certainly wasn't good for his bank balance. As always when business was slow, Rob worked out more fervently, spending at least two hours a day in the gym and an hour more running the trails that bordered the river near his condo.

His already-buff body became chiseled. He didn't aim for bulk, as some bodybuilders did. His goal was to have a beautiful, sculpted body with a clearly defined six-pack of abs and arm muscles that caught other beautiful men's attention when he entered a club, but that also fit into off-the-shelf men's shirts.

This night found him arriving at Dirty Mother's, a gay bar on a side street, half a block off Mill Ave. It was only ten thirty, which was early evening for a men's bar. Rob wanted to see a friend and sometime hookup partner of his, Phillip, there. He needed a diversion from the last seven weeks of nothing except working out and watching Tristin eat crickets. As it happened, Phillip was walking toward the entrance to Dirty Mother's from the opposite direction of Rob's approach. They met on the sidewalk, embraced, and chatted for a few minutes, catching up before entering the pounding beat of the current day's dance music inside.

The two men grabbed stools at the bar, ordered drinks, and took advantage of the relatively low volume of the music. This meant if they yelled, the other could hear each other over the music's throb. By eleven thirty, conversation would be virtually impossible over the blasting music. By the time that happened, Rob and Phillip had finished catching up on each other's lives over the past months since they last hooked up. They had also consumed several Red Bull-and-rum cocktails. The caffeine from the Red Bull had their nerves tingling; the rum provided a lovely buzz.

"Do you want to dance or come over to my place?" Rob yelled into Phillip's ear over the now-blasting music. Phillip answered by taking Rob's hand and pulling him toward the dance floor. After twenty minutes of clothed vertical sex masquerading as dancing, the two men left and headed to Rob's, where more rum and Red Bull awaited.

Two hours later, the men moved from Rob's bed to the living room for a brandy. Phillip knew from previous evenings with Rob that he would not be invited to spend the night, and that suited them both just fine. "You've got something on your mind, my friend. What's going on?" Phillip asked between sips from his snifter. Despite the casualness of their sexual relationship, the two men shared an authentic friendship. There was no artifice between them.

"Work has been very slow since before Thanksgiving, and that's given me a lot of time to think. I keep asking myself if this is what I want to be doing for the next twenty-five years of my life. When I'm busy and have interesting or challenging jobs, I really enjoy what I do, but I'm not convinced it's my life's passion. I'm too young for this to be a midlife crisis, right?" He added this last bit rhetorically.

"I have a friend, a straight guy," Rob said, "who I think is setting himself up for a big cash windfall in the next few years, and I think there must be a way to help him achieve his goal and share some of his good fortune. I think I'm getting obsessed with the idea, and that isn't healthy," Rob spoke more quietly, nodding his head to this last remark, as though hearing the truth in what he'd said. "Yeah, I guess that's the bottom line. I need to get busy with work again and stop obsessing on something that might not be real in the first place. Right?" Rob turned to Phillip for confirmation.

"Being in an obsessed state of mind is hardly the ideal position from which to make decisions about your long-term future," Phillip offered, his psychotherapist-day-job persona kicking in. "If you're asking for my two cents' worth . . ." He paused and inclined his head to Rob, raising an eyebrow in question. Rob nodded for him to continue. ". . . I'd say get a couple of jobs under your belt over the next few weeks and then revisit the 'What do I want to be when I grow up?' question."

"Yeah, I know you're right. I guess I just needed to hear myself say it out loud and get your wise counsel. Do you know anyone who needs a good PI?" he asked with a sad smile.

After Phillip left, Rick fed his obsession just a little. He checked the obituaries as he did every few days. It seemed the Cutler woman was still kicking. She was a big-enough name in the area that when she finally kicked the bucket, the big papers would all carry her obituary. Next, he checked out the San Amaro gringo Facebook group posts.

Stella and Molly were both regular posters. The only thing new in the last few days was a post from Stella with a few pictures of the beach and sea on a bright sunny afternoon. One included Simon standing near the shore, and another was a selfie of Stella and Simon sitting together on a multicolored Mexican blanket on the sand. They were looking very comfortable snuggled together. Rob slowly closed his laptop, a pensive look on his face. It was looking as if Simon might actually be able to pull off getting his hands on Althea Cutler's money. The lucky fuck!

The following Monday, Rob was hired to shadow the high school-aged daughter of a medium-level distributor of small electronic items of dubious origins. The father was concerned that his daughter's new boyfriend was involved in street-corner drug trafficking. Rob's remit was to track the daughter's movements and interactions to determine whether, in fact, the father's concerns were warranted.

So far, Rob had been tracking the daughter from home to school, school to the boyfriend's tiny apartment, and from the bus stop near said apartment back home. He'd spent one day tailing the boyfriend, and while Rob hadn't seen him selling drugs on any street corners, he had clocked the boyfriend meeting with a couple of guys who definitely looked the part of low-level dealers.

Teenagers, especially those whose senses were dulled by their raging hormones, were mostly oblivious to things happening around them, so Rob felt safe using his Triumph when tailing the girl and her boyfriend. He loved just cruising around town on his motorcycle, and having work again was a relief. It almost had the desired effect for Rob of getting his mind out of its obsessive thinking about how to get his hands on some of those $18 million. Almost.

Chapter 9—January 21, 2017, San Amaro

Sun winked off windshields and side mirrors of the ten or so cars in the parking lot of the only golf course in San Amaro. Half a dozen seagulls glided overhead traversing the quarter mile between the fourteenth-hole lake and sandy beach of the seashore, which edged several holes on the front nine. Simon could feel the sun's heat as he unloaded his clubs from the trunk of his Bimmer. January had been unusually cold, or so the locals and longtime residents said. To Simon, it was certainly cooler than Phoenix in January, but today was beautiful. Warm, no wind, perfect for golf.

Beside him, Stella's longtime friend Rick Worton pulled his clubs from the box of his battered old burgundy Dodge Dakota pickup truck. Many people in San Amaro had twentyish-year-old trucks or SUVs as runabouts for around town. Some streets in San Amaro boasted crater-sized potholes. Driving a nice car was not advised, as Simon was learning. "Hey, Simon, Jaime phoned me five minutes ago. He's running late. Should be here in thirty or forty minutes. Something about the restaurant and his daughter needing his help, apparently. Let's grab a beer while we wait for him."

San Amaro Golf Club was like so many places in San Amaro. Laid back. No one booked a tee time.

There weren't enough golfers to warrant scheduled tee times. A person just showed up, rented a cart, and went out. There wasn't a course marshal, either. Players were on their own. Golfers paid their 200 pesos, about ten dollars US, to rent a decrepit golf cart, and off they went. The course itself was in decent shape and had some very challenging holes.

"I can't believe I've lived here only a couple of months," Simon mused. "And that I've made such good friends already. Feels like I've been here for years. This town and the gringo community here just kind of wrap their arms around you and make you feel at home."

Rick was nodding his head. "I know what you mean. And it doesn't hurt that you and Stella seem to have made a significant connection. She knows a lot of people here, and everyone loves her. She's just that kind of warm, openhearted person. I connected with her right off when she moved here. Of course, it wasn't quite the same kind of connection she made with you." He winked at Simon, and the two men laughed.

"Even though I'd lived here longer than she had, she introduced me to lots of folks. Even got me connected with a few gay couples here. I wasn't sure what it would be like here being gay, but I quickly realized that no one here cares, gringos, or Mexicans. And now, with gay marriage being legal in Mexico, it really is a nonissue," Rick said.

"I'm a lucky guy," Simon remarked. "I know that for sure. Meeting Stella and your group is more than I hoped for when I moved here. I wish I'd come to San Amaro years ago. I wouldn't still be a bachelor," he said and laughed. "But hey, don't go sharing that with Stella. I kind of think I should be the one to tell her, don't you?"

The men were laughing and clinking their beer bottles when Jaime joined them. “Looks like I’m missing the fun. You guys ready to play golf?”

None of them was particularly serious about the game. Jaime had started playing only two years before, and this was Rick’s first game in months. It was simply a way to hang out, get some exercise, and enjoy the beautiful setting and sea views. As they stopped at the *baños*, bathrooms, at the sixth hole, Jaime said to Simon, “You’re a great new part of the group. I haven’t seen Stella this happy in a long time. Now we just need Rick to meet some awesome new guy. Right, Rick?” Jaime said, winking at Rick. “Anyway, Simon, it’s good to have you in the group.”

“Funny. I was saying almost the same thing before you arrived today. I can’t believe how quickly my life has changed since I moved here. I’ve always thought of myself as a confirmed bachelor until now,” Simon said, a solemnness overtaking his usual jovial demeanor.

“Shit! Don’t get too close to me, then,” Rick chided. “That might rub off. I still really like my freedom!” he exclaimed.

“Let’s go play some more golf,” Simon said, shifting the conversation back into neutral territory. He’d planted the desired seed.

Chapter 10—February 14, 2017, Four Miles North of San Amaro

Earlier in the day, Simon bought a couple of bundles of firewood and a very nice bottle of wine and stashed them along with a blanket, wineglasses, and fresh strawberries into the back of his new golf buddy, Rick's, RZR. He'd arranged with Rick to borrow his desert rig for a few hours that evening. He had been thinking through his plan for this day for a couple of weeks now. The time finally seemed right.

There was no good reason to wait.

The late-afternoon air was sweet with the scent of desert verbena and the unique fragrance of the creosote bushes' blazing yellow flowers. It had been a blessedly windless day, for which Simon was grateful. As he and Stella stopped the RZR near his chosen spot on the deserted beach, he made a silent prayer that he could pull off the events of the evening.

After smoothing the blanket, getting Stella comfortably situated close to the kindled wood and getting said wood alight, Simon uncorked the wine and handed her a glass. The sun was caressing the tops of the mountains to the west, and the sky was beginning to blaze as brightly as the fire with the colors of desert sunset. "What a beautiful evening!" Stella said. "This is really nice, Simon."

Simon got no sense that she guessed what he was planning. He wasn't sure if that was good or bad.

Regardless, he took advantage of her lead-in. "Good, I'm glad you like it. I wanted to do something special tonight." His eyes searched her face for any signs of weariness or concern. Seeing neither, he carried on. "Stella, I am so happy I moved to San Amaro. I knew it would be a nice place to retire, but I never imagined I'd meet someone who would make me want to give up my bachelor life. The past few months, meeting you, falling in love with you . . . It's been like a tidal wave sweeping me into an ocean of feelings I didn't know even existed."

It hadn't taken long, only two dates after the trivia game, for Stella to invite Simon to spend the night with her. Simon was pleased and relieved that she had initiated the start of their intimacy. She was an uncomplicated lover, an uncomplicated person. He found her pragmatic approach to life and loving quite refreshing. They had naturally fallen into a routine of him spending the night at her house three or four times a week.

Stella's expression now softened, and she was looking at Simon with inquiring, almost penetrating, eyes. He went on: "I have had plenty of girlfriends in my life, and I've always been happy to keep it casual. Until now." He was trying to keep as close to the truth as possible. And casual was not going to work for his plan.

"I can't believe I'm saying this, but, Stella, I want our relationship to be different. The way I feel about you is not like how I've felt about anyone in the past. It's important to me to acknowledge how different my love for you is. I want you to marry me, Stella. I'm not doing a very elegant job of saying this, but . . ." He sputtered to a stop, searching her face, trying to gauge her response.

Stella's eyes were scouring his face. They flicked over his features, bored into his eyes. She looked so serious Simon wondered what was going through her mind. He realized he was holding his breath and tried to relax enough to breathe. Something in that movement seemed to release Stella from a stupor. Her face grew soft again; her eyes focused on his. She placed her hands on his cheeks, lightly kissing his lips.

"I know it's Valentine's Day and this is very romantic, but why on earth would we get married at our age?" she asked, breezily. There was no rancor in her voice. It seemed a straightforward question of curiosity.

Simon was undaunted. "I know you and Don had a good marriage. And I imagine you think marrying again might somehow diminish your memories of him."

"No, it's not that at all. When Don and I married, it was because it was the societal norm then. Young professional people in the seventies were still expected to marry and not just shack up. Why would *we* get married? Now?" Again, her voice held a simple curious tone.

Ah, yes, Simon thought, *her question is pragmatic, not emotional.* He was ready for this. "Apart from the fact that I want to acknowledge, publicly, the depth of how I feel about you, Mexican law does not have quite the same domestic-partnership laws as the US when there isn't a child or children involved. If you were in the hospital or arrested, not that I think that will happen," he said, "I wouldn't have any rights to see or help you. Just thinking that makes me feel so powerless. I couldn't bear it."

He looked directly into her eyes as he spoke. The deepening colors of the sunset played across Stella's face, shading the contours of her cheekbones purple. He held her gaze as he could see her considering his words.

"Makes sense. That's as good a reason as any," she said at last. "And you do know I love you, too. Why not, then. Let's do it!"

Simon swept her into a deep embrace as the sunset sky darkened to a deep blue black. They made love on the blanket, their bodies rocking in a rhythm with the sound of the incoming tide lapping softly on the sand.

Chapter 11—February 15, 2017, Tempe

Rob was beyond frustrated. He'd been sitting in a rented black Nissan Sentra watching his current client's husband's car. It remained parked in front of a modest post-World War II bungalow of the kind found in almost every town and city across America. The tenant of this particular house was the husband's sister, according to Rob's research. The husband had been inside the house for almost three hours, and Rob had been sitting in his car for those same three hours.

His client, the guy's wife, suspected her husband of an affair, because every Wednesday evening he would leave their house and not return until the wee hours of the morning. Rob's remit on this case was to find out where the husband went every Wednesday and, if possible, catch him in the act of cheating on his wife. This was the first Wednesday Rob was on the man's tail. In the last three hours, his mind had roamed freely through myriad possibilities about what was going on. He assumed that the husband wasn't having an affair with his own sister, as that would be too weird. He'd considered that the guy came here, left his car out front, and then took off in his sister's car. If that were the case, Rob would need to put a tracker on the sister's car, in addition to the one under the right front fender of the husband's six-year-old Mercedes SUV. Rob walked up the alley and looked in the window of the detached garage in the backyard. There was a late-model Honda Accord still in the garage, so unless the sister had multiple cars, the husband likely hadn't left the house.

After he'd considered these and many other possibilities of what the husband might be doing, his mind slipped away to the persistent issue plaguing him for the last few months—how to get his hands on some of Althea Cutler's money. This morning, Rob noted that Stella Monroe had changed her status on Facebook to "in a committed relationship." This he interpreted as an extremely positive result for Simon, as all the posts he'd seen on Simon's feed showed pictures of Stella and him enjoying life in San Amaro. Simon's strategy appeared to be working.

It was time, Rob told himself, for a plan of his own. How could he persuade Simon to share some of those millions of dollars with him? It didn't seem as if Simon needed Rob's help beyond his initial work in finding Stella and providing Simon with details and photos that must surely have helped him get started. Unfortunately, he'd been paid for that work, and he couldn't think of anything else he could do to help Simon at this point that would entitle him to sharing in the coming windfall Stella would receive.

He'd thought of simply blackmailing Simon with the threat of telling Stella everything once the Cutler woman died and Stella inherited. That should be good for some significant payments, but he wasn't sure how he felt about blackmailing a friend. In the end, he supposed he could do it without very much trouble if he couldn't come up with anything better.

The ideal thing would be to find some way to set up a joint account with Simon, whereby Simon could deposit money in, and Rob could take money out. That might more easily facilitate the blackmail angle if he couldn't come up with a business idea that would make the joint account necessary. *What business could the two of them purport to have,* he wondered.

Maybe he could get Simon to include him in his will! But then, Rob knew, he'd just be really tempted to kill Simon to get to the money. Or, he pondered, he could get Simon to pay him to kill Stella. That would have to be expensive, he figured. Maybe he could get a couple of million for that and then blackmail Simon by telling him he'd set up the murder to look as if Simon were the killer and he'd send that information to the police if Simon didn't keep paying. Still, Rob wasn't happy with any of these ideas. He really didn't want to have to kill anyone, and blackmail could have an ugly way of coming back on the blackmailer. He'd have to keep considering other ideas, he decided.

Finally, at just before midnight, the husband emerged from his sister's house. Rob took copious photos of the pair as the husband left the house, in case the woman he was meeting was not actually his sister. Surely the wife would be able to identify her sister-in-law. Rob let the husband drive away and turn the corner before starting his rental car and pulling up the tracker app on the phone he had bought for this case. It took him a minute to catch up to the husband. Rob followed at a distance that would ensure the husband could see only car lights and not identify the car.

After tailing the car for twenty minutes, Rob watched the husband park on a dubious-looking side street in Phoenix. Two of the streetlights on the dowdy street were out, and as Rob looked up the length of the block, he speculated to himself that the business owners there might be quite fine with that.

Stallion's Gentleman's Club was nearest the north end of the block and Dancer's 24/7 was three doors in from the corner nearest where the husband had parked. Between these two illustrious establishments were a couple of adult bookstores and a frightening-looking, run-down Chinese restaurant.

To Rob's surprise, it was this restaurant the husband entered. Rob waited a minute before leaving his own car and sauntered up the street. He slowly ambled past the restaurant but couldn't see much inside because of the filthy windows. What looked from a distance like excrement rubbed on them turned out to be streaks of black and red paint that appeared to be remnants of Chinese New Year's decorations. It had moldered into the moisture build up on the inside of the windows from cooking in an unventilated kitchen. Fortunately for Rob, there was a menu taped to the window on the door, and he was able to stop and appear to peruse the menu while doing his best to see into the place.

He was surprised and disappointed to see the restaurant completely empty except for an old Chinese man sitting in the back booth, reading a newspaper, and smoking a cigarette. There were only six booths, three on each side of a narrow aisle with the open-style kitchen along the side opposite the door. At the end of the aisle between the booths was a single bathroom and a door to the alley. The door was closing. Rob stepped away from the front door and ran to the end of the block, around the corner, and then slowed down as he reached the entrance to the alley.

Whenever on a stakeout at night, Rob wore all black. Tonight, he had on a long-sleeved black T-shirt, black jeans, and black running shoes, with a black ball cap tucked in the back pocket of the jeans.

As he slowed and took a deep breath at the entrance to the alley, he yanked the ball cap from his pocket and pulled it over his blond curls and down over his brow. He slowly crooked his neck so only his head looked into the alley and let his eyes adjust to the darkness.

He could see only one other person in the laneway, but he cautiously crept around the corner and into the alley. Then, near the other end of the back street, he saw movement. He stopped and waited. Slowly another figure emerged from the shadows and walked toward the first. He recognized the shape of the second person as the man he was following. The man reached an arm out to the other person with trepidation. Rob could finally make out the other person to be a young, skeletally thin woman. As he watched, the couple slowly made their way back up the alley toward him. He slunk behind a disgusting-smelling dumpster and maintained a view of the couple by peering over the mounds of rotting rubbish.

When they reached the middle of the block, the man opened a door, likely the Chinese restaurant, Rob figured, and then they were gone. Rob reversed his path back toward the front of the restaurant and slowed as he reached its front door. Inside, he could see the couple sitting in a booth, the woman facing Rob. He dared not take a photo of her but tried to imprint her image in his mind. Back in his car, he waited.

It was a half hour later when the man trudged back to his car looking as if he were carrying the weight of the world. Rob followed him back to his home and watched as he unlocked and entered his front door at about two in the morning. Later in the day, he would report to the wife and ask her if they had a daughter or perhaps a niece, and if so, to show him pictures. He already had a story in his mind about what might be going on. If he were right, it was a family drama involving drugs, likely prostitution, too.

He was still sitting in his rental car making notes on his cell phone when the driver's-side rear window imploded, sending glass into the entire car. A second later, Rob realized the man he'd been tailing was accosting the car with a baseball bat and yelling, "Who the hell are you? Why are you following me?" Rob had previously started the car and now stomped on the gas and peeled away.

Goddam it, he thought as he pulled into a funeral-home parking lot a few blocks from the altercation and got his breathing under control. *That was too close for comfort. Thank God the guy went after the rear window.* He'd have to concoct a story for the car-rental agency. He sat there a few minutes to compose himself. During that time, a single thought pounded inside his brain. *I'm going to get some of that fucking old lady Cutler's money and retire into the life I deserve. Somehow.*

Chapter 12—February 16, 2017, San Amaro

A seagull caught an air current and was gliding over the liminal space between the *playa*, beach, and the azure sea's edge. It was a warm day with only moderate wind as Molly watched the gull absently from a table no more than one hundred feet away until she heard Stella's alto voice behind her.

"Beautiful, isn't it?" she said, placing a light, pure-white cardigan and her red purse on a chair. As usual, Stella was in a simple, but elegant outfit. Today it was white capris and scoop-necked blouse in pale pink. Her accessories, earrings, bracelet, purse, and slip-on flats were all deep red. Molly noticed at once that her friend was glowing.

"Wow! You look great today," Molly said as she watched her friend take the seat opposite her.

Before either woman could say anything more, a waitress was at their table with menus and asked if they wanted something to drink. Stella answered quickly, "We'll have a bottle of white wine and two glasses, please."

Molly raised an eyebrow and gave Stella a funny smile. "What's the special occasion? I can't remember the last time we had wine with lunch." As usual, Molly was bedecked in turquoise. Over an unfortunately form-fitting turquoise tank top, which showed every roll and crevice of her voluptuous torso, she wore an aqua-and-sea-green-patterned gauzy shawl. This was paired with a differently patterned floor-length teal-and-white peasant skirt. *Some of Molly's home sewing projects,* Stella surmised. Stella couldn't see Molly's shoes but was sure they would be one of her many pairs of bedazzled sandals. She loved her friend's eccentric fashion sense.

"I have news. An announcement, I guess," Stella said and then paused dramatically before going on. "Simon and I are getting married. He proposed on Valentine's Day." As she said this, she grinned and hunched up her shoulders while pulling her head down to her chest in a schoolgirl-like gesture of pure joy.

"Oh, my God!" Molly exclaimed. "When? Have you picked a date?"

"Not yet, but we want to do it soon, and you are going to help me organize it, okay?" Stella stated.

"Damn right, I am!" Molly answered. Her blue eyes shone as she took a moment to assess her friend. In the past, Stella had always said she'd never marry again. She didn't see any point at her age to make that kind of commitment. "So, what happened to the woman who said she didn't need to marry again?" She couldn't help asking.

"Oh, I know, but Simon made a good case for it, especially living down here. The laws aren't the same as in the US for common-law relationships, plus he said he wanted to make a statement to the world that I wasn't just another girlfriend. It was really sweet, actually, the way he said it."

By now the wine had been served. They toasted Stella's news and ordered their usual, a chile relleno with rice and beans. This little open-air café on the Malecon made the best chile rellenos in town, in their estimation. The view was unparalleled, with an unobstructed view of the sea and San Amaro Bay with its nearly-white sand. The tables and chairs were white plastic of the inexpensive kind found at any big-box hardware and gardening store. The tables were topped with plastic-coated red-and-white-checkered canvas. By San Amaro standards, it was a nice, casual restaurant. Molly was still surprised by Stella's announcement. "Well, tell me all about it," she said.

As they waited for their lunch, they enjoyed their wine and Stella told Molly about the beach, the fire, the proposal, and Simon's reasons for wanting to marry. It was obvious Stella was very happy, and Molly got swept up in her excitement. She was also relieved to hear Stella voice some thoughts she had had about Simon from the start.

"When we met him that first night at the Crown and Anchor, I thought he was a total player. I found him charming right off the bat, but he seemed too dashing, too sure of himself, you know?" Stella asked, and Molly nodded her head in agreement. "But also, right from that first meeting, I liked him. I liked that he invited you and Jaime to breakfast. I liked that he suggested I drive my own car and that he'd follow me. I think otherwise, I might have felt a bit pressured, but as it turned out, he was and has continued to be very considerate of my independence. I know this has happened very fast. I mean, my God, I've known him only a couple of months. But, I say, what the hell. I'm not getting any younger. I've been falling in love with him right from the start, and apparently, so has he. So why not, eh?"

"You are such a pragmatist, Stella. I love you for it, and I'm mystified by it at the same time. I don't know another person who makes decisions as fast as you do and with so little emotional angst. So, let's plan this wedding, girlfriend!" Over their delicious lunch and getting slightly buzzed from the wine, the two women came up with an outline for Stella and Simon's wedding.

With the basics of the wedding organized, Stella turned the conversation to other topics. "So, what's Jaime up to today?"

"That damned nephew of his called this morning and asked Jaime to drive a semi down to Loreto. Apparently, the normal driver isn't available or something," Molly answered with an annoyed tone of voice.

"Which nephew? Not that one who is always in trouble with the law, I hope. Doesn't he have links to the cartel?" Stella asked, anxiously.

"Yes, that nephew!" Molly's exasperation was very apparent. "Supposedly, he's doing legitimate fishing now, but who the hell knows. There were a bunch of photos and posts on Facebook since yesterday about all the totoaba carcasses littering the beaches north and south of town right now. I so worry that he's getting roped into something illegal because of his strong family ties. You know how closely knit Mexican families are. It is one of the wonderful things about Mexico. Only in this case, I wish Jaime could just say no."

"Is Jaime actually doing it? He's driving this truck down there now!? My God, Molly, please tell me he's not." Even usually calm, pragmatic Stella was getting upset and emotional. "Surely he knows once he starts doing anything for the cartel, he'll be stuck in their clutches."

"When he left the house this morning, he hadn't committed to helping his nephew. He was just going over to his house. I'm praying he doesn't agree to drive the truck."

"You know what will happen if he does it and gets caught. There are at least three military checkpoints between here and Loreto, and there is always a good chance one of them will do an inspection."

"There haven't been any arrests yet in Mexico for totoaba bladder smuggling. It's the ships taking them to Asia that bear the greatest risk since China started cracking down on the people bringing them," Molly said almost apologetically.

"Oh right, so that makes it okay for Jaime to break the law. You know how I feel about that, and you know the totoaba"—she stumbled over the name—"is extremely endangered, and so does Jaime." Stella paused and seemed to shift gears. "I hope you understand I'm not mad at you, I'm just worried for Jaime . . . and you if he does it and gets caught. I didn't mean to put a damper on our lovely lunch. Come on, let's pay and have a nice walk down the beach, and then I have to go start getting ready for my wedding."

Jaime climbed out of his Jeep and called out to his nephew, Ernesto, "*Hola mi sobrino. ¿Cómo te va?*" Hello, nephew, how's it going?

"Good, uncle. I'm glad you came. Have you got your driving hat on?" Hector asked jovially.

"First, let's have a coffee and catch up. I haven't seen you for weeks," Jaime said, not letting his nephew jump right into business. *These young people need to understand the importance of social connection,* he thought.

After they had discussed the family and how everyone was doing, Jaime turned the conversation back to the topic he knew Ernesto was anxious to discuss. "So, now, tell me how the fishing is going. Who are you working with?"

Hector adjusted his posture, sitting more upright. He even smoothed the front of his T-shirt over his lean frame. "Fishing is tough these days, Tio. The government still has a ban on commercial fishing for several kinds of fish, so everyone is going after the same shrimp, sierra, and corvina. The world is more concerned about the last couple of dozen vaquita porpoises left in the sea than they are about hundreds of fishermen trying to make a living. Now that a fisherman can get a hundred dollars US for every totoaba they catch, everyone is doing it. I've heard that on the black market in China, a totoaba bladder can sell for fifteen hundred dollars. Can you believe it?"

Jaime knew the totoaba fish, found only in the Sea of Cortez, was prized in Asia for its supposed fertility-enhancing properties and as a dowry item among the rich families of China—and that it had been fished almost to extinction by international fisheries in the previous decades. He was aware, as were all residents of San Amaro, that the fish had been protected by the Mexican government for years. These days the Mexican navy, Greenpeace, and other groups regularly sailed the sea to curtail poaching. Still, every year hundreds of totoaba were illegally caught, gutted of their bladders, and tossed back into the sea, only for their carcasses to wash up on beaches all along the east side of Baja and west Mexican mainland coasts.

"No, Sobrino, you've got your numbers wrong. A single bladder sells for between fifteen and twenty thousand dollars US in Asia. That's why the cartel is here in Baja and willing to pay you a hundred dollars for one bladder. Even at that, they are just using you fishermen. They could afford to pay several times that, but they don't have to. You and your friends see only the money you make today. You don't see the potential for danger, from the police, from the military, and from the cartel themselves, or any of the other problems you could encounter. Or that in the long term, the poaching guarantees the totoaba will be gone in a few years. Be very careful, Nephew. I don't want to have to visit you in Mulegé!" Jaime said emphatically, referring to the prison nearest San Amaro. "So, if the truck you want me to drive today has anything to do with totoaba, I'm not going to do it."

"No, Tio, no! I wouldn't ask you to break the law," Ernesto said placatingly. "It's a truck full of . . ." He was interrupted midsentence as his wife exited the house from the door near where Ernesto and Jaime sat talking.

"Hola, Jaime. *¿Que tal?* How are you? I'm glad you're talking sense to him. Someone needs to help him stay out of trouble," Hector's wife said, confirming Jaime's suspicion she was eavesdropping on their conversation.

"*Buenos días, Lolita. Estoy bien, y tu*?" Good morning, Lolita, how are you? responded Jaime, smiling at his niece-in-law.

"*Bien, gracias*!" Well, thanks. "I'm just heading to the market. *Hasta luego*!" See you later! she answered as she started walking up the street toward a grocery store a few blocks away.

The two men watched her go, and when she was out of earshot, Jaime said, "Okay, how much are they paying me to drive down there? And what's your plan to handle the military checkpoints?"

Chapter 13—March 8, 2017, San Amaro

It had been a chaotic three weeks for Stella, but with Molly's and Simon's help, she had managed to be ready for this day. It started off with their normal routine. Simon made fruit smoothies and toast for breakfast, and they even managed to sit and enjoy it on their outside patio before starting on the to-do list for the final preparations.

After Stella started looking into the legal processes required by the Mexican government for gringos to wed in the country, she quickly decided she needed help and found a wedding planner in San Amaro to handle the paperwork. She provided copies of her and Simon's passports; their birth certificates, which had taken two weeks to obtain from US registry offices in their birth states; copies of her residence card; and Simon's visitor's visa and a few other documents. The wedding planner also told Stella how her friend, Rick, could go online to become a certified officiant to perform the civil union, the only type of wedding officially recognized as legal in Mexico.

The wedding planner's cousin rented and delivered four long foldup tables, thirty chairs, and a trellis archway to the beach where the nuptials were to take place. Molly, who had taken care of organizing flowers, decorated the trellis with red carnations and white roses and tied red and white ribbons, Stella's two favorite colors, on the sides of the chairs forming the aisle.

The location they had selected was on a beach north of town that was part of the gated community where Jaime and Molly lived. There were tall palm trees, a row of palapas with tables built round their bases and soft, almost white, sand from the water's edge to the parking lot against the wrought iron fence separating the beach from the community homes. The tide was in, and the gentle lapping of water against the shore was as light a sound as the caress of the breeze was on the faces of the wedding guests.

At three that afternoon, twenty-four of their friends, most wearing brightly colored casual clothes, were seated on the rented chairs. Rick, a bit nervous about his role as officiant, was wearing a pair of white slacks, a bright, floral-patterned Hawaiian shirt, and red Converse sneakers, and he was trying to keep from wiping his sweaty palms on his pants. He was standing behind the trellis. He stepped forward in preparation when he could see the bride and groom were ready. Molly was standing to his right and Jaime to his left, acting in the roles of bridesmaid and groomsman. Rick pulled his cell phone from his pocket and ensured it was still connected to the Bluetooth speakers on either side of the archway. One tap on his phone and Pachelbel's Canon began playing, and the bride and groom walked themselves up the aisle to begin the ceremony.

Stella was wearing a simple white-and-red cotton dress and white sandals. Simon wore cream-colored linen slacks and a red golf shirt with hiking sandals. The ceremony was short and very sweet, as Rick ensured the legal requirements were fulfilled and Simon and Stella read their own vows. As they kissed at the close of the ceremony, their friends cheered and clapped.

Two of the rented tables had been combined to create a bar and were now holding wine, beer, vodka, gin, rum, and rye whiskey, along with a variety of mixers. A third table held the wedding cake, and the fourth had been transformed by the staff from Jaime's daughter's restaurant into a lavish buffet of Mexican food delights.

The party went on until sunset. Simon and Stella headed out for their honeymoon shortly before their celebrators called it a night. Molly, Jaime, and Jaime's daughter were left in charge of ensuring the rentals were returned and beach tidied up of plastic cups, cutlery, and paper plates.

The honeymoon location had been kept secret from their friends so that Simon and Stella could have a few days of uninterrupted time. They had privately both agreed they were already in paradise, so they felt no need to leave San Amaro. Instead, they spent several days together doing what newlyweds do in the comfort of Stella's, now their, home.

Chapter 14—March 12, 2017, Tempe

Just back from a two-hour workout at the gym, Rob was scrolling through his Facebook feed when a series of pictures showed up that surprised and then angered him. Rob had joined the San Amaro Facebook group when he'd been researching the area and Stella Monroe, and he hadn't removed himself. The pictures were of a wedding.

Simon and Stella's wedding!

He was surprised because Simon had been in Mexico only three months and already, they were married! The anger was because he hadn't heard from Simon since he'd left, despite a couple of texts Rob had sent him asking how things were going.

Since the altercation with the husband he'd been tailing the previous month, Rob's thoughts strayed more and more frequently into his growing obsession with what he had come to think of as Simon's windfall. As often happens with obsessive thinking, Rob's view of the situation was becoming further from reality every day. Rob now saw himself as the wronged party. In his mind, he had done all the work of finding Stella and gathering all the information that had allowed Simon to waltz into her life and sweep her off her feet. The fact that he received his usual fee for that service rendered seemed forgotten. Now he thought he was owed, that Simon was indebted to him, that some of that windfall was rightfully his. It was not a healthy state of mind.

Over the last four weeks, when he wasn't concentrating on a job, working out at the gym, or caring for Tristin, his mind was plagued with ideas of how he could persuade Simon to share the wealth. He didn't have any kind of a plan formulated, but somewhere in the recesses of his thinking there had been the vague notion that Simon was going to need his help snaring Stella into marriage. Now seeing these pictures, he realized he had been more invested in that notion than he'd realized. The reality that Simon had managed just fine without his help devastated Rob in a way he wouldn't have imagined possible.

His first response was to feed his anger. He could feel a rage settling upon him, like an enveloping fog on an English moor. All he could think of was breaking something or pounding his fists into something. But, before it could completely cloud his thinking, Rob pulled himself back from the brink, realizing his obsession was keeping him from the clear thinking he'd need to come up with a viable strategy. Instead of crushing his cell phone and the photos of a wedding that had taken place four days before, he shoved the phone into the leg pocket of his workout shorts and headed out the door to go for a run and clear his head.

Sweat was pouring off him when he returned almost an hour later. He'd run full throttle. He couldn't remember getting from his condo to the river walk, or from the river's edge to the far east end of the university campus, so murky was his awareness, but as he rounded the campus and cut through its athletic fields, his mind finally started to clear. He began to feel more present than he had in weeks. A different Rob stepped into the shower from the zombie version of himself who had been inhabiting the condo for the past weeks. By the time he was dried and dressed, Rob had completely distanced himself from the anger, frustration, and obsessive thinking that had been holding him captive.

Rob looked around his normally orderly and immaculate condo and shook his head. Because of the fog of obsession, he'd been engulfed in for the past few weeks, he'd let everything go. He acknowledged to himself that obsessive thinking and depressive thinking produce a similar result in a person's life. He started by going through the rather lengthy routine of cleaning Tristin's home, as that often resulted in a mess. Once Tristin was happily back in his clean abode, Rob began on his own home, putting dirty dishes into the dishwasher and stuff that was stacked on the kitchen counter in its place before turning to vacuuming, washing floors, and scrubbing the bathroom and kitchen fixtures.

It was suppertime when he finished. His newly regained sense of normalcy reinforced the state of his environment. He turned to his desk, where he started brainstorming ideas of how to move forward from his crazy thinking into making a firm and viable plan to persuade Simon to share his upcoming bonanza. In a short time, he had filled two sheets of lined paper with ideas, and his thoughts were beginning to coalesce into a course of action.

His first task, he began at once. He started the email to Simon with congratulations on his recent nuptials and then suggested that they get together the next time he was up in the Phoenix area. The conversation Rob envisaged between the two needed to be in person.

Chapter 15—May 10, 2017, Tempe

Simon had, of course, given up his little rental house when he and Stella married. He had been a bit trepidatious about living full-time with anyone, but so far, Stella had proved to be a fine housemate. He still couldn't believe he was married, and the idea of having a wife, when it flitted through his mind, still caused him to shake his head in incredulity.

He had plenty of time to think on the six-hour drive from San Amaro to Tempe, and he spent part of it evaluating his eight weeks of marriage. Stella was a solid, happy, and very social person. She was involved in several volunteer activities in the area, which gave Simon time alone almost every day. This, he decided, would be his saving grace. He found his own pastimes, such as golf, fulfilling the needs of his clients, and enjoying a few games of poker.

He'd learned that cockfighting was the local betting sport, but he didn't think he'd enjoy watching roosters try to kill each other, so he hadn't sought it out. The local casino was adequate and, along with online poker, mostly fed his gambling habit. His luck had been better than average for the last few weeks, and his line of credit was finally declining from his few new clients and lack of huge gambling losses.

As he'd already known before the wedding, they were compatible in bed. And since, he'd learned that Stella's sexual appetite was adequate to keep him satisfied but not so strong as to restrict his occasional evenings out at the casino. All in all, he felt that he'd be well able to keep up the ruse of the loving husband without too much difficulty.

Next, he turned his thoughts to his upcoming meeting with Rob. It had been over a year since they'd last seen each other, and, though Rob had texted on a few occasions during that time, Simon had never gotten around to responding. He pondered why that was as he paid his fee to enter the toll highway that led from Mexicali, east toward San Luis Rio Colorado on the border with Arizona, where he'd catch Highway 95 and then Interstate 10 north to the Phoenix area.

In letting his mind meander over his thoughts of Rob, he realized that the fact that Rob was the only other person on the planet, apart from Althea Cutler, who knew of Stella's upcoming inheritance made him afraid of Rob. In Simon's mind, Rob was very dangerous. He could easily ruin everything by letting Stella know that Simon had an ulterior motive. On the other hand, he'd known Rob for a number of years, and he'd never seen a vindictive side to him. Certainly, Rob was not afraid of anger or violence if he found it necessary, but he'd never seen Rob be intentionally mean or nasty for no reason.

Simon wondered whether he was being paranoid, but he also knew that it likely wasn't a coincidence that Rob had reached out to him for a face-to-face meeting just days after he and Stella had gotten married. He'd seen that a couple of their wedding guests had posted pictures of the event on the San Amaro Facebook group page, and he expected that Rob might still be a member of that group. So, his thinking went, that was likely the impetus for the get-together. And Simon conjectured further, Rob didn't just want to buy him a congratulatory drink.

With all these theories banging around in his head, Simon spent the drive from the border into Tempe trying to figure out what to do about it all and how to handle his meeting with Rob. The suggestion from Rob was that they would meet at a restaurant near his condo for a quick dinner and then they'd go over to Rob's, where they could catch up. In keeping with his lawyer persona, he'd imagined several possible ways tonight's conversation might go, and now he felt confident he knew how he'd handle any of them.

The first thing Simon saw was Rob's blond curls in a sidelong view. He'd changed its style in the ensuing months since their last interaction. Now the sides were shaved almost to his scalp, and the top was longer and curlier than Simon remembered, with a cascade of blond curls falling over Rob's forehead almost into his eyes. As always, Rob was impeccably dressed. Tonight, it was a vivid lemon-and-lime-patterned, button-down-collared shirt with the sleeves rolled to midforearm, pale-gray-green linen slacks, and light-gray, butter-soft leather loafers. He looked up just as Simon reached his table and stood up to first shake Simon's hand, then pull him into a bear hug, before they settled into their chairs.

The restaurant had high ceilings with huge blown-glass chandeliers in deep reds and purples dropping down to normal ceiling height. They reminded Simon of some of the work he'd seen of Dale Chihuly. Not Simon's taste at all, but he could admire the expertise that created them. The rest of the décor was modern chic. There was a lot of chrome and a sea of white. White marble floors, chrome-and-glass tables, and white covered chairs. Most of the contrast in the restaurant came from the light fixtures, the napkins, and the wait staff, who were all dressed in blood-red uniforms. Simon hoped the food was more colorful than the restaurant. And when the menu came, he was relieved to see it was.

Simon told him of life in San Amaro over drinks and the people he'd met and gotten to know. It was a weird conversation because, Simon realized, Rob knew who he was talking about as he spoke about Stella, Jaime, Molly, and Rick. Rob had cased all of them as he built his profile of Stella for Simon's client Althea Cutler. He was surprised yet not surprised when Rob asked specific questions about places and these people who were now Simon's friends. "Is Rick still dating the guy with the gray ponytail?" he asked at one point. Simon had no idea and said that must have ended long before he'd gotten down there, because none of them had even mentioned him.

They had both opted for a steak. Rob chose a salad with his, and Simon went for the baked yam and couscous. It was a delicious meal, and as they ate, Rob regaled Simon with tales of his various jobs, finishing with the guy that beat the crap out of the rental car. "It turned out that the guy was meeting his drug-addicted daughter, who was trying to get clean while working in a strip club in the closest thing Phoenix has to a red-light area. She wasn't having much success with the getting-clean part, but she was willing to see her dad every week.

"He was hiding it from his relatively new wife because she wanted nothing to do with the daughter and expected him to follow suit. The day after he took a baseball bat to my rental car, I called his house. I figured if the wife answered, I'd just update her on what I'd seen when I tailed her husband. But fortunately, the husband answered, and I explained what was going on with me following him. I thought I might lean on him for some money for trashing the car. Anyway, we met, and he poured out the entire sad tale to me. I felt like a priest hearing confession. If you can imagine that!" Rob chuckled at the thought. "Anyway, he told me, he'd finally fessed up to his wife about what he was doing Wednesday nights and that they would add five hundred bucks to my fees in hopes I wouldn't report him as the perpetrator of the damage to the rental-car company. I'd already made up a cock-and-bull story and insurance covered it all, so at least it ended well."

By the time they finally ended up at Rob's condo, they'd had scotch, wine, and a brandy, and Simon was feeling buzzed. He splashed some water on his face in Rob's beautifully appointed guest bathroom and took a couple of steadying breaths to try and get focused before they got down to the crux of it . . . whatever *it* would be. In good lawyerly fashion, Simon went through the responses he'd planned on the drive and believed he was prepared for whatever was to come.

Two hours later, as he made his way to the motel he'd booked for the night, Simon had to laugh at himself. The conversation they'd had was so far removed from any of the possibilities he'd planned for on his drive up, he wondered why he'd wasted his time on them. Rob had made a case for Simon's sharing some of the Cutler estate with him. His arguments all focused on the positive effect his work had done to lay the foundation for Simon's courting of Stella. Simon couldn't get past the underlying feeling he had that everything Rob said was really thinly veiled threats. Now, he had some serious thinking to do.

The next morning, Simon dressed in his best suit and again donned his Shibumi Firenze tie. He was heading to another meeting with Althea Cutler. It had been about nine months since he had finalized her estate, and he was curious about the state of her health.

"You're looking very well, Mrs. Cutler. Thank you for taking time today to meet with me." Althea Cutler simply gave a slight nod of her head in acknowledgment of his salutation and compliment. Simon was somewhat surprised that she did look so well. He was sort of hoping she'd be in more decline. She was ninety-four now. Surely, she wouldn't be around very much longer, but looking at her today, Simon realized that she was certainly not on death's doorstep yet.

"As I mentioned in my phone call, I wanted to check in with you and see if there were any changes in your situation that should be reflected in your estate plan." Simon smiled pleasantly at the grande dame before him. "I do this about this time of year with all my clients. Just part of the service," he said, lying easily while looking her square in the face.

Althea's blue eyes held his for several seconds, as though she were trying to discern if he was, in fact, lying. He held her gaze, not allowing himself to be the first to look away. "It's very considerate of you to stay on top of things, but I can assure you, nothing has changed in *my situation*, as you put it," she said graciously, and then added with much less warmth in her voice, "In the future, I think it will be unnecessary for us to have this conversation face-to-face. I would prefer you simply check in over the phone."

Simon could tell when he was being dismissed. "Very well," he said, standing. "Next year, I'll phone you. Have a lovely day, Mrs. Cutler. I will see myself out." He nodded slightly, almost feeling as if he should bow and walk out backward, like people did with Queen Elizabeth. Then he remembered, he knew one of her most guarded secrets, squared his shoulders, and walked out with his head held high.

He stopped at the administration office in a corridor to the left of the main entrance. He'd set up an appointment with the facility director. Since his meeting with Althea had been so short, he was a few minutes early, but the director was available, so he was shown into her nicely appointed office directly. Mrs. Huston was a tall, slender, almost emaciated-looking, stern-faced woman in her fifties. She was wearing a conservative royal-blue tweed suit, matching pumps, and a powder-blue, silk round-necked blouse.

Simon handed her his business card and took her offered hand. It was a tiny, dry hand with a firm, no-nonsense handshake. He got right to business, sensing anything else would be viewed as gratuitous by this rather formidable woman. "I am one of Althea Cutler's lawyers," he began. "And I am responsible for her estate plan. Having just met with her, she appears to still be in good health, which is wonderful. However, I realize that at her age, her estate plan may need to be fulfilled at any time in the next few years. I wanted to connect with you now to guarantee I'm contacted upon her death so that I can ensure her wishes are fulfilled as efficiently as possible. And to find out from you what your process is for contacting one's lawyer when they pass."

Mrs. Huston picked his business card from her desk, scrutinized it, and then set it back on her completely clear desktop. She tapped it once with a manicured, clear-lacquered fingernail and then raised her eyes to meet Simon's. "Mr. Wakefield, it's considerate of you to drop by," she said in a tone of voice that said she thought it was anything but considerate. "Mrs. Cutler has already informed us that you will be handling her estate. Our *process*"—she emphasized the word as though it were distasteful—"is to contact the person our clients have told us to contact when they die. As I've said, in the case of Mrs. Cutler, that is you. Was there anything else?"

Simon clenched his teeth and stood, then tried to put a smile on his face. He suspected the result was more like a grimace. "Thank you for your time, Mrs. Huston. That's all I needed to know," he said as he turned and left. He wanted to say, "You're just one of the staff here, honey, so get off your high horse!" But he didn't, of course. Being dismissed by two haughty bitches in less than an hour wasn't his idea of a good time, though. So, he headed to El Tapatio. He needed a drink. And, he thought, some afternoon delight, if possible.

Chapter 16—July 17, 2017, Kingman, Arizona

Rob had thought about taking his Triumph on a short road trip to visit his brother, but with the summer temperatures hovering in the low-hundred-degree range, he decided instead to rent a car for the air-conditioning. Hank was three years older than Rob, and while they were staunch rivals in everything from sports to grades in school, they had become closer as they aged. This was the first time in Hank's career that he was working outside of Alaska. He had just moved to Kingman, Arizona, and had started a new job. He'd invited Rob to visit for a few days before he was completely engrossed in his work.

Rob had arrived Thursday afternoon and stayed through the weekend. Monday morning, he headed back home. It was about a four-hour drive, and Rob enjoyed being alone with his thoughts. He and Hank had relished their time together, and Rob replayed some of their activities as he drove.

The highlight for Rob had been the tour of Hank's new workplace. A metallurgical engineer, Hank was now the engineering department manager. The mine itself was very new, having been in operation less than a year. It was an open-pit gold and copper mine with the crushers situated in the pit and the offices and processing facilities located about a quarter mile away. A series of conveyer belts and walkways joined the two.

Hank's office was located on the second floor of the office block, but as he explained to Rob, he spent at least half his time in the processing plant. He was responsible for all the processing, including processing materials. He had asked Rob to help him take an inventory of the stock of processing chemicals on hand, so he'd be able to properly account for the usage of the materials under his management, which officially started the coming Monday. Rob had been intrigued that cyanide was one of the main substances used in the extraction of gold from the ore. Their inventory showed there were four fifty-gallon drums full of cyanide and one partial drum. Rob, wearing the respirator Hank had given him, took off the lid of the partially full container and carefully peered in determining it was about a third full.

Hank used what looked like a very long-handled measuring cup to extract some of the white crystals from the open drum. He placed it in a small tub the size of a single-serving yogurt container. Next, he took Rob to a small lab and showed him how the cyanide, when dissolved and mixed into the crushed rock from the pit, pulled the gold out of the rock by making it dissolve. With the large debris removed, Hank's small amount of cyanide water slurry was then safely dehydrated using a Bunsen burner under a fume hood, leaving just the gold. It reminded Rob of some of the experiments they used to do with a chemistry set they jointly received one year for Christmas. They'd later laughed about it when Rob asked Hank why they hadn't had cyanide in that chemistry set.

For the remainder of his drive home, Rob occupied himself with coming up with ideas for a new business he might want to start or at least different work from what he'd been doing. His thoughts roamed from going back into emergency medical work and becoming an EMT again, to going to university and finishing his degree in chemical engineering, to using his photography skills for something other than snapping pictures of wayward spouses. By the time he returned to the car-rental agency to drop off the Mustang, he was no closer to coming up with a plan for his future, but he'd managed to fill the drive time with some interesting fantasies. He walked the five blocks back to his condo and was dying for a shower. But first he fed Tristin and put clean water into his terrarium.

After his shower, he was hungry, horny, and hankering for some hard-core action. He dressed in skintight jeans, no underwear, and a form-fitting tank top and headed to Dirty Mother's. He wasn't disappointed. All his appetites were sated, though the young man he partnered with may have gotten a rougher ride than he'd anticipated.

Chapter 17—November 23, 2017, San Amaro

Pippa Drummond was Stella's oldest and best friend. They had roomed together their first year in college and become fast friends. It was the nurturing kind of connection that was as fresh and close after even long periods of separation as it had been when they had shared the same dorm room or lived in the same city. Both women had graduated from the University of Wisconsin, in Madison. Stella got her degree in education and Pippa, several years later, completed a PhD in psychology. Having met and married a fellow student while finishing her graduate degree, Pippa and her husband, Gerald Drummond, opened a therapy practice in Madison, where they still lived after all these decades.

Stella had started teaching in Madison at an elementary school, but after two years, she determined that junior high school was a better age group for her. Trying to teach science to eight-year-olds was not as fulfilling as she imagined teaching young teens would be, so when a position opened at a respected junior high school in Helena, Montana, she jumped on it and made the move. Her intuition was correct. Her passion for her subject caught the interest of the older kids, and right from the start, she was a favorite teacher among most of her students.

It was after Stella's move to Montana that Pippa and Stella realized their friendship was built on a foundation strong enough to withstand distance. They visited each other when time and schedules allowed and spoke often on the phone. And, being women of that time, they maintained a regular letter-writing connection that survived the advent of computers and cell phones, and the instant communication they afforded.

Pippa's husband, Gerry, had begun developing muscle weakness, cramps, and twitches in his early fifties. Eventually, they got the diagnosis of the rare oculopharyngeal MD, a form of muscular dystrophy that initially causes weakness and wasting of the muscles of the eyes and throat but can progress to affect all limbs. When his difficulty seeing and talking became sufficient to keep him homebound, they had hired a live-in caregiver. This afforded Pippa a degree of independence they had both agreed would be essential to her mental stability during his continued decline. While the disease likely would not kill him outright, issues with swallowing and breathing could.

Pippa was in San Amaro staying with Stella and Simon for American Thanksgiving. She had flown to Phoenix to stay with her and Gerry's youngest daughter, Jessica, who was pregnant with her first child at age forty. Then after a week's visit, Jessica and her husband, Don, had lent Pippa their Range Rover so she could drive down and spend some time with Stella while Don's parents flew to Denver for Thanksgiving with Jessica and Don. When Pippa returned to Phoenix, it was her plan to stay with Jessica and Don until after their baby arrived and both were somewhat comfortable with their new parental roles.

It had been a couple of years since Stella and Pippa had seen each other, and Stella was shocked at the toll Gerry's illness appeared to be taking on her friend. Pippa's blonde hair had gone beautifully and brilliantly white in her forties, and she had never dyed it. It was part of her distinctive look, along with her statuesque body and piercing blue eyes. Now, however, her hair was looking tarnished and listless. Her usual tanned face from hiking, canoeing, cross-country skiing, and just taking long walks with their current black Lab now was replaced with a sallow pallor. Stella was determined to make Pippa's visit a restorative one for her friend.

Stella had put the turkey in the oven midmorning, and the intoxicating smell of the cooking bird filled the house. Pippa had taken on preparing roasted brussels sprouts and a green-bean casserole, which were both in the second oven cooking. Simon chose the role of bartender and had headed to the liquor store after lunch to stock up on wine, vodka, whiskey, and brandy. Since then, he appeared determined to sample some of everything he'd bought before the others arrived. Consequently, well before anyone showed up, he was already well on his way to being drunk.

"We have several hours of enjoyment ahead of us this afternoon and evening, Si. I'd like it if you slowed down the drinking so that we can all have a pleasant time together," Stella said to Simon in the corner of the living room where he'd set up his drink cart and was preparing to top up a scotch on the rocks.

"Oh, that's what you'd like, is it? What if that isn't what I'd like?" he replied, with a belligerent edge to his voice.

"Babe, I don't want a fight and I don't want to tell you what to do, and at the same time, if you keep drinking like you have been, you'll be passed out before anyone arrives. I don't want you to miss dinner or the fun you know we'll have when everyone gets here. It would be a real help to me if you could take Juba for a walk now. By the time you get back, everyone will start to arrive. How would that be?" she asked, in her disarmingly practical way.

Simon opened his mouth to argue, but realized she'd handed him an olive branch, so he shut it again. He took a deep breath and blew it out loudly, and that seemed to dissipate his angst. "Okay," he said as he walked over to the basket by the door in which Juba's harness and leash were kept. Before he'd even picked them up, Juba was at his side sitting ready to go. He looked over at Stella as he reached for the door handle. "I'll be back in half an hour . . . boss," he said to her with a wry smile and a slight nod of his head.

Stella and Pippa had set a very festive table. The long Mexican pine dining table was covered with a white tablecloth with orange and yellow leaves trimming its bottom edges. The good china place settings, white with a gold rim, were topped with orange, green, and gold linen napkins in wooden turkey napkin rings. The silver and stemware were gleaming, and trivets were placed strategically around the center of the table awaiting steaming serving dishes of delicious food.

A small turkey piñata hung from one of the mesquite trees in the yard and was filled with various individually wrapped chocolates, including Almond Roca and Ferrero Rocher. It would greet the others as they arrived and would provide sweet nibbles as they entertained themselves after dinner.

At five o'clock, a soprano "Yoo-hoo" rang out from the side-door entrance as Molly entered carrying a Pyrex casserole dish containing mashed yams. Jaime followed bearing a smaller crystal serving bowl full of homemade cranberry sauce. A few minutes later, Rick arrived balancing a store-bought pumpkin pie atop a six-pack of Mexican beer in his right hand and a plastic grocery bag containing whipping cream in his left. He managed to get everything safely onto the counter, much to the surprise of those in the kitchen watching.

"I have lots of beer, Rick. You didn't have to bring your own," Simon called out from behind them as he returned from his walk with Juba.

"No worries, Simon, I found this Mexican stout, and I thought we might want to see if it's any good. I haven't seen stout down here before. And, if it's terrible, we have your brews to fall back on. Are you watching any of the football games that are on today?"

"Not yet. But let's go into the living room, and we can see what game is on right now, if you like," Simon said.

Stella reacquainted Pippa with Molly, Jaime, and Rick as they arrived, and since dinner was still some time off, Rick, Simon, and Molly gathered in the living room to watch the Redskins play the Cowboys in Dallas while Pippa and Jaime stood around in the kitchen, watching Stella tend to the items on the stove.

"Not much of a football fan, eh, Jaime?" Pippa asked.

"It's okay," he replied, "but Molly is the real fan in our house."

"Jaime, have you been doing any more truck driving with your nephew?" Stella queried somewhat sternly, remembering what Molly had told her back before her wedding.

Jaime looked up abruptly, wariness in his eyes. "I fill in only when his company's regular driver is unavailable. How did you hear about my driving?" he asked, trying to keep his voice level.

"Well, I just hope your nephew isn't leading you into anything illegal. Especially if it's anything to do with those endangered fish. I can never remember their name, watoba or something," Stella said.

"Totoaba," Jaime said, providing the proper name. "And you know me better than that, don't you?"

"I just worry about you, Jaime. I know how strong family ties are for you, and you have a big heart and want to help people. I read on Facebook that the police and marines are really starting to crack down on the whole supply chain of the illegal poaching of those fish. So, I hope you're not getting dragged into it," Stella said as Jaime's normally even demeanor started to show signs of turning to dust under the weight of his wariness.

"What's this about?" Pippa asked, curiously. As Stella started to explain about the fish's bladder being worth thousands of dollars, Jaime slunk into the living room and, after getting a beer, sat beside Molly and turned his attention to the game. It took several minutes for his breathing to return to normal and his unease to depart.

When the halftime show started, Simon muted the TV and checked with Stella, learning dinner would be ready in about twenty minutes. He uncorked the dinner wine to let it breathe. He had heeded his wife's advice and hadn't had any more to drink after he returned from walking Juba. Now he accepted the Mexican stout Rick offered.

Rick also wandered out to the kitchen to chat with Pippa and Stella. “Hey, didn’t I see you with a young Mexican boy over by the baseball field? He seemed a little young even for you,” Stella said, teasing Rick.

Crimson rose from beneath the neck of Rick’s black No Bad Days in San Amaro T-shirt and crept up to the top of his shaved head. “What do you take me for?” he asked, more roughly than he’d intended. Then, trying to cover up both his blush and his inappropriate response, he picked up a tea towel and began fanning himself with it. “That was Israel. He’s the high school student I sponsor. I had bought him a baseball glove, and we were going to play catch. Completely harmless, I’m afraid.” Then looking at Pippa with a quizzical look, he asked, “Has she always been this much of a busybody?” Two could tease, he thought, and Pippa just shrugged in reply. But Stella’s question had stung him, and he wondered if she really did think he was preying on young boys.

The meal was wonderful, and everyone ate far too much, as is the Thanksgiving way. They polished off three bottles of wine with dinner, and Simon had opened a fourth as Stella and Pippa decided against an after-dinner brandy in favor of sticking with wine. Everyone adjourned to the yard for a few minutes and had some good laughs as each person, blindfolded and spun around, took whacks at the piñata, eventually resulting in Stella’s solid hit opening the papier-mâché turkey and revealing the goodies within.

Pippa had brought her daughter’s Pictionary game with her, and after she outlined the modified rules she used to play it, they spent a couple of hours playing in two teams of three. Simon, Pippa, and Molly were victorious against Stella, Rick, and Jaime, but much fun and laughter were had by all. Simon was reminded of the first time he saw Stella when she, at one point, tipped her head back and roared with mirth.

Everyone pitched in to help clean up the kitchen, and nine thirty, after the others had left, Simon, Stella and Pippa collapsed onto couches with an Earl Grey nightcap. Pippa had apparently been cogitating on the earlier conversation in the kitchen between Stella and Jaime. “What is being done here to try to save those fish you were talking about, Stella?”

“Not enough!” Stella answered passionately. “There are military ships, and a conservation organization has two ships out in the sea here patrolling, but the local fishermen go out in these tiny pangas with big outboard motors, with gill nets and often at night, and they are hard to catch. I just hate the decimation of the totoabas and other endangered species. I’d like to knock those fishermen’s heads together. I would turn them in to the authorities in a heartbeat if I knew anyone involved. It really is terrible.”

Simon placed his hand over hers in what he hoped was a loving gesture and in the hopes of diverting the conversation on to just about any other topic. “Pippa,” he interjected, “do you like fishing at all? If you have any interest, we could hire a fishing guide. It’s pretty fun, and you can take several pounds of fresh or frozen fish back into the US. The guides bait your hook, get the fish off the line, and clean and fillet them for you so all the dirty work is taken care of.”

It worked to change the subject, and while Pippa admitted she was not a fisherwoman, she said she'd go along to enjoy some time on the water if Simon was going out. And so, it was decided that he'd set up a fishing expedition for Saturday and see if Jaime or Rick wanted to join them.

Chapter 18—December 29, 2017–January 19, 2018, Tempe–San Amaro

The usual late-autumn dry spell at work had finally broken in mid-December. Rob had finished his latest job December 28, a fact that had garnered him a $16,000 bonus. He didn't often get corporate clients, but he'd done his usual "catch the wife cheating" work for Trevor Snodgrass a few months before, and Trevor had been very happy with Rob's work. As the owner of the large local insurance company of Southwestern Security Inc., Trevor had hired Rob in mid-December to determine which of the partners was providing confidential client information to a well-organized home-invasion gang that had been systematically burgling their high-end clients shortly after they upped their insurance. It was costing his firm a fortune.

Trevor strongly believed it was a partner because the clients who had been hit were wealthy and only those taken care of by the senior members of the firm. The partners' bonuses were paid out on December 31, and Trevor wanted to ensure that the culprit was found and fired before that date to avoid paying a large sum of money to the thief in their midst. He didn't want to get the police involved, as the publicity could break an independent insurance firm such as his and he'd promised Rob a huge bonus if the guilty party were found before the end of December.

Now that he had ready cash, Tristin was the only thing Rob had holding him in Tempe. He thought about just selling him, but realized he was emotionally attached to the scaly little guy. There was no way to take him along, as Rob would be traveling on his motorcycle. In the end, his friend Phillip had agreed to babysit him for a few weeks while Rob took a trip down into Mexico. They'd revisit the arrangement if Rob decided to stay south of the border longer.

When Rob crossed the border from Arizona into Mexico, he had over $40,000 in the bank. He figured he could live comfortably in Mexico for a year on that money. He had never rid himself of his fixation on Althea Cutler's fortune and how easily Simon was going to get control of it. He'd presented his ideas to Simon when he'd visited in March but hadn't heard anything from him since. He had eventually realized the only thing he could do was go to Mexico and see what happened.

Being someone who was well versed in tracking a person's movements, he decided to create a good backstory for himself as a precaution, should it ever be needed. Once into Mexico, he headed south to the popular weekend getaway of Puerto Peñasco. He planned to stay in a decent hotel on the beach for a couple of weeks, use his credit card in a few well-known restaurants there, and be sure to keep a few receipts. Anyone checking into his movements could easily be convinced he'd come to Mexico to poke around a few beach towns. He planned to get to San Amaro in a week or two after leaving Puerto Peñasco and could explain to anyone asking that he had intended to pass through but fell in love with its quaintness and stayed.

He really didn't care for Puerto Peñasco with its pushy street vendors and store reps who stood on the road in front of their shops and harangued passersby to enter. He was glad to see the back of it when he left after only five days. He also spent a few days in Mexicali and then went over to the Pacific side of the Baja peninsula to Ensenada and Rosarito before crossing back over the mountainous spine and heading south to San Amaro. He'd thought about getting in touch with Simon to alert him to his arrival, but in the end decided to play things closer to his vest. He found a casita in one of the smaller gringo communities north of town, as he would then be less likely to bump into Simon unexpectedly. He decided he wanted to do some covert reconnaissance of Simon and his new friends before he developed a game plan.

When he was in Mexicali, he'd met a couple of Canadians who were just finishing a motorcycle tour of the Baja. One of the men needed to get back to Vancouver quickly because of a family emergency and was trying to sell his bike so he could fly home immediately. It was an older BMW R1100GS. To Rob's way of thinking, it was the best dual-sport motorcycle made, and it was known to be the most popular Baja touring bike. He made the guy a lowball offer, which the guy surprisingly accepted, so Rob put his Triumph in storage in Mexicali and continued his travels on the Beemer. The Triumph would have been too conspicuous in San Amaro. The BMW would blend in perfectly. In fact, as he was merging on to Highway 5 from Highway 3 on his way from Ensenada to San Amaro, he saw three other men on BMW 1100s coming down Highway 5 and rode with them for the last thirty-five miles of his trip.

Once settled in his rented casita, Rob's first trip into town was to cruise past Stella's home to make sure she and Simon were still living there. He figured his full-face helmet would provide all the safety he needed should Simon be outside when he drove past. No one was in the yard of Stella's home, but seeing Simon's black BMW parked to the right of the garage was all Rob needed to confirm he had the right place. With that critical piece of information confirmed, Rob went in search of a bar that would be an unlikely location for his friend to visit.

Los Pescadores, The Fishermen, was exactly what he was looking for. It was a rough, mostly Mexican bar a block off the Malecon at the far west end of the beach. From the outside there was nothing to recommend the place. The building's external plaster was cracked, and hunks were missing. The bar's name had been painted on the outside wall at one point, years ago, but all that was left now was a faint outline of most of the letters and some fairly new graffiti over the "ores" portion of the name.

The inside was dark, and Rob stood just inside the door for a few moments while his eyes adjusted. It was midafternoon, and the place was mostly empty. He sauntered toward the bar, which was along the back wall. He had to weave among a few small tables of the white-plastic-lawn-furniture variety, though they were now mostly gray and pockmarked. A table in the far-left corner was occupied by three Mexican men in jeans and long-sleeved T-shirts. Rob, who was feeling warm in his tank top and knee-length cargo shorts, wondered how they could stand to be dressed so warmly. Then he considered that it *was* winter, and they likely thought it was cold.

At a table near the door were two gringos, most likely longtime residents, as there was nothing about them that said tourist. Apart from the bartender, there was only one other person there. The Mexican guy was leaning against the bar wearing a pair of avocado-green skintight jeans and an open-necked white shirt with only a couple of faded stains on the front that looked as if they'd been washed hard. He had tattoos covering his neck, chest, and hands. Rob went up to the opposite end of the bar to get a beer and nodded to the fellow. The guy seemed to take this as an invitation. He wandered over to where Rob was standing and asked him if he wanted a woman. Rob was surprised, but then realized the guy did look a bit like a pimp.

"Nah, not for me, amigo." Rob had chuckled, then added, mostly as a joke, "What else you got?"

The guy cased Rob then, looking him up and down with steely black eyes. Rob looked a bit like a tough guy with his taut muscles and tall, lean frame. He apparently passed the inspection. Whether despite or because of his looks, he didn't know. "I can get you guns, drugs, boys. What you want?"

Rob had been taken aback and stood up straight looking sideways at the guy. "Really?"

The guy nodded and asked again, "Sí, what you want?"

"I'd take some weed if it's any good." They had agreed on a half-gram bag for a tenth of what Rob would pay in Phoenix.

"Meet me behind de bar in five minutos," the guy said, his breath stinking of fish and beer. Rob did, taking his beer with him, which didn't seem to be a problem with the bartender. *Good,* he thought, *the bottle could be used as a weapon, if needed.* It wasn't needed, and in the end, he got the guy's number. He figured it didn't hurt to have connections.

He finished his beer and decided to take a tour around to Rick's to see what he was up to. It took him a couple of tries to find his house again. Since many of San Amaro's street signs were long gone from street corners, everyone in San Amaro navigated by landmarks. Rob remembered Rick's street intersecting one that had a burger place on the corner. Apparently, the food stall hadn't survived as the building now housed a clothing segunda, a secondhand store. After two passes, he recognized the street.

Finally getting to the right place, Rob's timing was perfect to see Rick coming out of his house and climbing into his ancient burgundy Dakota pickup truck. Rob drove past the house and did a U-turn at the end of the block. He was then able to follow Rick. Rob hadn't planned on tailing him, but then he couldn't think of a good reason not to. In the end, it was a very short trip. Rick went to the main supermarket in town, favored by gringos because it stocked so many American products. Again, Rob was grateful to have bought the BWM in Mexicali because there were four motorcycles, two of them the same model as his, parked together in the store's side parking lot. He pulled in beside them and fit in perfectly. He sat on his bike waiting for Rick's return and looked, to anyone passing by, as if he were watching the bikes of his fellow riders. Rob followed Rick as he left and, when he realized he was just returning home, headed back to his own little casita.

Over the next two weeks, Rob watched Simon and Stella, Rick, and occasionally Jaime and Molly. He quickly realized they all saw one another regularly. The guys golfed a couple of times. Stella and Molly went out to lunch frequently, sometimes with a couple of other women. Stella walked her dog twice a day for about forty minutes each time, and Simon went to the casino in town two nights a week. Apparently, he hadn't kicked his gambling habit. It didn't take Rob long to establish everyone's routines. He didn't know if that would be useful, but he bet it might be.

In his third weekend in San Amaro, he was thrilled to see literally hundreds of motorcycles of all types and makes arrive in town. He followed a small group of Harley riders from a motorcycle club from San Diego, all wearing the same colors. They ended up on the Malecon, which had been transformed from its usual sleepy little road fronting the beach into a festival of motorcycle clubs, vendors selling bike paraphernalia, and the ubiquitous street-food and T-shirt vendors. Rob parked his Beemer in a group of other BMWs and wandered up the street admiring all the different bikes, everything from choppers to dirt bikes and even a few ATVs.

He was a bit surprised when he spotted Rick chatting to a fellow with a beautifully custom-painted, though older, Harley. He decided this was the perfect way to "meet" Rick and then, if that worked out, the perfect way to insert himself into Simon's circle of friends. He wandered along, slowly admiring each motorcycle as he went. When he came to the one painted with elaborately dressed lady skeletons, he stopped and admired the bike.

"That's a Bassani exhaust system, isn't it?" Rob asked, looking between Rick and the other fellow, as though trying to determine whose bike it was.

"Yeah, good eye," said the other fellow, who went on to introduce himself as Cliff and his friend, Rick.

The three chatted about bikes for a few minutes. Rob could tell Rick's gaydar was pinging.

Perfect, he thought and then said, "I'm ready for a beer and a taco. You guys interested?"

The three men enjoyed a few beers and tacos and shared a conversation centering on their shared love of motorcycles. Rob played it cool with Rick, but he could tell the other man was interested in him. As they walked back to where Cliff's bike was parked, Rob casually mentioned he was living in San Amaro, at least for the next few months. Rick took the bait and said as Rob turned to go, "Why don't you give me your cell number. I can show you around a bit and introduce you to some people if you'd like."

"Yeah sure, that would be good," Rob said, handing Rick his phone with the Add Contact screen up. "Put in your number, and I'll call you." That put Rob in control in case Rick got cold feet and decided not to reach out.

Earlier in the day, Simon had seen a Facebook post about the motorcycle clubs gathering on the Malecon. Since he didn't have any other plans for the day, he parked his car over by the casino and walked to the Malecon to see what was going on. He was surprised to see well over 200 bikes of all kinds lining the beach side of the street. Not being a motorcycle buff himself, he was walking up the opposite side of the street, checking out the numerous vendor tents selling T-shirts, food, and motorcycle paraphernalia.

He'd just bought himself a small bag of churros, a guilty pleasure of his and was savoring his first bite of the sugary, cinnamon-dusted, fried-dough treat when something caught his eye by a beautifully painted Harley. It took his brain a second to register that he must have subconsciously noticed Rick standing with a couple of other guys. He started crossing the street to say hi when he realized one of the other men talking with Rick was Rob. He stopped and then stepped back behind a tent to fully process what he'd seen.

His heart was beating wildly in his chest, and his breath was shallow. *Rob. Here. Talking with Rick. What the fuck!* Waves of panic washed over him. Rick was handing a cell phone to Rob, and Rob clicked a couple of keys and then stuck it in his back pocket. The implication struck Simon like a blow. He spat the mouthful of churro back into the bag and dropped the bag into the trash. It suddenly tasted like sawdust. He staggered back to his car trying to quell the dread he was feeling.

All he could think of was that Rob was here in San Amaro. He had not reached out to Simon, yet he was making friends with Rick, who Rob knew was a close friend of Stella's. No matter how Simon put those thoughts together, the outcome was the same. And it chilled him to the bone.

PART 3—Conclusion

Lead-Up to the Hike . . .

Chapter 1—February 17, 2018, San Amaro

"Hey, Simon, it's Rick. Are you doing anything tomorrow? I was thinking it would be a good day to golf. The wind is supposed to be light."

Simon hadn't been golfing for a week, and the thought of spending some time on the course sounded pretty good. He hadn't seen Rick for a couple of weeks, not since he'd spied him talking with Rob at the motorcycle rally. He still hadn't heard from Rob and continued to be plagued by fears of what he was doing in San Amaro. But golf did sound fun.

"Yeah, sure. What time did you want to go?" Simon asked.

"Let's meet at the clubhouse at ten o'clock, okay? And I'll see if Jaime wants to play, too."

"That sounds good. See you then," Simon agreed.

The next morning, Simon was just unloading his clubs from the trunk of his car when Jaime pulled his Jeep in beside him. Simon had already rented a cart and loaded it with water and a large bag of tortilla chips. Jaime was heading to the clubhouse to get a second cart when Rick's purple Dodge truck parked beside Jaime's Jeep. Simon, busy tying his golf shoes while leaning against the passenger side of his car, didn't see him pull in. He was completely caught off guard when he heard footsteps and looked up to see Rick, followed by Rob rounding the end of his car.

"Simon, I want you to meet Rob, a new friend of mine." Rick's voice hardly penetrated Simon's instantly addled brain as he tried to think how to respond.

The decision was made for him when Rob stepped forward with his hand out. "Hi, Simon, it's great to meet you." Rob's penetrating blue eyes never left Simon's as Simon shook the offered hand.

Simon's mind was whirling, but with his best poker face, he responded almost by rote. "Yeah, nice to meet you, too." Then, mostly to avoid Rob's intense gaze, he turned to Rick and said, "Good to see you, Rick. You didn't tell me you had a new buddy."

Jaime returned with the second cart. Rick introduced him to Rob, and they decided Rick and Rob would take Jaime's cart. Rick handed Jaime the 200-peso, ten-dollar, cart-rental fee.

"I met Rob at the motorcycle rally a couple of weeks ago. He's new here. I thought this would be a good way for you guys to get to know each other," Rick explained to Jaime and Simon as Rob went into the pro shop to see about renting clubs.

Simon, beginning to get his spinning mind back in control, took advantage of Rob's absence to query Rick about the situation. "So, are you two an item, or is he just a friend?"

"Hey, your gaydar's getting pretty good for a straight guy!" Rick kidded him, causing Simon to panic for a moment until Rick went on. "I guess you could say we're dating. I don't know if it will lead to anything more, but we're having fun."

When the four men teed off from the third hole, both Simon and Rob sliced to the right and ended up in the rough beside the fairway. They found themselves separated from the other two as they located their balls and prepared to take their shots. As they walked back to where their cart partners had left the carts, Simon got his chance to ask what he'd been dying to since he'd seen Rob two weeks ago. "What the hell's going on, Rob? What are you doing here? And why the subterfuge of pretending not to know me?"

"Don't get your panties in a wad, Simon. I'm on your side. I'm just here in case I can help you. I thought it would be easier if no one knew we had history," Rob said smoothly in a casual voice.

They were almost to Simon's cart, where Jaime was already seated and waiting for Simon, so their conversation ended with Simon no less nervous about Rob's presence in San Amaro.

It wasn't until they stopped at the sixth-hole bathrooms that Simon got a chance to continue the conversation with Rob. "I don't see how you can help. I have everything in hand. I'm married to Stella. We have a joint bank account in the US that we draw on and into which the Cutler lady's will directs the monetary portion of her estate to be deposited. I'm Stella's sole beneficiary. All I have to do is wait until Cutler dies. What exactly do you think I need help with?" Simon spoke quietly but intensely as the two men stood side by side behind the restroom building ostensibly looking at the beautiful seascape before them.

"Hey, you never know how things play out, right? I'm here for an extended vacation. I like Rick well enough, so I'm close by if something does come up. Don't sweat it, okay . . . Oh, hey, Jaime. This view is really beautiful!" Rob covered nicely as the others prepared to continue the game. "Everybody ready to go?"

Simon stood alone for a moment before following the others to the carts. He watched Rob's back and for just a second, an image of a knife in a back flashed through his head. Even though it was gone almost as soon as it came to him, his mind formed the question *Who's stabbing whom?* He was glad no one was looking at him, because he wasn't sure how he could explain, if asked, why his body was trembling. A deep breath and a slight shake of his head banished the shakes and some of the foreboding he felt.

At least for the time being.

Chapter 2—March 3, 2018, Pleasant Valley

Althea Cutler was seated in the sumptuous dining room of the retirement home. Although The Villas housed only fifty-six residents, this room had seating for eighty. The chef at The Villas was renowned in the Phoenix area, and The Villas' residents often entertained guests for luncheon or dinner. Floor-to-ceiling windows covered the west wall, framed by gold and mint-green brocade drapes. The wall sconces and chandeliers were gold gilt with delicately fluted alabaster shades. The north wall was a floor-to-ceiling mullioned mirror, giving the room an expansive, open feel.

Ivory linen tablecloths covered square tables set for two, three, or four diners. Exquisite stemware specially made of lightweight, virtually unbreakable high-quality plastic, looked like Waterford crystal and graced each setting. The tableware was simple and elegant white china with a thin gold rim and a small version of The Villas' tasteful logo in the center. Louis the XIV replica chairs, luxuriously padded and covered in dark-burgundy velvet, provided comfort and the convenience of reinforced arms to aid the elderly in taking and vacating their seats. Many tables provided space for wheelchairs, and it was at one of these Althea was entertaining her guests. The vanity of not allowing people other than caregivers to see her in her motorized wheelchair was finally gone. The Abelsons, visiting for dinner, were friends with whom she and her late husband had years of close friendship. Their two daughters were like dear nieces to Althea.

Ari and Rina had been telling Althea of recent adventures of their younger daughter, Judith, over a rich crème brûlée. At fifty-eight, she had retired from the CPA firm where she had been a partner for twenty-five years. She and her husband, Will, had bought a small Mercedes-Benz motor home and, with another couple, were currently caravanning down the Baja peninsula of Mexico. Ari had his cell phone out and was providing pictorial references for Rina's stories of their travels.

Althea did not follow technology trends, but she could see the appeal for people, like her friends, to have the latest gadgets to be able to get instant access to photos and messages from their children and grandchildren. Althea had seen several photos of Judith on the beach in shorts and sleeveless blouses. She'd commented how carefree both Judith and Will looked. Rina went on to say they were in a small fishing village on the Sea of Cortez.

Rina next told Ari to show the photo in the pub. Ari handed Althea his phone again to show her a photo of Judith and Will in what looked like a shabby English pub. "This is one from a quaint place they found in San Amaro. It's Mexico, not England," Ari said, laughing, pointing out the dartboard behind his daughter's head.

At the mention of San Amaro, Althea's senses quickened. *Damn that lawyer for telling her the location of her heir.* She leaned forward and brought the picture closer. It was a shock then when she looked over Judith's shoulder toward the aforementioned dartboard and saw a familiar face at a table over her friend's daughter's shoulder. It was none other than her lawyer, Simon Wakefield. She almost dropped the phone when she saw the woman around whose shoulder the lawyer had his arm. She felt was as if she were looking at herself twenty years ago. Her mouth went dry, and Ari reached out for his phone to keep it from slipping into Althea's half-eaten dessert.

"Are you all right, Althea?" Rina asked, laying an age-spotted and crepe-paper-skinned hand on her friend's arm.

"I am getting a little tired. Perhaps we could call it a night?" Althea said, trying to cover her dismay. Her mind was whirling with the implications of what she had just seen.

Chapter 3—March 5, 2018, San Amaro

Stella and Simon were meeting her old friend Rick and his new boyfriend for dinner at the Mexican seafood restaurant Jaime's daughter ran on the Malecon. Simon had said the boyfriend was a nice guy after they golfed together a couple of weeks before. Rick had arrived on his own, saying his new beau would be along shortly. Simon and Rick were deep into a dissection of the latest news about Phoenix baseball camps and teams for the upcoming season. Stella, who always had her phone on vibrate when she was out socially, felt her phone pulsate. "I'll be right back," she said as she pressed the Accept button on her phone and moved toward the back of the restaurant to take the call.

It was not a number she recognized, but it had a prefix she identified as being from the Phoenix area. She knew her old pal Pippa was visiting her kids and new granddaughter there. Perhaps it was her.

"Hello," she said brightly into the phone, the image of her friend in her mind. The responding voice quickly disabused her of the notion of Pippa, and she exited the back door of the restaurant, choosing to stand in the loading-bay area where she could better hear the wavering, elderly female voice on the other end of the line.

"Is this Stella Monroe?" the voice had said, sounding at once commanding and frail.

"Yes," Stella responded, her brow furrowed as her mind tried to think who this was and what this call could be about.

"Do you know a man named Simon Wakefield, a lawyer from Phoenix?" the old lady asked.

"Yes, he is my husband," Stella answered, the hairs on her neck starting to tingle. "What is this about? Who are you?"

"My name is Althea Cutler, my dear. I am sorry for getting in touch with you this way, and at this time, but it is urgent and critical that you listen to me. I think I may have put you in danger." Stella heard the old woman's words but couldn't bring her mind to make sense of this out-of-the-blue call. "How long have you known Mr. Wakefield? When did you marry?" the old woman asked.

Stella was getting anxious and a bit angry. "We met about fifteen months ago. We have been married almost a year. Now, please, tell me what this is about, or I am going to hang up," she said, frustration colored with fear putting an edge on her words.

"So, my name doesn't mean anything to you?" the old woman queried.

"No. Who are you?" Stella demanded, fear now her dominant feeling.

Althea Cutler believed her. She hadn't given too much credence to the wave of suspicion that hit her when she first saw a picture of Simon Wakefield in the tiny Mexican town he'd told her was the home of her long-ago abandoned daughter. The woman he was with looked so much like Althea herself. She was not likely to be a scammer pretending to be Althea's deserted child. However, there was still the chance that she and Simon were somehow in cahoots. The woman with whom she spoke sounded bewildered and frightened, not like someone trying to swindle her.

"I am your birth mother, dear, and you are my only heir. Two years ago, I hired Simon Wakefield to locate you so I could leave my not insubstantial estate to you upon my death. At that time, I was adamant that you were not made aware of either your relationship to me or your upcoming inheritance." Over the next few minutes, Althea finished her story and provided answers to the inevitable questions Stella had for her. Althea was stoic throughout the conversation, speaking dispassionately, though kindly. Stella was incredulous at the whole situation.

When Stella hit the End Call button, her head was swimming, her heart was pounding, her breath was coming in pants, and she felt a sheen of sweat covering her face and back. After a moment, her mind kicked into gear, and she started thinking through all the implications of what this woman had told her. She looked through the loading-bay door into the dining area and could see Simon and Rick still engrossed in their conversation and, for the first time since meeting him, Stella felt a wave of terror wash over her at the thought of rejoining Simon and carrying on as if nothing had happened.

At that moment, a handsome, younger blond man came up the loading-bay steps toward her. She hadn't seen him walk through the rear parking area to the steps, but he must have. "Hey, are you Stella, by any chance? I'm Rob, Rick's friend." He didn't look at the phone, which she still held in her hand. And he didn't ask if she was okay or why she was standing in the loading area at the back of the restaurant. He simply placed his hand lightly on the small of her back and said casually, "Let's go join those two handsome guys in there." Stella, still in a stupor, went with him.

Stella pasted a smile on her face and allowed herself to be guided to their table. For the next hour, she mostly allowed the men to chat through topics ranging from baseball to fishing to golf. At one point, Jaime arrived, saw them, and came over to say hello. He explained that the walk-in cooler was on the fritz again and his daughter had requested he come and fix it, as he seemed to have the knack. He didn't stay at their table for more than a couple of minutes before heading into the kitchen, complaining that the stupid cooler had been a problem ever since he'd had it installed. For her part, Stella responded as best she could to questions and remarks addressed directly to her, but mostly, her thoughts were focused on trying to figure out what to do.

By the time dessert was ordered, she had a rough mental outline of a plan. "I'm going to go powder my nose before dessert comes," she said, excusing herself from the table. The *baños*, were at the back of the restaurant beside the propped open door to the loading area. She again stepped outside onto the loading dock and dialed the number to a person she hoped she could trust.

"Oh, Martín, thank God you answered!" Stella's words rushed out of her like a relieved exhalation. "It's Stella Monroe. Remember, I know your wife quite well. We both volunteer at the dog rescue. You have taken me flying a few times. We also shared a table at the last Rotary Steak in the Park event?" When Martín indicated he remembered her, she went on. "Are you and your little plane free this Wednesday, the eighth?" Stella said without preamble, and then held her breath waiting for the man to check his calendar.

"Aye, *sí*. But not past. I go to España the next day to see my *madre*," mother, he answered.

"You are available! Oh, thank goodness! I know this will sound crazy, but I really need your help." Stella spent the next five minutes outlining her request. By the end of the call, Martín Robles had scribbled a page of notes. What Stella had told him for the reason she needed his help seemed impossible, and somewhat bizarre, but the strain in her voice was information enough for him to believe that this was important. The poor woman sounded panicked. He reassured her that he would do as she had asked for a modest price to cover the fuel, and they rang off.

Stella was surprised to see Rob washing his hands at the sink outside the water-closet bathrooms. He was only a few feet away from where she was standing, but he turned toward their table without giving any indication he had even seen her. She had a creepy feeling, nonetheless. She quickly used the women's room, and as she exited the tiny room to wash her own hands, she spotted Jaime standing beside their table again. The four men were talking intently, and Rob seemed to be the center of their attention. As she watched, Simon glanced over his shoulder, and upon seeing her watching them, leaned back in his chair, a warm smile transforming his face. She tried to name the look that had been there for a millisecond before the smile. Anger? Fear? Hatred?

Had she imagined it? She shuddered, then put on a smile of her own and walked back to the table. Jaime said his goodbyes as she was sitting down. For the remainder of the evening, she was able to choke down only a couple of bites of flan. Fortunately, no one seemed to notice.

Chapter 4—March 6, 2018, San Amaro

Again, the phone went to voice mail. Stella was beyond frustrated and beginning to feel desperate. She had already left two voice mails on Pippa's cell phone. This time, as she had the previous three tries, she simply hung up. She was filled with paranoia after having had time to mentally revisit the call from her mother. *Her mother, how incredible!* She felt as if there were no one she could trust in her circle of friends. She knew that was probably irrational, but she was terrified to talk with anyone in San Amaro other than Martín about what she was planning in case that person betrayed her to Simon. It was so outlandish anyone would think she was making it up.

Stella was starting to feel as if she were going crazy. It had been sixteen hours since she'd received the call from Althea Cutler. Just trying to wrap her head around the concept of her birth mother and the inheritance was crazy enough, but that wasn't the issue with which she was grappling. Simon was acting just as he had since she had met him fifteen months ago. He was sweet, attentive, funny, and affectionate. That was the problem. Stella now knew that he had known about her for months before he arrived in San Amaro. He also knew her birth mother and that Stella was soon going to inherit a small fortune. Stella was no longer under any misconceptions that he had married her for love. He was after only the money she would inherit.

Over the past day, Stella had replayed instance after instance of Simon's deceptions. His insistence that they marry. It wasn't because he wanted to acknowledge the deeper relationship that he had with her than with his previous girlfriends. It was so he'd have easier access to the money once she got it. She also now doubted his claim that having their finances in a joint account was to protect her in the event of his death. Oh yes, and the wills they had both created leaving everything to the other. The list went on!

She could barely stand to be in the same room with him. She had a plan, and that gave her some reassurance. She had thought several times in the last few hours about jumping in her car and just driving away. She could be in Arizona in three hours, but that wouldn't give her much of a head start. And, if she took off in her Jeep, he'd know that she was driving somewhere. She'd be easy to find. He'd found her once already with very little to go on. She needed to go through with her plan. It would give her several days before anyone started to suspect that she hadn't just gotten lost in the desert. Yes, she was confident in her plan. She just had to be patient for another day and her plan would unfold, giving her the time she needed to take care of herself before Simon guessed anything was amiss.

That he had no idea that she knew of his duplicity worked in her favor. Still, she really didn't want to be around him. She called her favorite spa and booked a facial, manicure, and a massage for the next day. She was not a great liar and no kind of an actress. Yet, she believed that she must be a consummate pro of both to get through the day and a half until their desert trip, when she could put her plan into action. She needed to create enough of a diversion for Simon and the others to really believe she was lost in the desert so she would have enough time to get to Phoenix, get a new bank account and credit card, put a new will in place, and fly somewhere safely away from the man whose lies she had fallen for.

She didn't think she could confide in Molly, who would normally be to whom she'd turn. Their social circle was small, and she was well aware that Simon had established very close friendships of his own with all her friends. Would they believe her if she told them of the call from a woman identifying herself as Stella's birth mother? She had no way to prove that the woman was legitimate, except her own gut feeling it was true. Could she convince anyone else she wasn't crazy? Hell, she was having trouble convincing herself of that. She was ashamed she had been so easily duped. Talking with Pippa seemed like the only thing that would help calm her. But she couldn't reach Pippa. She didn't have Pippa's daughter's phone number or email address, either. She knew Pippa's husband was in a resident physical therapy program at a university hospital to help him deal with his severe muscular dystrophy, so there was no point in calling their home in Madison.

Finally, she decided to write to her friend. They had kept up regular correspondence with snail mail ever since they first lived in different places and, while it wouldn't provide her the opportunity to hear her friend's counsel, at least it would give her the chance to document what was happening, and that alone might help her see things more clearly.

It wasn't a long letter, and it took Stella only a few minutes to write it. She told Pippa about the phone call from Althea Cutler and her future inheritance. She spelled out Simon as the lawyer who had created the old woman's estate plan. She mentioned their own wills ensuring Simon was Stella's sole beneficiary, Stella as the sole beneficiary of her mother's estate, and her fear of Simon now as someone who was with her for the express purpose of getting his hands on the Cutler fortune. She also laid out for her friend her proposed plan to escape San Amaro and Simon on the first anniversary of their wedding when they were all on a hike in the desert. She'd then go to Phoenix, meet her birth mother, and take care of all the other things needed to ensure Simon could neither benefit from the Cutler estate nor find her. Althea Cutler had told her she would make sure she had enough money to live comfortably until she received her inheritance.

When she finished the letter, she did indeed feel more in control of herself. She was sure that Simon had no way of knowing she was aware of his subterfuge or that she had a plan to escape him. All she had to do was keep up a façade of the happy wife looking forward to their anniversary for another day and night. As she walked to the office of the service she used to get her mail to and from the US, Stella began to relax slightly. She told herself over and over . . . *you can do this, Stella.* By the time she returned home, she felt confident she'd be able to pull off her plan.

Walking also reminded her she had bruised her toes when she dropped a frozen roast on her foot a few days previous. They were black and blue and sore, but not terribly. The fact they didn't hurt badly was something only she knew. As she approached her house, she began to limp slightly. She could easily pass off her discolored toes as broken and use that as the excuse she would need to leave the group on the hike.

Martín would meet her about a kilometer south of the mouth of the canyon they planned to hike. He would fly her to his uncle's cattle farm west of San Amaro, where she would borrow Martín's wife's car. She would drive to Calexico on the US side of the border and leave the car in the parking lot with the keys locked inside so Martín and Lili could pick it up later. She'd rent a car in Calexico and drive herself to Phoenix and meet her mother. From there, the plan was very loose. Once she was safely away from Simon, had a new bank account, and had some money from her mother, she would figure out where to go and what to do.

Simon was sitting in the yard reading as she returned home. "Hey, you, are you limping?" he asked, with a note of concern in his voice as she came into the yard.

"You remember when I dropped that frozen roast on my foot last Saturday. I think I may have broken one or two of my toes," she replied.

"Oh no," he exclaimed with what sounded like real concern. "Do we need to postpone our hike?"

"Absolutely not," she reassured him. "I'll tape them, and in my hiking boots, I'm sure I'll be fine."

Stella watched him carefully to see his reaction, but he simply said, "Okay, great," and went back to reading his book. Her heart was pounding as she went inside. She realized that getting through the next thirty-six hours was going to be more difficult than she'd thought. She needed to be away from Simon as much as possible in that time if her nerves were going to survive. She was so glad she had her spa day tomorrow.

Chapter 5—March 6, 2018, San Amaro

It was almost midnight when Chuey's cell phone rang. He was getting ready to leave The Fishermen bar, *Los Pescadores*, having just finished his beer. He grabbed his phone, noted the caller's name on his phone's display, and sauntered into the alley as he answered it. "*Bueno*."

"*Hola, amigo*," hello, friend, came the response. "I have a job for you if you are up for it."

Over the next few minutes, the caller outlined what he wanted done, with Chuey asking myriad questions throughout the explanation. Chuey knew he'd do the job after the first couple of minutes, but he wanted to make this man sweat a little before he agreed. It was the best way to bargain a better price for his services.

There were very few things that Chuey considered taboo when it came to his work, but this request would be challenging to pull off and was skirting very close to the edge of where he drew the line.

"This is dangerous job you ask me do. I could go to Mulege for years if police catch me. You no give me much time to get what I need to do it. And I no have vehicle that go into the desert so far. You need get me one, or I no can do it. You need get me one!" Chuey restated emphatically.

The other man had expected that Chuey would give him some pushback about his request. Just good negotiation tactics. He hadn't considered that he'd need to provide a vehicle, however. He gave the situation some thought and then had a brainstorm. He remembered something he'd seen earlier that evening.

"That shouldn't be a problem. In fact, I think I can get you one tonight if you have somewhere to keep it out of sight until you need it," replied the caller.

"I can do it. When tonight? I going have to meet you and take it to my safety place." Chuey was mentally adding up the amount he figured he could ask for this crazy and dangerous, spur-of-the-moment request. It was a lot!

"I'll call you when I have it, and you can come meet me. I'll give you a good desert vehicle, but whoever brings you to meet me will have to drive me home after, okay?"

The remainder of the call was spent verifying that Chuey knew all the details of what he needed to do and haggling over the money. The caller was thrilled at what he considered the bargain price Chuey quoted him, but he still argued for several minutes to make Chuey think he was getting more than was reasonable. Half the money would be handed over with the desert vehicle and the remainder once the job was done. The vehicle itself would be part of the overall payment.

When the call ended, both men felt like victors in the negotiation, and both were anxious about what they had agreed to do. They had to trust each other. That wasn't something that came naturally to either.

After the hike . . .

Chapter 6—March 16, 2018, Mexicali

It had been ten days since Ted Blair's RZR had gone missing from his home in Campo Cristal. Luis was frustrated that the investigation was stalled because Sergeant Garcia was so engrossed in looking for the missing woman. She wasn't putting any time into their robbery case. Finally, he'd pinned her down, and she agreed that he should do whatever he could to find the owner of the shed they suspected might house the missing RZR.

Luis had spent an entire day trying to find out who owned that garage in the Punto de Cono Ejido. The nearest Property Public Registry to San Amaro was in Mexicali. Luis had driven the two hours to get there and, after standing in line for forty minutes, explained his situation to the clerk. Because he had police credentials and a specific need, he was allowed into the back where the registry documents were maintained in myriad filing cabinets. The clerk had bemoaned to Luis the fact that a project to digitize all the documents got through only four filing cabinets before being scrapped when the funding for it was cut. By the time Luis had been educated on how the documents were filed, it was nearly noon.

He spent four hours in the stuffy, dusty, and poorly lit filing room digging through masses of files to find the ones pertaining to the Punto de Cono Ejido.

He read every file but learned nothing useful. If the garage where he suspected the missing RZR was being kept was on a privately owned plot, he found no record of it. He was left believing the building must still be part of the communal portion of the ejido. On his two-hour return trip, Luis mulled over several questions. He hoped Sergeant Garcia would be able to enlighten him about what the ejido communal ownership laws might mean for a police search of the building. If it wasn't privately owned, he hoped the police would be able to search it with less need for formal warrants and the like.

After arriving back at the police station and returning the cruiser he had used for his excursion to Mexicali, Luis spent twenty minutes writing up the meager results of his day in a report for Julia. He popped a hard copy into her in basket and emailed a copy to her. He was hoping she would make time for him the following morning to address the questions he had posed in his report.

Luis was not disappointed. At eight the following morning, Julia was sitting at her desk. By the look on her face when she saw Luis arrive, she was waiting for him. She had already spoken with her papito about the legalities of searching a building on communal ejido land. Apparently, it was a gray area in Mexican law. He had advised Julia to speak to the current comandante about the situation. If he felt confident in the need for the search, then he would have Luis and Julia's back if there were repercussions resulting from their examination of the place.

Julia had already made a request for the earliest possible appointment with their comandante.

She relayed all this to Luis. Then, it was just a waiting game until she got a call with an appointment time. She found out from his assistant about eight thirty that the comandante was at the local Rotary meeting. He wouldn't be back until noon.

"We have over three hours until I can meet with the boss," Julia said to Luis. "I should have a look at this place myself before I speak with him. Grab us a truck, and let's drive out there. You can show me the building".

"*Sí, jefa*" Luis said easily as he hurried to the front desk to sign out a vehicle. He was pleased that she was going to try to get them access to the building based on his information.

Luis arrived in the back parking area in less than two minutes and unlocked a late-model, white Ram pickup truck with blue and yellow reflective police decals. The San Amaro Police force did not have undercover vehicles. There would be no covert arrival into the ejido for the pair today. It wouldn't matter. Luis and Julia were both uniformed officers. They could hardly fool anyone no matter in what vehicle they arrived.

Less than ten minutes later, Luis parked the pickup in the same place he'd parked on his previous visit. He led her to the garage. She pulled out her cell phone and walked around the building taking several photos of each side and a close-up of the lock holding the two large doors shut tightly. She had even given the lock a yank to verify it was locked. It was.

As Luis had done on his circumnavigation of the building on his first visit, Julia tested the joints between the pieces of siding covering the garage. And like Luis, she found no weak spots that would allow the curious to see within. Despite the shabby appearance of the place and its sheath of aging RV siding, it was sturdily built and impenetrable without either a key or a metal saw. Even a couple of holes drilled through the skin might give them the ability to see what this enigmatic place contained.

Breaking into Julia's thoughts, Luis pondered out loud as he and Julia walked back to the pickup. "I wonder if el Señor Blair knows a man with yellow curly hair?"

"Que?" Julia asked. What? She had stopped abruptly and now stared at Luis.

"The truck driver who saw a RZR type of desert rig turn up this road the night el Señor Blair's was stolen said the driver had yellow curly hair. It was in my report." Luis looked at Julia with a scowl and an edge of frustration in his voice.

Dammit, Julia thought. She had forgotten. And this was likely the cause of the little niggle that had been surfacing occasionally over the last few days. "Right. Thanks for the reminder. Let's go see if he knows anyone who matches that description."

As Luis drove to Campo Cristal, Julia phoned Ricardo's mobile on her cell. "Hola Chica," he said, seeing her name on the caller display. "Que pasa?" What's up?

"Ricardo, where does Rob Gurenburg live? Is it Campo Cristal?" she asked without preamble.

"Ha, and I thought this might be a social call!" Ricardo laughed. "Yes, he is renting a casita there. Do you need the house number?"

"Yes. There might be a connection between the missing RZR case Luis and I are working on and Gurenburg. Wouldn't that be interesting?!" she exclaimed.

"*Sí, muy interesante*!" Yes, very interesting. "I'll text you his address," Ricardo responded.

Chapter 7—March 17, 2018, San Amaro

Julia was not surprised that even with the dog barking within, it took several minutes of banging on the door and calling out before Ted Blair's fuzzy white head flickered behind the curtain. It gave her a sense of déjà vu as she recalled her and Luis's first visit to interview el Señor Blair. Both she and Luis already had their identification cards open. Just like the previous visit, Ted Blair simply opened the door and waddled into his kitchen, leaving Luis and Julia to close the door and follow.

The place actually looked tidier and cleaner than on their previous visit. There were no dirty dishes lining the countertops, and the dog hair coating the floors last time was no longer in evidence. Julia would wager money that he had a local woman who came in to clean for him. She mentally sent the woman her sympathy.

"Ya find my rig?" Ted Blair asked, as he reached his kitchen and plopped himself on a stool. He did not offer the police officers a seat.

"Not yet, Mr. Blair," Julia began, "but we are following up a lead and need your help." This caused the old man to lift his head from his apparent perusal of his socks and look at her. "Do you know a fellow living in a casita here in Campo Cristal, by the name of Rob Gurenburg?"

"I don't think so. Name doesn't sound familiar," Blair responded, a disappointed tone creeping into his voice.

Julia pulled out her phone and brought up a photo of Rob that had been taken the day of the hike. It showed Rob and Simon from a distance, so wasn't the best, but she passed her phone to Blair, anyway. "He's the taller blond fellow on the right," she said, watching Blair's reaction carefully.

He looked at the photo for a few seconds and then spread his thumb and forefinger over the screen to enlarge the picture. He looked again for a few seconds before handing the phone back to Julia. "Nope, never seen him before. You think he stole my rig?"

"At this point he is a person of interest, but we have no evidence linking him to your missing RZR. Thank you for your time, Mr. Blair." Julia kept the disappointment out of her voice as she took back her phone.

As they buckled themselves into the police pickup, Julia's phone buzzed with a message. Her appointment with the comandante was scheduled for noon. She glanced at the time on her phone. She had over an hour. "Let's give Mr. Gurenburg a visit. Ricardo texted me his address. It's on Calle B, so should be just the next street toward the beach," she said.

The casita was small, likely constructed of cinder block, but finished with a thick coating of parged plaster stucco, painted a rich mossy green. The red-tiled roof of the overhang above the door gave it a welcoming appeal. The landscaping around the property was a mixture of local cacti, ice plant, and a paloverde tree that had created a carpet of yellow as it disgorged its flowers across the sand.

Julia stepped up to the dark-brown, mission-style door and rang the bell. "Just a sec" came an almost instant response. Rob Gurenburg's lanky frame filled the doorway a moment later. He had obviously expected someone other than Julia and Luis as the smile on his face disappeared in the two seconds it took him to look from Luis to Julia.

He opened his mouth to speak, but Julia beat him to it. "Good morning, Mr. Gurenburg. Sorry to drop in unannounced. We just have a couple of questions. May we come in?"

"Yeah. Ah, sure. Do you have some news about Stella?" he asked, with a sincere look of interest. He led them into the home's main living area. It reminded Julia of her own casita, though this one was larger and better furnished. The inside walls were a lighter version of the exterior mossy green. The couch and chairs were upholstered in a soft yellow. It seemed decidedly feminine and a contrast to this tall, muscular man before them. Rob gestured to the couch and seated himself in one of the chairs.

"This is not about Stella. Corporal Flores and I are working a case of stolen property, from one of your neighbors, Ted Blair. Do you know him? He lives on Calle C, almost right behind this place," Julia asked smoothly.

"No. I haven't really gotten to know any neighbors. What was stolen? Do I need to be worried?" Rob asked, his brow furrowing in concern.

"His RZR was stolen from in front of his home the evening of March 6 or early morning of March 7. Were you here that evening, Mr. Gurenburg? Did you happen to see or hear anything?" Julia kept her voice even and friendly.

"That was the last day of the Baja Two Fifty," he said, to help himself place the date into the framework of his own actions. "Yeah, I was here, but I went to bed early that night. I'd been out to the desert watching the racers come in earlier in the day. I was exhausted, and I sleep with earplugs. I didn't hear a thing." Julia thought his answer came pretty quickly. Most people had to think about what they had done yesterday, let alone almost two weeks previous.

"So, you weren't out driving around in a desert rig at four the morning of the seventh?" Julia asked, watching him closely.

"No, I just told you I was asleep." For a second, Julia thought he was going to continue, but she watched as his eyes flashed darkly and he clamped his mouth tightly, muscles flexing along his jawline. She waited. After a moment, his face lightened. "Anything else?" he asked, breezily.

Julia waited another couple of beats before standing. "No, that's it. Thanks." Luis jumped up, too, and they walked the few steps to the door. "If you remember anything from that evening, please give me a call at the station. The number is on this card." She left a business card on the small table by the door. It was printed with San Amaro State Police and a phone number.

"He has yellow curly hair," Luis excitedly stated the obvious as he maneuvered the truck out of the small street and headed back up the main road toward the highway.

"Yes, he does. And his alibi *brilla por su ausencia.*" She used the colloquial phrase "shines by its absence" to indicate her own suspicions of the alibi's validity.

With forty minutes to wait before her appointment with the comandante, Julia found

Inspector Martinez and Ricardo. She needed to bring them up to speed on her suspicion that the stolen RZR might factor into the missing woman case and that the inspector also knew about her upcoming meeting with the comandante.

Inspector Martinez sat at the head of the war-room table. He was flanked on the left by Julia and Luis and on the right by Ricardo. He had not spoken for several minutes. Instead, he had been flipping through Julia's pictures of the garage from that morning. Before he spoke, he laid seven of the photos out on the table as if he were laying out a game of solitaire.

"Walk me through how you think these two cases are connected," asked the inspector, looking wearily at Julia.

Julia felt Luis shift forward in his chair as though he were going to speak and looked briefly at him, willing him to sit back and be quiet. He did. "Corporal Flores got a lead from a neighbor of the man whose RZR was stolen in the early hours of the day before Stella Monroe went missing. The neighbor mentioned she heard a noisy vehicle leaving Campo Cristal at about four o'clock in the morning. He took the initiative to set up a vehicle check at four a.m. the following week in the hopes that someone traveling that stretch of road on a regular basis might have seen something that would further the case." Luis had his eyes glued to the side of her head. He had fully expected her to take the credit for the vehicle check.

"He was richly rewarded for his motivation. He spoke with a water-delivery truck driver who did see a 'desert rig' driving along the highway away from Campo Cristal toward Punto de Cono Ejido, where it turned. The truck driver described the driver of the desert rig as being 'a gringo with curly yellow hair.'"

She stopped for a moment to underscore the importance of this last piece of information. She was rewarded as she saw the inspector turn to look at the photo board, directly at the picture of Rob Gurenburg.

"Mr. Gurenburg is renting a casita in Campo Cristal right in front of the house from which the RZR was stolen," she said, continuing. "Corporal Flores drove into the ejido later that day and discovered this sturdily constructed building that appeared to be a garage." She pointed to one of the photos in front of the inspector and went on. "It didn't have any windows, and the two large doors on one end were padlocked. He spoke with a resident of the ejido, who appeared to be warning him that it was dangerous to be investigating that building, and Corporal Flores, wisely, left. That night when I read the corporal's report of his findings, I began to suspect that the missing RZR and the disappearance of Stella Monroe might be connected. Then, when the Amundsen brothers gave us their statement of seeing a desert vehicle, which they identified as being either a RZR or a Can-Am, in the desert in the timeframe when Stella Monroe went missing, my thoughts of a connection were reinforced."

When Julia paused to take a drink of water, the room was silent, waiting for her to resume. "Corporal Flores reviewed the records in the Property Public Registry office in Mexicali and was unable to find any private registration of the land on which the garage sits, leading us to believe that it is still part of the communal ownership. I am hoping the comandante will authorize us to search the building." As she was speaking, Julia had sat forward in her chair, her back rigid and her eyes trained on the inspector. Now finished, she allowed herself a deep breath and sat back in her chair.

Martinez shifted his gaze to Luis. “Thank you for your help, Corporal Flores. I’m sure you would like to continue to be involved in determining whether the RZR stolen from Campo Cristal is involved in the missing woman case.” Luis looked like a puppy that was going to get a bone. His eyes shone with excitement. “Unfortunately, Semana Santa starts in just a few days, and your involvement in the policing of that event takes precedence. If that weren’t the case, I’d invite you to stay.” Luis made a valiant, but unsuccessful, effort not to look disappointed. “Yes, sir.” He stood and left quickly. Julia’s eyes followed him to the door. His shoulders sagged as he left the room.

Through Julia’s report, the inspector had maintained an aloof expression, looking more at the photos in front of him than Julia. After Luis left, he sat silently for several moments. He finally nodded his head twice, as if confirming something with himself. He brought his hazel eyes into full focus on Julia. “Okay, thank you. That helps pull things together,” he said. “I can see how you think the two cases may be connected. Good luck with the comandante. Let’s see what he says about searching the garage.”

Chapter 8—March 18, 2018, San Amaro

Julia was hunched in the flip-down jump seat that pretended to be a back seat in the pickup's extended cab. Luis and Ricardo occupied the two front seats. The atmosphere in the truck was one of excitement and anticipation. Luis was hoping to find the lost RZR, and Julia and Ricardo were eager to discover if there was a link to, and therefore, a new clue in their missing woman case. The comandante had deliberated for the afternoon and overnight before giving Julia the go-ahead in a phone call shortly after she arrived at the station that morning. He had agreed that there was sufficient cause to open the garage in the ejido and see if it contained the missing RZR. If, in fact, it had been Rob Gurenburg driving it the morning of March 7, it may still show his fingerprints. And, though it was a stretch, it might also be possible that it had evidence of the disappearance of Stella Monroe.

Beside Julia on the floor of the cramped back seat were a large bolt cutter, a cordless drill with a variety of bits, and a hacksaw. One way or another, the three would be viewing the interior of the shed within a few minutes.

Ricardo was the first to see it. They had just turned off the highway onto the bumpy track that led into the Punto de Cono Ejido. "¡*Mierda*!" Shit, he cried. Ahead, rising above the hills leading into the ejido was thick, black smoke—the kind of smoke that comes from burning gasoline and burning tires.

Luis sped ahead. Julia felt every rock and pothole in the road jackhammer through the hard jump seat, against her tailbone, and up her spine. As they crested the last hill, more curses filled the truck cab. They could clearly see flames leaping from the garage they were planning to investigate.

Ricardo radioed for a fire truck, but they all knew it was hopeless.

The heat from the inferno kept them back fifty feet from the building, but already, the roof had collapsed, and one wall was completely gone. Bits of siding were lying about, some smoldering where the framing lumber was still attached. Inside the remains of the building the burned-out shell of a RZR sat, its tires still smoking, causing noxious black smoke to obscure the fire site and then scud along the ground as winds from the incoming tide alternatively blew and subsided through the area.

Among the fifteen or so onlookers, Luis noticed the old man from his first visit to the ejido standing beside his ramshackle trailer. Luis walked his way. The old man started to climb the steps to his home, but his lame leg slowed him enough that Luis reached him before he could disappear behind the strip of canvas that acted as his door. "*¿Amigo, que pasó aquí?"* What happened here?

The old man looked up at Luis; his small black eyes burned into Luis like lasers. Holding Luis's eyes, the old man spat. "¡*Estúpido cerdo*!" Stupid pig! He then dragged his bad leg up the final step and disappeared into his hovel. Luis, knowing he wouldn't get anything useful from pursuing the old man, turned back to the fire. It was starting to burn itself out. It had likely been started no more than a half hour before they arrived, almost exactly when they were preparing to leave the station.

Julia was taking pictures on her cell phone of the destroyed building, what remained of the RZR, and the crowd that had gathered to watch the blaze. The smoke was making picture taking very challenging, and she worried that none of her photos would be of any value.

The fire truck lumbered into the camp about fifteen minutes after the three police officers had radioed for it. They set about trying to extinguish the remaining fire, but their efforts were far too little and far too late to make any difference in the outcome. What remained when they had succeeded in putting out the last of the fire was a blackened shell of the desert rig sitting in a hardening pool of smoldering, reeking rubber covered with water.

Julia knew from her training that tires burned at about 750 degrees Fahrenheit. The heat from the congealing remains of the tires was still very intense, and Julia was not able to get very close to what remained of the RZR. She had to content herself with taking her final pictures from many feet away.

The fire department would call in an expert from Mexicali in the next day or so. He, as the inspector would certainly be male, would create a report on the probable cause of the fire and provide any details that might assist the police in their own investigation. For now, there was little left to learn from the building, and Julia held faint hope for useful information from the fire investigator's report.

The excitement and expectancy that had buoyed the trio as they headed out this morning was long gone. It was replaced with frustration, anger, and a sickening sense that their unknown quarry was several steps ahead of them.

Chapter 9—March 18, 2018, San Amaro

Shortly after his appointment time of ten o'clock, Martín Robles rushed into the police station and asked for Inspector Martinez. He had phoned the station the evening before, saying he wanted to come forward with information about Stella Monroe. The inspector wanted to do this interview himself.

In her role as liaison to the Americans involved in this case, Julia had no reason to be involved in the interview of Robles, as he was Spanish and a longtime San Amaro resident. Her curiosity, however, was just too great. She was seated at her desk sporting earphones and watching a currently vacant interview room on the monitor before her. As she watched, Ricardo escorted Martín Robles into the room and turned on the recording equipment. A loud pop in her ear made Julia jump, and she smiled and shrugged at the officer her abrupt movement had startled at the desk beside her, pointing to her earphones. Martinez also entered the room, and the formalities for the recording began. Names were spoken for the tape and Martín's address was noted. Martín was originally from Madrid and was bilingual, but this interview would be conducted in Spanish.

He made his living giving people, mostly gringos and weekenders from Mexicali, rides in his ultralight plane at one hundred dollars US. Even one ride a week was enough to allow him to get by. He usually gave several rides a week during the winter season and multiple rides a day during Semana Santa and Baja race weeks. He lived comfortably.

"Do you know Stella Monroe?" Inspector Martinez began the questioning, showing a picture of Stella on her wedding day that Simon had provided.

"Yes. I know her. Not really close friends, but more casual. She has ridden in my plane a few times, and she and my wife both volunteer together for some dog thing," Martín answered earnestly.

"Tell us why you were flying your plane at the time and near the location where she went missing March 8," Martinez said. At her desk, Julia felt her pulse quicken in anticipation of learning something specific that might move this case forward.

Martín, who had been sitting forward with his hands on the table in front of him, took a deep breath, leaned back, and began. "I got a panicked phone call from Stella in the early evening of March 6. She asked me if I could, very early on the morning of March 8, fly out to an area about a kilometer south of where people leave their vehicles to hike into Cañon Del Demonio. She said she would hike over to where she asked me to park the plane. Said she'd meet me there about quarter to eleven. She asked me to wait until at least eleven thirty, in case she got held up. She told me she'd have her dog with her, which seemed weird to me, but she said she had to get him out, too. She told me her dog is well trained and would sit on her lap in the passenger seat. So, I went along with it. She sounded like her life depended on my help."

"And didn't you think it was a strange request?" Ricardo interjected, his voice ringing with incredulity.

"Ah yes. Very weird!" Martín answered and quickly went on. "When she called me, she sounded scared to death. I asked why she wanted to do this thing and where I was to fly her. Then it got even weirder. She said she was pretty sure her husband planned to kill her. She asked me to take her to my wife's tio's farm in the mountains up toward Tecate. You know, he has a few rooms he rents to tourists now and then. Apparently, she has stayed there a few times and knows my wife's tio. She also asked me to lend her my wife's car so she could drive into the States with it and leave it across the border for us to pick up. I said yes, and my wife drove her car to her tio's. I was planning to fly my wife back to San Amaro after I dropped off Stella and her dog."

Julia tried to suppress her shock and surprise. She had been a police officer long enough that she thought very little could surprise her anymore. But this caught her totally off guard. She wasn't sure what she thought they would find out from Martín, but it certainly wasn't this.

"This is a fantastic story, Señor Robles. Is it true?" asked the inspector.

"I know. It sounds crazy. It is crazy. It is also true," Robles answered in the same earnest way he had spoken since his arrival.

"Please continue with your account, Señor Robles. What happened the day of March 8?" Martinez said.

"I flew my little plane like she asked and landed south of the parking area. I arrived shortly before eight thirty that morning. I waited like she asked. About nine thirty, I thought I heard their vehicles arrive and park. The rumble of their rigs traveled through the air to where I waited. I had brought a sheet with me that I used to make a shaded area under the wings of my plane. I stayed there until almost noon. She never arrived."

Ricardo shifted in his seat as though he wanted to ask a question, but Robles continued before Ricardo could speak.

"While I was waiting, I heard another vehicle arrive. I looked at my watch. It was ten forty. At the time, I just thought it was more hikers. Then I heard it drive away again about fifteen minutes later. I hadn't really thought much about it until I heard it drive away. But then I started to fear they might have intercepted Stella. I walked over the boulders to a place where I could see the vehicles. There were only three there, but there was still some dust in the air and receding engine sounds. Stella and her dog were nowhere to be seen. I went back to the plane and waited. But like I said, she never arrived, so I flew back to San Amaro. When I got back on the ground, I phoned my wife and asked her to return to town in her car. I asked her *tio* to call me if Stella showed up there. He hasn't seen her."

"Why the hell haven't you come forward sooner? She has been missing for ten days. She obviously trusted you to help her. Why haven't you tried to help us find her?" Ricardo sounded furious. Julia was surprised by this outburst and wondered how the inspector felt about it.

"I left Mexico the next morning to visit my mother in Madrid. I just got back yesterday, so I didn't know until last night that she was missing," Martín answered. He sounded like a scolded little boy afraid he'd get a spanking. He hung his head, looking at his boots, and added in a quiet voice, "She told me not to talk to anyone about what she was planning, no matter what happened. But when I got home and found out she had been missing since that day, I phoned to make an appointment to see you, even though I was afraid you would not believe me and say I harmed her." Police corruption was unfortunately not a rare occurrence in Mexico. Martín had no way to know if the policemen before him were looking for a Mexican scapegoat so they could close their case, or if they were legitimately seeking the truth. He was truly frightened.

"And did you harm her?" The inspector's voice sounded strained and angry. His frustration was also evident.

"No. No, I didn't. I would never." Martín's voice trembled as he spoke.

The inspector and Ricardo continued questioning Martín for three hours. In that time, he repeated his story several more times. He was able to provide the information that the single vehicle he heard sounded very loud and rumbly. He didn't think it was a conventional vehicle like a Jeep or a pickup truck. Very little else of value came from the further questioning. In the end, he was released, but told not to leave San Amaro.

After the second time through his version of events, Julia tired of watching the interview of Martín Robles on her computer. She pulled off her headphones at about the two-and-a-half-hour mark, massaged her ears, and closed her eyes. They were beginning to feel gritty from staring at her computer screen uninterrupted for so long. She was sitting at her desk like this, eyes closed and hands rubbing her ears, when the on-duty desk sergeant came to her desk.

"There is a phone call from an American woman who doesn't speak any Spanish. Can you come to the front and talk to her?" asked the desk sergeant. Julia asked what it was about, but the desk sergeant had no idea. Julia rose and followed the man into the foyer.

"Hello. How may I help you?" Julia said in her excellent, only slightly accented English.

"Hello, my name is Pippa Drummond. I am a friend of Stella Monroe, and I'm calling from the United States. I just received a letter from Stella that says she thinks her husband is going to kill her. I didn't know who to call . . ." Pippa's words exploded across the phone lines.

"Ms. Drummond, I'm going to stop you for just a moment and transfer this call to my desk, where I can take all the time we need to get the information you received from your friend. Please stay on the line, even if it sounds as if it goes dead. But if I'm not back on the line in two minutes, please phone back to this number." Julia told her the number of her direct line at her desk. And then she and the desk sergeant tried to remember how to transfer the call. It took at least a minute, but by the time Julia returned to her desk and depressed the HOLD light, she was again speaking with the American woman, Pippa Drummond. On her way back to her desk, Julia had grabbed a small digital audio recorder from the tech cupboard and was relieved to see that the batteries were good. She turned it on as she walked to her desk and introduced herself on the tape, so she was able to begin recording the conversation with Pippa immediately, with the American woman's permission.

Julia started by getting Pippa's name spelled properly, her phone number and address in Wisconsin, and details of her relationship with Stella. She asked several general questions about when she had last seen Stella and learned that this woman had been in San Amaro less than six months ago. Then they moved on to the purpose of Pippa's call. It turned out she had just returned home from a trip to visit her daughter, son-in-law, and three-month-old granddaughter in Phoenix and found a letter from Stella waiting for her. The letter was dated March 7. Pippa explained that was about a typical amount of time for a letter from her friend to reach her in the US, given that it had likely been delivered a couple of days before her return. Julia had Pippa read the letter to her.

Dearest Pip,

I have tried unsuccessfully to reach you on your cell phone, and I'm at my wits' end with fright and worry. I thought I'd write to you in hopes it will help me think more clearly about the situation I find myself in. This came as a complete surprise to me, and I'm still in shock. Two days ago, I got a phone call on my cell from a woman named Althea Cutler from Pleasant Valley, Arizona, which apparently is part of the metro Phoenix area, maybe you know it. She claimed to be my birth mother and told me she had hired an estate lawyer two years ago to locate me so she could make me her heir, her sole heir! She is supposedly very rich and old, ninety-four, she said. The lawyer she hired was my Simon. Some friends of hers were showing her pictures of their daughter's travels down the Baja peninsula and in one of them the old gal spotted Simon with his arm around a woman, me, who Mrs. Cutler said was her spitting image

from when she was my age. She wanted to warn me that he might be up to no good.
You can imagine how that freaked me out, even steady old me!
I have devised a plan to leave Simon tomorrow and get far away before he realizes I've left. You remember me telling you about taking a plane ride from the beach several years ago in one of those ultralight planes? Well, the pilot is a casual friend, and he is helping me escape, in his plane and then in his wife's car to the US. I'm going to go to Pleasant Valley and meet my birth mother, and she has promised me sufficient cash to comfortably start again until I get the remainder of my inheritance.
Please don't call me at home. Use my cell if you need to call me, but know that I'll reach out to you once I have my feet under me again. As you can imagine, this has me pretty scared, but I'm virtually certain Simon has no idea I know what his end game is. The bastard!
I hope that you and Gerry are doing okay. I'm sorry to dump this on you, but I'm really scared.
Love,
Stella

Julia updated Pippa to the fact that Stella had gone missing during a hike in the desert and on the status of their investigation, saying only that their search had not turned up any sign of Stella or her dog in the desert and that the investigation was ongoing. After thanking Pippa for calling and reassuring her that they would update her with new information when that was possible, Julia hung up the phone and verified that the recording she made was clear enough to be transcribed. Before she set about that task, she logged back into her sleeping computer and discovered that the interview with the pilot was finished. She headed upstairs to update Ricardo and the inspector on this latest information. At last, they had the motive that had eluded them for the last week and a half. Stella Monroe was set to inherit a large amount of money.

As expected, Julia found Ricardo and the inspector in their war room. She wanted to blurt out what she had just learned, but the men were standing at the topographical map in deep conversation about the route Martín had flown in his ultralight and Stella's revelation to Martín about needing to escape her husband. They had looked up briefly when Julia entered but had not stopped their discussion of these new details.

After a minute, Julia realized they weren't planning to stop and include her, so she cleared her throat and said in a clear, steady voice, "Sorry to interrupt, but I have new information you need to hear. We finally have our motive." She then went on to tell them about Pippa's call and the contents of Stella's letter to her friend. "Pippa's cell phone was stolen while she was at a food court in a shopping mall in Phoenix the first week in March, and she decided not to replace it until she returned home to Wisconsin. So, she wasn't able to receive the calls Stella mentioned in her letter."

"Finally, we are getting some breaks in this case," the inspector said. "The letter gives us the why and perhaps even the who, but we are still no closer to knowing *what* happened that day or how." Even with this still-missing information from the "who, what, where, when, and why" ensemble, the inspector exuded an air of excitement for the first time since the case had begun. There was real eagerness in his voice as he continued, saying, "We *are* going to figure this out. What happened that day?"

Chapter 10—March 19, 2018, San Amaro

It was Saturday, and the inspector and Ricardo had the day off. Julia was sitting in the war room. She had been staring for a half hour at the white board displaying the photos of the missing woman and the five friends with whom she had been hiking and notes of other information relevant to the case. The inspector's final remark from the previous day was rattling around her head. *What had happened that day?* Her attention was caught by the photo of the extra set of tire tracks that appeared to show a vehicle had stopped north and just out of sight of the parking area where the hikers had left their desert rigs, and that it had then proceeded to the exact location of where the hikers' vehicles had been parked.

As instructed by Inspector Martinez, Ricardo, had noted the GPS coordinates and the mileage from that spot where the unknown vehicle had stopped to the place the hikers left their vehicles the morning Stella disappeared. Julia had been fascinated by Günter Amundsen's description of GPS notation and the calculations that would convert the notation of hours, minutes, and seconds from the fixed point of Greenwich, England, into a decimal number used by computers and in-vehicle GPS systems. Suddenly, thinking of her own dyslexia gave her an idea. She pulled up the calculator app on her phone and used her new knowledge to check something.

After a few minutes she had proved to herself that the difference in distance between the location where the unknown desert rig had stopped initially and the location of the parked hikers' rigs was caused by a transposition of the last two numbers in the latitude—eighty-two instead of twenty-eight. If a person had been given GPS coordinates of the location where the hikers were leaving their rigs, but had transposed those last two numbers, that person would have ended up exactly where the unknown vehicle had first stopped. It was circumstantial, at best, because the police couldn't prove the tracks had been made the day Stella went missing, but it implied that someone had been given GPS coordinates to where the hikers parked and sat next to a large boulder for a few minutes before realizing an error had been made and drove farther to find the proper location. And, given that the Amundsen brothers had seen a RZR drive toward the hikers' parking spot, it implied that someone sent the rig driver to a specific location, which that person wrote down wrong.

Excited by this discovery, she wanted to see if she could figure out more. She decided to pinpoint on the topographical map in the war room, where Günter Amundsen estimated that same rig veered east on its return trip. Perhaps it might help her figure out where the unknown vehicle was headed, since it wasn't back the same way from which it arrived. After more calculations, using Günter's GPS coordinates of his campsite, and Google Earth, she had some valuable information. She was able to mark where the brothers had been camping and the location of Günter when he observed the returning vehicle turn. When viewed on Google Earth, she could see a dirt track that the rig may have potentially taken. That track ended at a small, secluded cove with a small section of sandy beach. It appeared to be about fifty miles south of San Amaro. Julia decided to pay it a visit, though what might be left there after ten days was anybody's guess.

The drive south had taken her past several small, mostly gringo, communities where little houses and parked RVs studded the seafront. There was no electricity in that area, but solar panels glinted in the sun from most rooftops. Were she close enough to hear, she surmised the drone of generators would be heard on hot days when air-conditioning consumed more power than solar batteries would provide. Perhaps most of the residents of these tiny communities were seasonal inhabitants, returning to other homes in cooler climates for the late-spring-to-early-fall months, when temperatures in this area of the Baja rose to over one hundred degrees Fahrenheit.

Less than two hours later, Julia arrived at the cove and took photos of the sandy track between the highway and the beach before she destroyed any existing tracks by driving over them. The beach was hidden behind a series of low, rocky, and cactus-covered hills. It was a perfect smuggler's cove. The hills were high enough to provide both cover and lookout spots. The cove itself was small, composed of only about fifty feet of curving beach bracketed by high, rocky outcrops that provided shelter and obscurity. She explored the beach, the track in, and the hills. While there was nothing to see, no discernible tire tracks, and certainly no indication Stella had ever been there, it did leave Julia with a new line of thinking about where the missing woman might be.

When she returned to the police station, she fired up her computer and researched prevailing currents and tides in the Sea of Cortez. Later, she checked into police activity on the opposite side of the Sea of Cortez, in Puerto Peñasco, specifically, as it was almost directly across the sea from San Amaro. What she learned both excited and depressed her.

Although it was the inspector's day off, she decided her news was important enough to call him. After apologizing for interrupting his family time, she launched into her news. "The body of a woman washed up on a beach about seventeen miles north of Puerto Peñasco two days ago. Its description matches that of Stella Monroe. Dark hair, five foot four, slight build. The Puerto Peñasco police haven't finished the autopsy yet, so we don't know how the woman died. I sent them Stella's picture, but with the condition of the body, they can't verify it's her. There are no visible signs indicating cause of death, but the body had been in the warm seawater over a week and had extensive bloating, skin loss, and predation by fish. Their coroner should finish the autopsy tomorrow. At my request, they put a rush on it, so we should know more then or by Monday at the latest. I'm going to try to obtain her dental records, but I'm hesitant to ask her husband about who her dentist is, as he might figure out that we have found her body," she explained.

"First, clarify how you made the leap from missing in the desert to possibly floating on the currents over to the other side of the sea," said the inspector.

Julia spent several minutes explaining her theory of the GPS coordinates being transposed by the mystery vehicle driver and how that inspired her to revisit the GPS information she'd received from the

Amundsen brothers about the possible route taken by that same vehicle on its return trip. She described using the topo maps and bringing up Google Earth and told him how that route could have taken the driver to the small cove she'd visited earlier and how that discovery got her thinking perhaps this case involved a body dump at sea.

She also explained that the prevailing currents on the Sea of Cortez are clockwise in winter and counterclockwise in summer, so if the body had been dumped, it would most likely end up on the opposite shore at the north end of the sea rather than somewhere south, thus her call to the Puerto Peñasco police. The inspector listened to her recount her discoveries with few questions until she was finished. She ably answered his queries, and when their discussion was complete, the inspector surprised and embarrassed her with lavish praise for her initiative and deductive reasoning. She blushed deeply and was grateful they were on the phone.

The inspector's decision was to wait until the autopsy was completed and they had more information before informing the husband, given the high probability Simon was involved in his wife's death. She decided to call Ricardo, too, and bring him up to speed. "Chica. Calling me on my day off! Should I be flattered?" he said, with a chuckle in his deep voice.

Julia told him the same information she'd given the inspector. Ricardo listened to her without interruption, finally saying, "Wow, Lucy, that's impressive. Guess you're not just a pretty face after all." Julia was surprised and a little embarrassed by his praise, but very proud that she'd made such an important leap forward in the case. "It's pretty close to quitting time for you, right? Why don't we meet for a taco and a beer to celebrate?"

Julia's initial reaction was to say no. She knew Ricardo would be very happy to be more than friends. And she really liked Ricardo. But she couldn't get past her emotional scars. The damage done by losing her father when she was a teen made it extremely hard for her to believe that she could trust her heart to any man. Aside from that, she carried the fear of being discounted as a serious police officer if she started dating a coworker on the force. Julia also knew that Ricardo respected her enough not to push her into a romantic relationship, although he flirted with her constantly. In the end, she realized it was just tacos and a beer, not a big date. Julia agreed, and they decided to meet up at a hole-in-the-wall place near the sea with the best fish tacos in town.

Chapter 11—March 20, 2018, San Amaro

It was Palm Sunday and the first day of Semana Santa. San Amaro's Malecon, like most of the beaches in Mexico, was transformed into a throbbing mass of people from landlocked parts of Mexico. The number of Mexicans traveling for the Holy Week was second only to those traveling at Christmas. It is a time to visit family, make pilgrimages, and have a vacation on the beach. Over 30,000 people had descended on San Amaro over the last few days, and more would be arriving today.

For the San Amaro Police department, it was all hands on deck. Julia had therefore been surprised and delighted when Inspector Martinez had called her the previous night to tell her she didn't have to report in for her scheduled desk-duty shift as shown on the roster. She, Ricardo, and the inspector were to meet in their war room at seven that morning.

Julia was the first to arrive, getting into the building at six thirty. She had made a fresh pot of coffee and made some notes on one of their whiteboards about the latest, significant information the team had uncovered over the past few days.

As she waited for her male teammates, she reflected on the circuitous course this investigation was taking. In less than two weeks, they had gone from believing a woman was lost in the desert, after separating from her fellow hikers, to learning her husband had knowledge of a future windfall she would receive and had potentially facilitated her death to get his hands on the money. That provided "motive." Hopefully, the autopsy being done in Puerto Peñasco on Stella Monroe's corpse would help explain or give them clues to the means. As far as she could see, they were still in the dark about the "opportunity" any of the hikers had to actually kill her, since they were all at the cave drawings.

She was pondering this point when Ricardo plopped himself down in a chair across the table from her. "Morning, Lucy," he said with a smile. "Hope you had a good time last night. I did. I wonder if the inspector realized we were together when he called us about this meeting."

"Well, *Ricky*," she said, emphasizing his nickname, since he insisted on calling her by hers, "he's a detective inspector, and the restaurant's boom box was playing the same song when he called me as it was when he called you. I'd say the chances are good." This was not something that pleased her. Rumors were rampant at the academy about her and Ricardo, even though they were only friends, and not friends with benefits. That was bad enough, but they had managed to leave the small talk behind in Mexicali when they were both hired on to the San Amaro Police department. She didn't need that kind of attention here in San Amaro. She liked Ricardo a lot, and that scared her emotionally. But equally important to her, she didn't want anything to become a roadblock to her goal of one day being the town's police comandante.

Ricardo didn't seem worried, but he wouldn't be. He was a man. He could have a fling or a relationship with a female police officer, and no one would bat an eye . . . about him. For the female officer, however, it would be a different story. It could mean the end to a career. *So unfair,* Julia thought to herself. Her thoughts along those lines were abruptly displaced by Inspector Martinez's arrival.

After hellos, he grabbed a coffee, and sat at the head of the table with Julia on his left and Ricardo on his right. Without preamble, he began, "I suspect we are now investigating a murder, as I think it's highly unlikely Stella Monroe found out her husband had an ulterior motive in marrying her and left their hike to go and throw herself in the sea." He smiled at his little joke and then got more serious. "I see one of you started a list of new information. Let's start with that and see if we can refine our theory of what happened."

Julia, who had fallen into the role of scribe during their previous brainstorming sessions, stood and moved to the whiteboard where she had started her list earlier. She was holding her phone on which she had the list of things they had previously developed about this case.

"March 8, Stella Monroe went missing from a hike in the desert. On March 10, two days after Stella went missing, we speculated this could be an abduction, a plan by the missing woman to leave an unhappy marriage, or a conspiracy among the five remaining hikers to cover up something like a murder or suspicious death of the missing woman." Julia started to draw a timeline on the whiteboard starting with the date of the hike. "The search of the hike area failed to turn up any clues about what might have happened, except for a set of tire tracks that may or may not have been made on the day in question that were several hundred yards away from the area where we believe the woman disappeared and then moved to that same area." She extended her line farther to the right and drew a squiggly line along a short distance of it, writing "Search" under it.

Ricardo had been flipping through his notebook, finally finding what he was looking for, and added, "We interviewed all five of the remaining hikers on March 15 but didn't really learn much."

"Yes, and I called off the official search on March 17," interjected the inspector. Julia added those two dates to the timeline, bracketing the wavy line indicating the search.

Julia then made a demarcation for March 16 and added "Learned about another RZR and a plane in the vicinity of the hike," saying, "The Danish brothers camping a few miles north of the hike location witnessed the coming and going of the desert rig and the departure of an ultralight plane the morning Stella disappeared." She then turned to the inspector and asked, "Do you want to include anything on the timeline about the stolen RZR case Luis and I have been working?"

He suggested adding that information in another color. So far everything was in black, but there was a blue whiteboard pen downstairs in the lunchroom that was used for writing up daily assignment changes. She quickly ran down and retrieved it, hoping no one would miss it. When she returned to the war room, she added "March 6 Ted Blair's RZR-stolen from Campo Cristal," and she underlined with the blue pen the March 16 mention of "another RZR seen" by Anton and Günter, to show a possible link between the two things. She then added "March 19 garage on Punto de Cono Ejido suspected of housing the missing RZR burns."

Julia then wrote, in black, under March 19, "Learned that a woman's body had washed up in

Puerto Peñasco matching Stella's description." After retrieving her notebook from the table and flipping to her last entries, she continued the timeline to the left a bit and added March 6, "Stella gets phone call from birth mother and contacts Martín Robles," and then added to March 19, "Learn of letter from Stella to Pippa."

The inspector looked pensive for a moment and then said, "We need to get the husband back in here for a proper interrogation. We can inform him then that we suspect it's murder, that we know about Stella's mother and the inheritance. We need to get the mother's contact information so we can inform her of her daughter's death once we get confirmation. Hopefully, with the results of the autopsy, we can also let the husband know we know how she was killed. Perhaps he will admit his guilt."

After a couple of more moments spent contemplating the timeline, he went on. "How did the husband know about her plan with the pilot? At this point, I'm still concerned about the new guy in the group"—he looked at the photo board and then went on—"Rob Gurenburg. If he stole the RZR and if it were used by the people seen by the Danish brothers, he and the husband must have been working together. We need to talk with the hikers again, but we have to be careful. I really doubt that all five of them were involved, but I don't think we can completely rule it out. Rick has that expired arrest warrant for child sexual assault that Stella may have found out about, and Jaime and Molly's argument may have been about Jaime and Stella having a fling, but we have nothing to substantiate that.

"And didn't we find out that Jaime Lopez could be driving illegal product for the cartel down the Baja? Ricardo, see if you can verify if there's anything to that. If he has cartel connections, he'd certainly be able to facilitate getting a body dumped into the sea and killed, too, for that matter. It seems any of them may have had a motive."

Ricardo chimed in, asking, "Since he and Stella have been good friends for years, it doesn't seem likely to be Jaime, though, does it?"

"No, it doesn't. Unless he and Stella did have a relationship that threatened his marriage," the inspector said emphatically. "Julia, talk with the Lopezes and Rick Worton and see if they know what Simon and Stella were doing on March 5. Maybe we can find out if the husband overheard the call between Stella and her mother."

"Will do," she said, writing in her notebook. When she looked up, her forehead was furrowed, and her mouth looked as if she'd just sucked on a lemon. "If the husband knew that Stella had found out about her mother and the inheritance, what does he gain by killing Stella? Why not just leave? Or if he were going to kill someone, or have someone killed, why not the mother? Then there might still have been a chance that Stella would inherit the money so he could get his hands on it."

They all pondered these questions for several minutes in silence. It was Inspector Martinez who broke the quiet. "We still don't know how this was done or even who did it." There was a hint of frustration in his voice. "Was Stella already dead when the two people in the RZR arrived? And who were the people driving that RZR that the Danish boys saw? Are they the killers, or did they merely transport and dispose of her dead body? We need to review all the witness statements from when the missing person report was filed and the interviews with the hikers on March 15. See who was first back to the vehicles. I seem to recall it was the new guy, Rob. Did he have time to kill Stella and put her body somewhere for the RZR drivers to pick up? And how does that timing line up with Danish brothers' account of seeing the RZR?"

Ricardo was scanning back through his notebook. "No, the timing doesn't work. She would need to have been dead long before the other hikers returned. It *was* Rob who was back there first, but it was at least an hour after the Amundsens saw the RZR leaving the area. Also, since the husband wrote the mother's will, he likely put in a provision that Stella's estate passes to her beneficiary in the event of her predeceasing her mother. And we know from Simon that he was her only beneficiary, so, with Stella gone, he would likely still get the money when Mrs. Cutler dies unless she learned about Stella's death and changed her will."

They spent another couple of hours reviewing all the statements and notes they had, trying to come up with a theory of what might have happened. Once they thought they were on the right track, they developed a plan of how and when to speak with their witnesses and suspects again. The inspector decided he wanted to wait until the autopsy was complete and they knew the cause of death before proceeding with any of the interviews. It was almost two in the afternoon when they wrapped up their meeting. Julia and Ricardo had their assignments. There was little they could do until they got the results of the autopsy the next day, they hoped. So much was hinging on it. They were like horses in the starting gates, raring to go, just waiting for the starter's pistol to fire.

Chapter 12—March 21, 2018, San Amaro

It was almost midday before Inspector Martinez received an email with the autopsy results. The three officers were in their war room at the time, reviewing again the timeline they had developed the previous day. The inspector read the entire report before discussing the findings with his team.

"I've just received the autopsy results. It's not good news for us, I'm afraid. They haven't found a conclusive cause of death," he said with frustration to Julia and Ricardo. "So, we have to wait for the toxicology report. The coroner suspects it may be a poisoning, but so far hasn't found specific evidence to support his suspicions. He did find some burning in the gastrointestinal tract that raised his curiosity, so he has requested a specific blood-tox test looking for some specific marker that will help confirm or shoot down his idea of what may have happened. They are rushing the tox report, and hopefully we will have something by tomorrow.

"If it turns out to be death by poisoning, that opens the door to it having been any one of the hikers on the trip. If the unknown desert rig is part of this situation, which I think it must be, then the job of its occupants could just have been body retrieval and disposal. What are your thoughts?" he asked his team.

Ricardo was the first to speak. "I think it's a good thing we haven't told any of the hikers that we believe Stella is dead. As you say, poisoning opens the door to any of the five being our killer. Isn't poison usually the method of choice of women? Should we be looking at Molly Lopez more seriously? I seem to remember she gave Stella a sandwich or something before she headed back to the vehicles. Right?"

Julia was madly flipping through the notes from Molly's interview. "That's right. Tuna with pickles. Sounds awful, but the strong tastes of fish and vinegar might mask some of the taste a poison might have. Either Jaime or Molly could have added a little something." She thought for a moment before continuing. "For that matter, Rob Gurenburg's drink might also have masked an odd flavor. Since he makes them himself, the others would have no expectation of how it *should* taste. And don't forget, Simon handled the drink, the sandwich, and her walking stick before she left the group. He could have sabotaged any of them. Maybe he did something to the leather hand strap on her walking stick before they left for the hike, to make it rip apart. Remember forensics said it had evenly spaced pinprick holes where it tore."

"Yes, we are back to having too many suspects. I think we have to be very cautious about how and when we inform the five hikers about Stella's probable death. We need to know the exact cause of death before we can rule anyone out, and I also think we need to keep them separate when we tell them. I don't want any of them getting the information when one of us is not there to observe their reaction. Let's spend some time figuring out the best way to handle this," the inspector said, as a lead-in to the next three hours while they debated the best approaches for each suspect.

The next day, the Puerto Peñasco coroner phoned. The team was in the war room. The inspector answered his phone and, on hearing who it was, put the phone on speaker.

"It was cyanide!" the coroner said excitedly, with a slight lisp. "Up until a couple of years ago, there was no way to test for cyanide any more than two days after death, and then the only test was that you might be able to smell it on the body. Then we found out about two-aminothiazoline-four-carboxylic acid. Its presence indicates cyanide. It lingers in the liver for a few weeks and in the blood for up to two weeks. Your body got to me just in time. We were able to identify it in her blood. I still need her dental records to give you certainty it is your missing woman."

All three pummeled the sibilant coroner with questions about how it may have been administered, time efficacy, symptoms, and more, keeping the man on the phone for almost twenty minutes. By then, an email copy of the toxicology report had been received and printed.

After the call ended, the inspector and Julia began reading the hard copy of the report. Ricardo was on his computer in no time doing research. "There are several types of cyanide, but the most common are two gases—hydrogen cyanide and cyanogen chloride—and two solids—sodium cyanide and potassium cyanide. Does it say in the report which one caused her death?"

Julia scanned the report, finally saying, "It was sodium cyanide. Apparently, a massive dose. It says she would have died in less than two minutes if the solution were strong enough."

"Where would someone get it?" the inspector asked no one in particular.

Ricardo typed and then read, answering, "It's used in a lot of industrial processes, but it's not readily accessible by a person on the street. You can't get it in a pharmacy. It is used in gold mining, though, so I guess anyone working at the gold mine north of town could have some chance to get it there." He paused for several moments, typing, and reading some more. "Like the coroner said, it's usually administered in food or a drink. It has a bit of a smell . . ."

"Of almonds," Inspector Martinez interjected.

"Right," Ricardo agreed. "But not everyone can smell it and, apparently, the smell can be masked by other food smells."

"Does this get us any closer to knowing how, specifically, Stella Monroe was killed or by whom?" the inspector asked. "Other than the possibilities of an electrolyte drink or the sandwich, that is."

"Okay, let's say Rob made a beverage containing cyanide and gave it to Stella as she was leaving the group to go back to the vehicles. What would have stopped her from drinking it immediately and dying somewhere on the trail? How would the two guys who transported her to the sea know where to find her if she wasn't at the vehicles?" the Inspector asked. "And, why would Rob have any reason to kill a woman he's known for only a few weeks? Maybe Simon spiked her drink."

"Maybe Rob and Simon were working together. They could have known each other before, in the States," Julia interjected.

"Yes, I think that's highly likely, Julia," Martinez agreed. "Okay, before we inform the husband about his wife's death and how she died, let's put a priority on getting the dental records. I want to proceed on the assumption that the poisoned woman in PP is Stella, but we need to get her dental records to the coroner just to tie off that loose end. We also need to talk to them all again tomorrow. When we bring Simon in, we treat him like our prime suspect. Let's bring Rob in, too, just so they can't communicate with each other."

Chapter 13—March 23, 2018, San Amaro

The inspector had used the remainder of the previous day to obtain the warrants his team would need to move ahead with their investigation. Even though it was right in the middle of Semana Santa, he had also been granted the use of three additional constables for the morning. The comandante had agreed with the inspector's evaluation that they were closing in on the person or persons responsible for Stella Monroe's death.

Ricardo and Julia decided to interview the Lopezes together. As they drove out to Jaime and Molly's home, they discussed the best way to approach the situation. They decided Ricardo would take the lead with Jaime while Julia spoke with Molly.

It was an uncharacteristically cool and cloudy day that hinted at rain. A Gila woodpecker clung to the trunk of a paloverde tree in the front yard of Jaime and Molly Lopez. Its one-note song was punctuated by irregular taps of its beak on the tree's delicate green bark.

Molly and Jaime's home was in a gated, primarily gringo community, on the mountain side of the highway. They had a view of the sea from their front yard and the large, covered porch that ran the full length of the west side of the house. The casa itself was a single-story, two-bedroom, two-bath, open-floor plan. From the outside, Molly's hobby crafting skills were evidenced by a dozen hand-painted clay pots placed strategically around the front yard, each overflowing with a vast array of purple, turquoise, and yellow plastic flowers. It was eye-catching, Julia thought, though not particular attractive to her taste.

When they knocked on the turquoise front door, it was Molly who answered. She seemed a bit startled to see police officers at her home, but invited them in. "Do you have news?" she asked, as Ricardo and Julia stepped into the living room.

Julia responded by diverting her away from that question. "We have some questions for you and Jaime. Is he also at home?"

"He's in the garage, working on his truck, I think. Shall I call him in?" Molly inquired.

Julia raised an eyebrow at Ricardo, and he picked up on her cue, turning to Molly, saying in his best English, "I can talk to Jaime there. Can you take me to the garage?"

Julia added, "Molly, Sergeant Hernandez can speak to Jaime in the garage, then perhaps you and I can have a coffee, if that's okay?"

The garage was behind the house and consumed a good portion of the backyard. It was clear this was Jaime's refuge from the color explosion that was Molly's interior-decorating style. One wall of the garage displayed a full complement of mechanic's tools. In one of the two bays was a long workbench covered with parts, tools, grease guns, oil cans, and dirty rags. In the other was an aging dark-blue Jeep Rubicon with the hood up. Jaime's body was hunched under it. He turned at the sound of the door opening.

"*Hola*, Jaime," Ricardo said as he entered the garage.

Julia turned to Molly and escorted her from Jaime's domain, back to the kitchen. Molly looked a little bewildered, but left with Julia, closing the door behind them.

Jaime removed his torso from under the hood of his vehicle, wiped his hands on a rag from his workbench, and leaned back against the bench with a neutral look on his face.

Ricardo started by saying he had a warrant to search their property and that he would be looking around the garage while they talked. Jaime looked shocked that a warrant had been issued for them and opened his mouth to question Ricardo, but the police officer began the questioning at once. "Do you know anyone who works at the mine north of town?"

The question was a complete surprise for Jaime. He looked surprised but answered quickly. "One of my grandsons runs the crusher out there. Why?"

"Does he have access to any of the chemicals used in the gold-extraction process?" Ricardo asked, probing.

Jaime chuckled and said, "No, all he does is break up the rocks."

"What was your profession in the United States, Mr. Lopez?" Ricardo asked.

Whatever Jaime may have been expecting, this question was clearly not it. His head jerked back slightly, and his face took on a perplexed expression. "At first, I worked in a Mexican restaurant, then I got my CDL and was a truck driver, long haul mostly, not just around town, you know?"

"Do you still drive trucks, sir?" Ricardo's tone held a note of curiosity with just a hint of sternness as he checked all the tools on the workbench.

"No," Jaime replied, "I'm retired." Ricardo noticed he shifted his body slightly so that he was no longer facing him directly. *He's hiding something,* Ricardo thought.

"I think one of your family is a fisherman, right? A nephew, Ernesto Lopez?" Ricardo asked this quickly after Jaime's last answer. Jaime blanched. He reached for a bottle of water on his workbench and took a sip.

"I have several family members who are fishermen. Half the men in this town fish to feed their families and for cash." Jaime gave a nonanswer.

"I'm sure you know that too many of our local fishermen are illegally poaching totoaba for the cartel. We think Ernesto is one of them. Has he involved you in moving the totoaba bladders down to Loreto, Mr. Lopez? Did Stella find out and threaten to expose you? Did you have her killed to keep your secret safe?"

A bead of sweat ran from under Jaime's ubiquitous truck-manufacturer ball cap. It wound around his left eyebrow and down his left cheek. He swiped at it with his left arm.

"Stella is dead?" He looked as if he might collapse but steadied himself against the workbench. "How?" Jaime looked imploringly at Ricardo, perhaps hoping he would explain what was happening. "I would never hurt her. Never."

"Yes, Mr. Lopez, a body was found on a beach near Puerto Peñasco. She had been in the water for nearly a week. We have every reason to believe it's Stella. Do you need to sit down, sir?" he said, moving toward a stool at the other end of the workbench.

Jaime waved him away. "No, I'm okay, just shaken. This is terrible news. I know nothing about it. Nothing. Nothing!" he echoed emphatically.

Ricardo picked up the thread again. "With your cartel connections, it would be easy for you to arrange her murder and disposal. Tell me what happened!"

Finally, Jaime turned to face Ricardo and stood up straight. "I would never hurt Stella. I didn't know she was dead, and whatever happened to her, I don't know anything about it. And neither does Ernesto. You have just told me one of my dear friends is dead. Please let me and Molly grieve our loss. She will be devastated. We both loved Stella dearly. Please go." It was clear that he was about to start crying.

Ricardo had done a cursory search of the garage, but there were no containers of white powder or anything else not expressly used in car repair. He turned and left the garage and headed to the squad car, while Julia continued talking with Molly in the house.

Julia had also informed Molly of their search warrant and did a thorough search of the kitchen while Molly made coffee. Once Molly was sitting at the kitchen table, Julia sat and asked her about the argument Rick had mentioned hearing between Molly and Jaime on the return part of the hike. "Oh, my goodness, that is funny that Rick heard us. Jaime really wants a dog, and every time we are around Stella and Juba, he can't take his eyes of Juba. I told him that I see the way he looks at her, and if he really wants one that badly, we can get a small dog from the rescue place. I don't really want a dog, so I do get a bit testy when the topic comes up. Jaime has finally agreed it can be a small dog, so I have relented."

As they finished their coffee, Julia informed her of the body in PP. Molly began weeping immediately. Julia left her to her grief while she searched the rest of the house. She found nothing in the living room, either bathroom, or the master bedroom.

The second bedroom was clearly Molly's crafting room. There were two long worktables in the center of the room. One was for sewing and the other for various other crafting pursuits. Julia's attention was grabbed by a small tool on Molly's sewing table. It looked like a riding spur on a handle. The spikes of the "spur" were tiny, sharp needles. She took it into the kitchen. "What is this, Mrs. Lopez?"

Molly tried to blot the stream of tears from her cheeks. Taking the tool, she looked at it as if it were a mystery to her. Then she answered, "It's a tracing wheel, for sewing." And then she showed Julia, using the newspaper sitting on the table and the lid of the sugar jar how the needlelike spikes on the wheel left a dotted outline of tiny holes in the paper when the wheel was used to trace around the lid. "It has several different heads with different types of needles for different materials."

"Is there one for leather?" Julia asked, trying to keep her voice even and conversational.

"Yes. I've never used it because I don't do leatherwork. I gave mine to Stella. I think she used it when she was re-covering a footstool a few months back," Molly replied as a fresh series of sobs racked her ample frame at the thought of her friend, dead.

"I need to take this with me. Don't worry, you will get it back. Also, do you know the name of the dentist Stella used in town?" Julia asked.

Molly gave her the dentist's name just as Jaime came in, and Julia took that as her cue to leave and let the couple mourn their friend. She left them with the admonishment that they were not to talk of Stella's death for the remainder of the day, with anyone, including the other hikers, and to do so would result in a charge of obstruction of justice.

As they drove toward Rick's home, Ricardo said, "Jaime's emotional response could be remorse. He never responded to any of my questions about him driving for the cartel. He has a relative who works at the gold mine, so it's possible he could get his hands on cyanide. He's still on my list of viable suspects, even though we didn't find any cyanide."

Julia didn't disagree with him. She was wondering about a leather tracing tool in Stella and Simon's house and whether the hole pattern would match the holes in the thong of the hand strap of Stella's hiking stick.

Rick was in front of his house, watering his trees. His yard had several mature acacia trees creating shade over a vast majority of the yard. With the water pooling in the tree wells, there was a sense of instant cool as the two police officers entered through the front gate.

Rick stopped spraying water and set down the hose as they approached him. "Hi, officers. What's up?" he asked.

"Mr. Worton, could we please sit and talk with you for a few minutes?" Julia asked, glancing toward a table and four chairs on a brick patio in one portion of yard. Once they were all seated and having declined the offer of drinks, she went on. "Did you see Stella at all in the days leading up to the hike? Say from about March 5 onward?"

"Hmm, let me think. The hike was on a Tuesday, the eighth, right? So, the fifth would have been, ah, Friday, no Saturday. Okay, yes. Stella and Simon and Rob and I went for dinner that Saturday night. We went to Jaime's daughter's restaurant on the Malecon."

"Did you all arrive together?" Julia asked.

"No, I got there first, then Stella and Simon came, and Rob arrived about ten minutes later. Apparently, he had trouble finding a parking spot. I remember he came in the back door, from the loading dock, and Stella must have been back there on the phone. She got a call just a couple of minutes after she and Simon arrived, and she left the table. When she came back to the table, Rob was with her. He said they'd met on the loading dock," Rick explained.

"And how did Stella seem that evening? And Simon?" Julia prompted him to continue.

"Actually, Stella was kind of quiet. I never really thought about it at the time. The three of us guys were talking baseball quite a bit, so maybe she just didn't have anything to add. And I noticed she hardly touched her dessert, which is totally not like her. Simon was his usual self. He's pretty easygoing."

"Did Stella have any other calls that evening that you remember?"

"Not that I remember. Oh, but I think she made a call between dinner and dessert. She went to the little girls' room and was gone for a really long time, and I think Rob said he'd seen her talking on her phone then," Rick answered. "What is all this about?"

Ignoring the question, Julia, at prompting in Spanish from Ricardo, asked, "Mr. Worton, did Stella have concerns that you are a pedophile?"

"What? No!" he answered immediately, his face flushing, though his memory of her questions to him about the young man she'd seen him with at the baseball field came to mind. He reddened even more at the thought that perhaps she did.

Julia and Ricardo both noticed the man's physical response to Julia's question. "Don't lie to us, Rick," Julia responded, using his first name to rattle him a little.

"I'm not. Sorry, your question just shocked me. Stella and I are good friends and have been for a long time. She's known all my boyfriends over the past ten years, and they have all been adults. She knows I'm not interested in young boys. That is a horrible misconception some people have about gay men." Rick looked as if he'd been punched in the stomach. His blush of a moment ago was gone, and now he was pale. He looked as if he might be sick.

Julia and Ricardo spoke briefly.

"I'm sorry to have to tell you we learned that a body, which we have every reason to believe is that of Stella Monroe, was found washed up on a beach near Puerto Peñasco a couple of days ago. We were waiting for the autopsy results before letting you all know. She had been poisoned," Julia said to him. Then seeing the look of devastation that came over the man in front of her, she added, "I'm so sorry for your loss."

After giving him a few moments to take in the news, Julia went on to tell him two officers would be arriving shortly with a warrant and would be searching his property and that he was not to speak with anyone that day about Stella's death. Rick simply nodded his head in acknowledgment as the two sergeants left. They still had two more stops.

As Ricardo and Julia drove toward their next destination, they discussed this new information. "March 5 was the day Julia told her friend Pippa that her mother phoned her. It's possible that was the first call Stella got at the restaurant," Ricardo mused.

"Yes, and the call she made after dinner could have been the one Martín Robles said he received from her that evening," Julia added. "Things are starting to fit together . . . finally."

Chapter 14—March 23, 2018, San Amaro

The inspector had taken a team of constables to Simon's house, telling him they wanted to speak with him at the station. "Please get dressed. We go to the station. We will talk there." The firmness of the inspector's brief sentences spoke volumes to Simon. He was a lawyer. He knew what this meant. It wasn't good.

When Simon realized he was sandwiched between the two constables in the back of the police car, his face blanched. "Something has happened, hasn't it? Have you found Stella? Just tell me, please." It came out like a whine. The inspector ignored his request.

The ride to the station took only a few minutes and was silent except for the crackles of the police radio. It was all in Spanish, of course, and it underscored for Simon just how fragile he felt. He was in a country in which his knowledge of the law was nonexistent and his understanding of the language equally so. He tried to steel himself for what might be coming.

Once Simon was ensconced in an interview room with a constable to keep him company, the inspector had taken the remaining two constables to Rob's, telling him much the same thing he'd said to Simon. Rob had been belligerent, but the constables got him into the squad car. He and Simon had been cooling their heels in separate interview rooms all morning.

Since Rick's house was in town, Ricardo and Julia headed to Simon's house, which was nearby, for their next search. They left a copy of the warrant on the kitchen counter and proceeded with their investigation. It took them over an hour to go through the place. Julia found the spur-like leather tracing tool in a sewing box in the closet in the second bedroom. It was in an evidence bag and would be scrutinized by the forensics guy at the station for Simon's prints and the pattern of the holes it made to the piece of leather from Stella's walking stick.

It was after lunch when they made their way to Campo Cristal. Once gloved, they entered Rob's casita. Julia headed into the bedroom, and Ricardo began with the closet by the main door.

Ricardo was the first to find something interesting. He'd called Julia to get her thoughts on his find. "I found this bag," he said, holding out a narrow nylon drawstring bag with a mountain-hiker logo on it. "It had a collapsible hiking stick in it, which makes sense, because Rob mentioned he gave one of his to Stella when she left the group. I also found these two small disks in the bottom of the bag. It says 'Dog Traks' on them. He doesn't have a dog. What do you suppose they are for?" he asked, as he handed one to Julia.

She looked at the small plastic disk and then pulled out her phone and searched "Dog Traks." "They are GPS locator beacons you can put on a dog's collar, so you don't lose your dog. Apparently, you use an app on your phone to see where the dog is once the tracker has been synced to the app. I wonder why they were in with his hiking poles?" She pondered this question for a couple of minutes, then had an idea. “Can I see the pole?”

It was a very nice walking pole, she thought. The hand grasp was generously sized and was ergonomically designed. It had a neoprene cover to keep sweaty hands from slipping. As she held it, she noticed the neoprene was removable by unscrewing the cap at the top of the pole. “Hmmm. Looks like it has a small storage area in the handle. Likely for matches or something. That’s kind of cool.” She was about to hand it back to Ricardo when a thought occurred to her. She picked up one of the Dog Traks and compared its diameter with the size of the handle chamber. The tracker disk fit inside the handle. Ricardo was watching her, and the significance of this find occurred to them both at the same moment. Julia said what he was thinking, too. “Oh my God! He could have set Stella up with a GPS beacon so she could be tracked by someone who had the app on a cell phone. Of course, we don’t have the other pole to prove that, but I think the inspector will be interested in this. It answers one of his questions about Stella being found by the two people who transported her body.”

They placed Ricardo’s find into evidence bags and went back to their search. The bedroom produced nothing of interest, so Julia headed to the kitchen. Under the sink, she found a metal box that looked like an old ammunition box. She unclipped the side lock and was surprised to find nothing inside except a small plastic container that looked as if it once held yogurt. When she picked it up, it rattled as if it contained seeds or nuts. She carefully took off the lid and found a white, crystalline, saltlike substance. The smell of bitter almonds hit her nose almost immediately. She quickly pushed the lid back on the container.

"Ricardo. I found cyanide."

The team of three convened in the war room once all the searches were completed. They looked over the evidence bags on the conference table: two tracing tools, one from Molly's house and one from Simon's; two Dog Traks GPS beacons; a hiking pole; the ammo box; and the small container of cyanide. They were still surprised that the most incriminating items were found in Rob's possession. As they had previously speculated that Rob and Simon may have known each other in Arizona, it took no time before they agreed that the two men were working together to abscond with Stella Monroe's upcoming inheritance. Otherwise, what motive could Rob have to murder a woman he had supposedly known for less than two months?

They spent a few minutes discussing their approach to interviewing their two main suspects. All three believed the next few hours would be the most important in their investigation.

Chapter 15—March 23, 2018, San Amaro

The commencement of the interrogation followed a similar procedure to the previous interview of Simon just days after Stella went missing. Julia introduced herself and Inspector Martinez for the recording and had Simon say his name before anything else occurred. Ricardo was watching and listening from his desk, using the same translation software as before.

Martinez spoke in rapid guttural Spanish to Julia for over a minute. Julia then began the interview. "Mr. Wakefield, the body of a woman matching the description of your wife, Stella Monroe, was found washed up on the beach near Puerto Peñasco several days ago. We learned of it sometime later and needed the postmortem to be completed to be able to officially inform you of her death and the manner in which it occurred. Do you know where Puerto Peñasco is, Mr. Wakefield?"

"Oh my God!" was all Simon said.

"Your wife died from cyanide poisoning. Her body was dumped in the sea and, because of the currents, was carried across to Puerto Peñasco in about six days. Apparently, whoever you hired to kill and dispose of her body didn't weigh down the body when they dumped it." Julia maintained her calm, easy tone, but the intent of her words was clear. The gloves were off.

"What? Poison?" Simon sounded bewildered. He shook his head. "I didn't kill my wife." His torso was leaning against the table, his arms extended, palms up. It was the body language associated with pleading. His voice was scratchy.

"Mr. Wakefield, we know you've been lying to us from the beginning. We know about Mrs. Althea Cutler being Stella's mother, that you were her estate lawyer, and her estate was to be inherited by Stella. It is obvious that you orchestrated a marriage with Stella to gain access to the Cutler fortune. Stella found out your plan and was trying to leave you in a way that would give her several days' head start. Somehow you found out her intention and you hired two men to stop her. Did you give her the poison, or did they?" Julia was unrelenting.

"I didn't kill my wife," Simon repeated. There was sweat on his brow, and his eyes were red and bulging slightly.

Julia placed an evidence bag on the table in front of Simon. It contained the leather tracing wheel. Forensics had not found his prints on it, but that could simply mean he'd worn gloves. The forensics guy was currently comparing the pattern of holes left by the tool with those found on Stella's walking-stick strap.

"Mr. Wakefield, do you know what this is?" Julia asked.

"I'm not really sure. Stella used it on a project she was doing, but I don't know what for. Why, is it important?" He sounded confused.

"It appears to be the tool used to make evenly spaced tiny holes in the strap of your wife's walking stick, causing it to tear when she put more and more pressure on it during the hike," Julia explained. "Did you use it to sabotage her hiking stick?"

“No, of course not. I didn’t kill my wife,” he reiterated. He was not pugnacious, more just confused, as if he were in shock.

The inspector leaned toward Julia and spoke briefly to her. So far, he’d been able to keep up with the interaction between Julia and Simon. He wanted Julia to turn the screws even more.

“Sir, we already have enough evidence to charge you with your wife’s murder. Why don’t you just tell us what happened?” she said firmly, pressing. At least now he knew where he stood. “It will go better for you if you do.” Julia’s voice shifted into a more conciliatory tone.

Simon didn’t so much sit back in his chair as sag into it. He appeared to deflate in front of her eyes. Julia and the inspector simply waited. At his desk, Ricardo realized he was holding his breath. Finally, Simon looked into Julia’s face and then into the inspector’s. “I didn’t kill my wife” he said again, then plunged his face into his hands. Finally, he continued speaking into his palms, “But I think I know who did.”

Over the next hour, Simon admitted he had planned to wed Stella to get access to her inheritance when Althea Cutler died. He also told them he had grown to like her. Apparently, not enough to tell her the truth, to come clean and try to make an honest life together, but he wouldn’t have condoned her murder. At first, he hadn’t wanted to say who he thought had perpetrated the crime, but with Julia’s relentless prodding, he finally admitted to having known Rob in Phoenix and his suspicions that Rob had orchestrated the events that took place the day of the hike when Stella left her group.

"Rob kept suggesting he come down here 'to help me' with my plan to marry Stella, but I kept telling him I didn't need help. When I found out he had come here, anyway, I was shocked and a bit concerned, but I've known Rob for a long time, and I never thought he'd do anything as drastic as having Stella killed. I honestly don't know how he made it happen." Simon spoke with an edge of frustration and anger in his voice, but, to Julia's eye, he looked broken, sad, and very afraid.

"I never wanted her to get hurt. I was a decent husband. I just wanted to share in her windfall when her mother died," Simon said, lamenting.

"But she did get hurt, Mr. Wakefield. We believe you had foreknowledge of it. The laws here are not so different from those of the United States on that point, sir. We will be keeping you in custody while we investigate the allegations against you." Julia informed him on the inspector's instruction. "But you are, at a minimum, an accomplice to her death."

The interrogation eventually concluded, and Simon was placed in a cell.

Chapter 16—March 23, 2018, San Amaro

"I've been sitting here for over four hours. I'm not staying here any longer," Rob Gurenburg blustered when Julia and the inspector entered the interrogation room. His face was red, and as he stood up as though to leave, Julia could see he had been sweating, as there were stains in the armpits of his T-shirt. Julia thought he'd likely spent the last few hours working himself into a state of righteous indignation. It was time to knock the wind out of his sails.

"Sit down, Mr. Gurenburg. You are here, in this room, because we wanted you to be more comfortable than you would have been in a cell for the last four hours." Julia looked at the inspector, and at his nod, she continued. "Rob Gurenburg, you are under arrest for the murder of Stella Monroe. You aren't obligated to say anything during this interview. However, this is your chance to tell us your side of things."

"What the hell? You mean Stella is dead? Did you just forget to tell us of that interesting piece of fantasy?" *Oh yes,* Julia thought as Rob ranted, *he's definitely been working himself up*. "It must have been her husband, Simon. I hardly even know the woman."

"Yes, the body washed up on the other side of the sea. Her autopsy was completed yesterday in Puerto Peñasco. She died of cyanide poisoning, but of course you know that. We found the identical type of cyanide in your casita. A tiny bit in your custom-made electrolyte drink given to Stella when she headed back to the vehicles would have done the trick in a couple of minutes. We also found GPS tracking devices of the kind you placed in the walking stick you gave her because her walking-stick strap broke. That was in case she died before she got back to the vehicles. Then your friends could find her if she died on the path."

At this point, she pulled out an evidence bag with the piece of leather that was found the first day of the search. "The strap on her walking stick had been weakened with holes at one end, according to our forensics team. Seems you thought of everything. Too bad the two men you hired to dispose of her body didn't do a better job! And you even provided them with a RZR, stolen from your neighbor, to do the collection." Julia stopped for a moment to confer with Inspector Martinez. As she listened to his directions, she watched Rob closely. His rage was evaporating. His flushed coloring had drained away, leaving a pallor even his tan couldn't cover.

"I never touched Stella's walking stick, let alone did something to make the strap break," he said angrily, seemingly gaining back some of his confidence. "And I have no idea what you're talking about. I didn't hire anyone, or steal a RZR, or whatever else you think I did. I got that container from Simon. He asked me to keep it for him. It has nothing to do with me." His bravado was returning with every sentence he uttered.

Rob watched Julia and Martinez talking, almost as closely as Julia was watching him. He'd opened his mouth a couple of times as though to interrupt them but remained silent until they were finished. His sharp intake of breath cued Julia to cut him off before he tried to continue with his rebuttal. She followed the inspector's instructions and continued letting him know the evidence they had against him.

"We have your fingerprints all over the container of cyanide, Mr. Gurenburg, and none of Simon's, so your excuse isn't going to . . ." Rob started to say he had only checked out the container's contents, but Julia continued before he could complete his argument. "We know about Mrs. Cutler being Stella's mother and the inheritance that Stella was to receive. We know about the escape plan Stella had to leave your hike and get picked up by a friend in an ultralight plane. Her mother learned that Simon had married Stella and warned her she was in danger. But neither her mother nor Stella knew about your long friendship with Simon. We also have your fingerprints all over the ammo box. So, you see, Mr. Gurenburg, we have everything we need against you. Getting the arrest warrant issued was no problem, and we feel confident, with Simon's testimony against you, your conviction will be as easy.

"Now, it's your opportunity to give us your side of things. Tell us to whom you gave the stolen RZR. Tell us what happened to Stella's dog. Admit your crimes, and things will go easier for you with your sentencing, perhaps even in prison." Julia spoke in her usual easy, matter-of-fact tone. Her last sentence, though, was said with more emphasis and with a note of finality. She was obviously finished speaking. She sat back and waited.

Rob sat very still. Only his eyes were moving. They darted back and forth, like a caged animal's looking for an escape route. The two officers waited. Eventually, he spoke. "I don't know what Simon told you, but he is not innocent of any of this," Rob said insistently. Then it was his turn to wait. He was hoping to see uncertainty in the faces across from him. He was disappointed.

"Don't worry, Mr. Gurenburg, Mr. Wakefield is also under arrest. But he was not the poisoner. You were." Again, Julia finished and sat waiting for Rob to speak again.

Instead, Rob sat quietly looking at his hands. He was sweating again. Julia could see small beads on perspiration on his forehead and on his upper lip, and she could smell his fear. He appeared to be thinking. After a minute or two, he looked at the ceiling and took a deep breath. It came out as a long sigh. His shoulders sagged as he brought his head down into his hands. A moment later he scrubbed his face with his palms and then leaned forward, elbows on the table. He began to speak in a low voice.

"Simon hired me to find the abandoned daughter of a client of his. It was an inheritance thing for the estate plan he was doing for Althea Cutler. It took me a few weeks, but I finally tracked her down. Stella Monroe. She was here in San Amaro. I came here to gather information on her, so I knew she had a group of friends and that one of them was gay. I gave all the information to Simon and then I went on with my life. I wouldn't have given it another thought except that Simon said, off the cuff one day, that he was thinking of moving to San Amaro to see if he and Stella had any chemistry.

"After he'd moved here, I started to get obsessed with all that money. Stella was going to inherit it, and she didn't even know. It seemed too bizarre. Why was she getting money from someone she didn't even know? Why couldn't that happen to me? It was insidious. I couldn't get my brain to focus on anything else. It was like a malignancy. It only got worse when Simon and Stella got married. Eventually, I had to come down here and see if I could persuade Simon to give me a cut of the money when Stella inherited. I know now there was no reason he should, but I was intoxicated with believing there was some way I could benefit from the situation.

"It was like a drug, and I was addicted. I've never done anything really illegal before, but when I learned that Stella was planning to leave Simon with some elaborate plan involving a plane, I just lost it. I figured that this being Mexico, there was little chance the Cutler woman would learn of Stella's death, and her estate would just go into Stella and Simon's joint account and then I could blackmail Simon into sharing it with me. I had some cyanide from a gold mine where my brother works and I just . . ." He couldn't go on. His head sank into his hands, his shoulders began to shake, and Rob began to weep.

It took another hour for the full story to come out, including whom he had hired to dump the body. Rob spewed it at them as though he were trying to rid his body of some affliction that had him in its grip. As Julia sat watching and listening, she realized the truth of that. Greed had overwhelmed him like a disease and caused him to commit murder. It truly was a deadly sin.

When Rob was finally taken away to the holding cells to await transportation to Mexicali, where his trial would be held, Julia, Ricardo, and the inspector met again in their war room. "Just over two weeks . . . It's two weeks and two days since Stella Monroe died in the desert. You two have done an exceptional job on this case," the inspector said. "Obviously, we still have some loose ends to clear up, but I'm impressed with your work to figure out what happened to her. Ricardo, will you please bring in

Chuey Alverez. We can get him for receiving stolen property and improper disposal of a body. I'll see what I can do to persuade the comandante to include accessory after the fact to murder into his arrest warrant as well. And see if you can find out what he did with the dog. I hate loose ends.

"Julia, you take young Luis with you and go inform the gentleman whose RZR was stolen that it was incinerated in connection with another crime. He will likely be able to get his insurance to cover the loss, and I want Luis to be part of wrapping up that investigation."

Ricardo and Julia stood to complete their late assignments on this case. As they headed out the door, they called in unison, "*Hasta mañana*, see tomorrow, Inspector Martinez." The inspector called after them, "Call me Hector. You've earned it."

Chapter 17—March 23, 2018, San Amaro

Julia and Luis were on Ted Blair's doorstep at nine o'clock. Julia suspected they'd get him out of bed at that hour, but Ted surprised them by answering the door after the first knocks. He had a coffee mug in hand, and definitely wasn't sleeping. As usual, he left the door open and shambled down his hallway to the kitchen, leaving them to follow.

On the car ride to Campo Cristal, Julia asked Luis to explain to her the outcome of their investigation as if she were Ted Blair. He began a little shakily, but he gained in confidence as he went. "Mr. Blair, we, um, have, ah finished our investigation into your missing RZR. It was stolen by a man renting a casita in the next street up from yours. Unfortunately, sir, it was used in the commission of a crime, and the person who stole it had it burned in an attempt to hide evidence. There is nothing left of your rig, sir." Julia chose to honor Luis's approach and said almost the same words to the man when they were all seated in his kitchen.

Blair took a moment to absorb this information and then looked from Julia to Luis, perhaps in hopes of getting a different answer from him. When Luis didn't respond with new or different information, Blair sagged visibly. Julia did add, "I've brought you a copy of the police report and photos of the burned remains of your RZR to help you with your insurance company. It is in Spanish, but I'm sure they will be able to get it translated."

"I use a local company, so translation won't be necessary," he responded. "Isn't that a bugger! Used in a crime, you say. Isn't that a Goddamn bugger!" He paused then, apparently considering if he needed to know anything else from the two cops in front of him. "Well, I guess that's that, then. Thanks for letting me know. Thanks for this copy of the report and photos. I can't think what else I need from you. Nothing, I guess." He scratched at his fuzzy white head, then headed back to his front door with Luis and Julia following behind.

What a funny little man, Julia thought as they drove back to the station. Luis was thinking the same, but he was also excited that he'd successfully helped solve his first robbery case and been involved, even peripherally, in solving a murder case. As he headed down to the Malecon to start his shift patrolling the area where the Semana Santa celebrators were camping, Luis felt pleased and proud.

Julia headed to the war room to begin the mountain of paperwork that closing this case would require.

Chuey Alvarez was well known to San Amaro Police. He was often on the wrong side of the law and had spent time in the Mulegé prison on several occasions, but never more that eighteen months in one stretch. If they could get him on accessory to murder, that would change. It would mark his transition from being just a low-level thug. Ricardo was considering this as he prepared to knock on

Chuey's door. The more likely it was that Chuey had been involved in anything more than transporting a dead body, the more dangerous he would be to pick up.

When the door opened, Chuey came barreling out of the door like a charging bull. He sprinted past Ricardo headed down the street. Ricardo chased him about forty yards before tackling him into the sandy road.

As Ricardo pulled a handcuffed Chuey from the dusty street where he'd landed when tackled, he said gruffly, "Seems like you've got something to hide." Chuey spat a dusty wad into the sand and tried to wipe his caked face on his shoulder. A grunt was his only response as he was placed into the back seat of the cruiser. Ricardo pulled the front door of Cheuy's home closed before climbing into the cruiser.

It was clear in a matter of minutes inside an interview room that Chuey held no loyalty to the person who had hired him. Within a half hour, Ricardo and Hector had a full confession from Chuey to having moved and disposed of the dead body. From his explanation of the events leading up to that day, he confirmed several things the team had already surmised. He'd known Rob for several weeks before being hired to pick up the body and drop it into the sea. Rob had procured for him a four-seater RZR and had given him the GPS coordinates of where he could expect to find a dead body. Chuey had transposed some numbers in the coordinates causing him to be stymied for several minutes when he got to the place where he was expecting to find several vehicles and a dead woman. Rob had, however, also given him a burner phone that had a tracker app installed and programmed to track a small beacon stowed in the handle of a hiking stick. It was checking this app that caused Chuey to move the RZR around the hill beside which he had parked, where he found the hikers' vehicles. By following the tracker app up the path, he found the location from which the beacon was transmitting, thus finding Stella's body.

Throughout the interview, Chuey had been cooperative and forthcoming. He spoke easily and at length when answering their questions. Julia, who was watching the camera feed from her computer, was surprised at how relaxed and conversational he was. It appeared to her that his life of crime was one in which he viewed the cops as a necessary evil. They did their job, and he did his. The times he got caught, he was prepared to pay the price exacted by the law. Clearly, it was not a price too high for Chuey as he appeared to have neither regret nor contrition for any of his actions.

Chuey became cagey only when questioned about his accomplice. He insisted he acted alone, but from the statements given by the Amundsen brothers, they knew he was lying. Ricardo and the inspector suspected a relative of Chuey's had assisted him, but never got Chuey to admit to it. Neither would he implicate anyone in disposing the body in the sea. His story was that he'd borrowed a boat from a relative and left it on a secluded beach south of town. He then used it to take the body far enough from shore that he was sure the body would not drift back to San Amaro.

When asked about the garage in the Punto de Cono Ejido, Chuey's demeanor changed drastically. Julia thought for a minute that he was going to cry, which completely surprised her. "It is so sad. I built that garage for my uncle. I built it strong. With good wood. It was storage for his important supplies, for his business. When I got the RZR from the gringo, I put it in the garage, to keep it safe and out of sight. Then I hear you are looking into it, and I have to burn it. My uncle was not happy. I was not happy, but I get extra money for getting rid of the RZR in a fire. Too bad, really, I would have been able to sell it this week with all the people here for Semana Santa. Very, very sad. I wish you hadn't found it." Chuey expressed regret for the first time and looked from Ricardo to Hector with recrimination in his eyes. Clearly, he felt they were at fault for this tragedy.

This gave the inspector the opportunity he'd been awaiting. "How did you learn that we were going to open the garage the day you burned it?" This was an outstanding, and critical, question the team needed to have answered. No one outside the police force had known of the trip to the ejido to open the garage. The decision was made, and within the hour the team had driven the ten minutes to its location. The clear implication was that there was an informant at the station who had contacted whoever started the fire.

Ricardo, Hector, and Julia all held their breath. The answer, when it came, was a complete surprise and was the source of many more questions, none of which Chuey would be able to answer. "The gringo, Rob, phoned me and told me he'd pay me more money to go immediately to the garage and burn it. So, I did."

The idea that someone in the police station had informed Chuey the garage was about to be searched, no matter how uncomfortable it made these three police officers, was so much more palatable than the idea that a gringo, relatively new to town, had been given closely guarded information by one of their own. Because of close familial ties in Mexican culture, it was not surprising that police secrets found their way into the ears of cousins, sisters, uncles, and wives. It wasn't surprising when first loyalty was to family. This situation, however, implied there was someone in their midst at the station who was actively selling secrets to outside buyers. That was a surprise and a shock!

Hector recovered first from this news by shifting the questions to something that had been bugging him from the start. "What happened to the dog?"

Chapter 18—March 23, 2018, San Amaro

Inspector Martinez sat at his desk looking at the list of names he'd written on a sheet of lined yellow paper in front of him. It contained five names: his own, the comandante's, Julia, Ricardo, and Luis. One of them had either called Rob Gurenburg and told him about the plan to break the lock on the garage in the ejido or had told someone else who had then made that call. He hadn't done it, and he was pretty sure the comandante hadn't, either. He didn't think either Julia or Ricardo would have done it, so that left Luis. He was young and new to the station. It could have been a boast made to a friend without thought for potential consequences. Or it could have been intentional. But sitting here staring at his name on the pad wasn't going to give Hector any answers. He picked up his phone and called dispatch.

It was almost six in the evening when Luis got off his patrol shift on the Malecon. It had been pretty quiet. A couple of drunks had gotten into a fight he'd had to break up, but that was the most excitement he'd had. He was feeling curious and a bit nervous that he had been instructed to visit Inspector Martinez before leaving for the night as he made his way upstairs to the inspector's office.

"Hi, Luis, come in. Take a seat. Do you know why I've asked to meet with you?" The inspector got straight to the point.

"I think so, sir. You want to know how the guy who stored the RZR in the garage in the ejido knew we were coming. Is that it? I've been thinking about that since the fire," Luis said, speaking plainly. At the inspector's nod, Luis continued. "I figured. The only people I spoke to about what we were doing that morning were three constables who were getting coffee as I was waiting to get the keys for the vehicle we drove out to the ejido. They wanted to know where I was going . . . Javier Bustamante, Chalo Guerro, and Juan Trujillo. Oh, and I guess Ana Maria Verde. She was the constable making vehicle assignments."

After Luis was excused, Hector sat pondering the additional four names on his list. Finally, he ripped the sheet from his pad and walked to the comandante's office. It would be in the comandante's hands whatever would happen next.

"Is this Mrs. Althea Cutler?" Julia had finally persuaded Simon to give her the contact information for the mother of their deceased hiker. She lived in a city that was part of the metro Phoenix area. "My name is Sergeant Julia Garcia of the San Amaro Police." As she said this, she heard the woman on the other end of the line make a small, strangled sound deep in her throat. Julia suspected the woman knew what was coming and so delivered the sad news quickly and compassionately. As she told her the story and answered the woman's questions, which were few, she wondered what it must be like to have not seen her daughter since birth and to then learn she was dead and that she had been instrumental in setting in motion the events that lead to her daughter's death. Sad. She sounded very sad. And Julia found herself feeling sad for both Stella and her mother.

Althea was very surprised to learn that it wasn't Simon who had committed the murder but that he was only an accessory. Julia had given her Molly's contact information, as Mrs. Cutler wanted to pay for the funeral expenses and Julia thought Molly the most likely person to be involved in making the arrangements.

Julia's next call was to Pippa. Another sad conversation. She was just finishing up the call when the inspector came into the bullpen of the officers' desks. He lurked by the door until Julia hung up, then walked over to her desk. "Sergeant Garcia, I'd like a word with you upstairs, if you have a minute." They walked up the stairs and into the war room in silence. Once they were both sitting, the inspector went on. "Julia, I have been very impressed by your work on this case. I brought you on because of your excellent English skills and I thought you'd make a good liaison, and you did. But that's not what impressed me. Throughout the case, you were an active member of the investigation, making insightful suggestions, and taking independent initiative to check out ideas that proved instrumental in solving the case."

Julia was surprised and flattered by his remarks. "Thank you, sir. That means a lot to me," she replied.

"Have you thought about taking the detective exam, Julia?" he asked.

"Not at this point, sir. I thought you had to be a second-level sergeant to take that exam?"

"Not if you're sponsored by a detective inspector. I would like to sponsor you if it's something that interests you. I think you have many of the qualities that make a good detective." Hector smiled at Julia, trying to gauge her reaction to his suggestion.

Julia was blown away with excitement at this idea. She was ambitious. She had a career plan that she saw taking her to the comandante's chair. She hadn't seriously considered her path veering into the detective cadre. That was a club almost exclusively made up of men. But she had really enjoyed the mental stimulation of trying to solve a murder. Being a detective would be challenging and exciting, she thought . . . and it would certainly also give her a route to the big chair. "I am very interested, Inspector Martinez, and honored that you'd be prepared to sponsor me. Thank you!"

"Call me Hector. And you've earned it. I've just spoken to the comandante about it, and he is also supportive. You'd have to go to Mexicali to take the exam, and it's offered only twice a year. The next sitting is in four months. Do you think you can be ready by then?"

"I think so. Does that seem reasonable to you?" she queried, watching him closely.

"Yes, it does. You'll have to study hard, but I think you can do it." The inspector finished and then headed back toward his office. He stopped a few steps outside the doorway and then came back and stuck his head in the war room. "Did you hear that Chuey left the dog near a farm out in the desert? Apparently, the farmer has a son who has been wanting a dog to help him bring in their cattle. Chuey figured they'd find each other. I hope they did. I have a soft spot for dogs."

"So do I, sir. Thanks for letting me know. Goodnight, Hector," she answered.

Julia sat in the war room for a few minutes basking. The inspector's suggestion was a surprise. A wonderful surprise. She couldn't wait to tell her abuelo. He would be very proud. Ricardo tromping into the room with an arm full of filing boxes broke her reverie. He unceremoniously dumped them on the table, saying with a laugh, "You just taking a nap up here?"

Julia told him about her conversation with Hector and that she was going to do it. "Well, that is really great, Julia. You deserve it. You made some of the key mental leaps on this case. I don't know if we'd have found the body in Puerto Peñasco if it hadn't been for you," he said with all kidding aside. Then a moment later, he went on. "Hey, I'm already a level-two sergeant, which means I can take the exam without sponsorship. Maybe we should do it together. We can be study buddies, just like we were in the academy. What do you think?"

"I think it's a great idea," she said immediately.

They continued talking about becoming detectives for the remainder of their shift as they dismantled the war room and boxed up the evidence, photos, and reports that had accumulated in the conference room over the past two weeks. By the time the room was back to its normal condition, they were both excited about becoming detectives and decided to have dinner to celebrate. Ricardo reasoned that with the Semana Santa celebrators downtown, it might be better to go to one of the restaurants north toward the gringo communities.

They ended up at La Placa de Oro, The Gold Plate, and shared a seafood platter for two and a bottle of good red wine. It was a fine end to the day and to the case. Just as Ricardo raised his glass and made a toast to the successful end to their case, Julia's phone vibrated on the table.

It was the station. She answered.

"Sergeant Garcia, can you come to the station as soon as possible? There is a woman here who says she is Stella Monroe."

Chapter 19—March 23, 2018, San Amaro

Inspector Martinez was just pulling into the staff parking lot of the station as Ricardo and Julia leapt from Ricardo's car. All three rushed into the station and were told the woman claiming to be Stella Monroe was in Interview Room Two. Before they entered, Hector asked Ricardo if he still had the cameras and translation equipment they'd used earlier in the day up and running. On getting a positive answer, he requested Ricardo watch and video record the conversation from his desk.

Julia did her best to hide her shock upon seeing the woman facing the door as they entered. She was gaunt and filthy, and her skin appeared to be hanging from her bones like clothes several sizes too large. Her hair was matted and greasy with a half inch of white roots showing at her scalp. Her face was bruised in several places, some old and yellowish-green, others newer and still purple and blue. She was still wearing the hoodie and red-and-white-striped shirt she'd worn the day of the hike, though now there was blood down the front. There were cuts on her lips and chin. She smelled terrible.

"Do you speak English?" the woman asked with a pleading tone. Her words were slightly slurred, her eyes not completely focused as she looked up at Julia and Hector. Julia wondered if she'd been drugged.

Then Julia remembered something from the first day of the search.

"Mrs. Wakef . . ., ah, Stella," she said, changing her approach when she saw the distress in the woman's eyes at her married name. "Do you need your heart medicine? What strength of digoxin should we get you?"

Hector called the only late-night pharmacy in town and relayed the urgent need for the medication Stella needed for her heart problems. He, too, remembered Wakefield had said she could faint and have breathing problems without it.

Stella did not want to wait until the medication arrived before telling these people her story. She had been desperate for this moment for over two weeks. Through her fatigue and fogginess, she began her shocking narrative, stopping only to gulp water, nibble a tortilla, and take her digoxin when it arrived. She started at the beginning, and though they had already pieced together much of the story, no one stopped her.

"Three days before the first-year anniversary of my wedding to Simon Wakefield," she said spitting out his name, "I received a phone call from my birth mother. At first, I didn't believe it, as I had never had any contact with her prior to that call. But she convinced me and warned me that Simon was not the nice guy I thought he was. He knew I would inherit a lot of money, and that's the only reason he married me. I was out to dinner with Simon and my friend Rick and his new boyfriend, Rob, when I got that call. After dinner, while the guys were busy talking, I phoned a friend of mine who has a plane and asked him to meet me in the desert the day of the hike and fly me to safety so Simon wouldn't realize for several days that I was gone and not just lost.

"When I was finished with the call, I saw Rob near where I stood and realized he may have heard my side of the conversation. I had a creepy feeling but put it down to my own nervousness. Now that I've had time to think about it, I realize that Rob and Simon must have been friends in Phoenix and that they were conspiring against me. At the time, though, I had no idea, so I didn't worry." She stopped for more water.

"I had over two days to keep my secret from Simon, but I didn't ever get the idea he knew that I knew he was a fraud or that I was planning to escape from him. The day of the hike, everything went as planned at the start of the hike. I walked a way with the group and then started limping. I had used a sewing tool to weaken the strap of my walking stick the day before, and when I was ready to leave the group and make my getaway, I put extra pressure on the strap and it broke, as I had hoped it would. I persuaded the others to let me go back to the vehicles alone. Rob gave me some kind of drink he'd made and one of his walking sticks and Molly gave me a sandwich, and I headed back down the path.

"I didn't get very far when I realized how thirsty I was. I reached back for my water bottle in the side pocket of my pack, but Simon had put Rob's drink there. I didn't want to waste time taking my pack off to get my own bottle, so I opened Rob's bottle and took a drink." Stella stopped and took a couple of deep breaths. She appeared to be gathering her strength before she went on.

"My mind registered the smell of bitter almonds a few seconds later. I was a science teacher. I knew what that smell was. It was cyanide. And I'd just drunk some of it. I tried not to panic, but I was instantly terrified. I moved off the trail and made myself throw up. I didn't stop until I had nothing left. I felt limp. I was still terrified. I had no idea how strong the cyanide solution in the bottle was, but I did know that, if it were strong enough, even a small amount of the stuff could kill me, and quickly.

"I lay in the sand for a few minutes to gather my strength before I moved on. I must have fainted briefly, because I came to and registered that I hadn't died. I pulled a Kleenex out of my pocket to wipe my mouth, and the torn strap from my hiking stick fell into the sand near my vomit. I'd kept it as a talisman to give me strength to get through the rest of my escape plan. But I was pretty foggy, and I guess I must have left it there. Juba, my dog, was standing over me. I was so happy to see her. We started back down the trail toward where we'd veer off to meet my friend with the plane. I was weak from vomiting and likely some poison, too. I remember stopping to sit on a boulder, and then I guess I fainted again, and I must have hit my head against a rock." Stella had stoically told her story up to this point. Now, however, she faltered. A tear slid out the corner of one eye and trickled down her cheek. She didn't wipe it away.

"The next thing I knew, I was tied into the back seat of a RZR that was speeding away from the parking area where our vehicles still sat. My head was throbbing, and it felt like there was dried blood on my forehead. Juba was on the seat beside me. Her harness was tied to a roof-support post. A Mexican man was driving. A woman was in the passenger seat. She was about my size, but much younger. They seemed oblivious to me. They were wearing headphones, and I realized they were talking to each other through an onboard communication system. After a few minutes, I figured maybe they thought I was dead. I guessed that Simon and Rob had made a plan, even more elaborate than mine, to ruin my escape. I felt so angry and scared. I kept trying to untie my bonds. The trouble was, I kept fainting.

"When my next lucid moments came, I saw the woman eating half the sandwich Molly gave me. Then I watched in horror as she took a large gulp from the bottle Rob had given to me, the poisoned one. For a minute or two, nothing happened. Then she put her hands to her throat as if she couldn't breathe. It happened so quickly after that. It couldn't have been more than a couple of minutes, and she was dead.

"The man freaked out. He'd stopped the RZR. He tried to revive her, but there was nothing he could do. He didn't cry or even seem sad, so I guessed she meant nothing to him. He just seemed angry. He was swearing and lashing out, punching and kicking the RZR. I stayed very still, afraid he'd turn his anger on me if he knew I was alive. Eventually, he calmed down and got some more rope like that holding me upright in my seat and tied the dead woman to her seat the same way. I realized he wanted it to look as if he and two other people were out for a drive in case anyone saw us from a distance." Stella took another drink of water. Hector, Julia, and Ricardo were almost holding their breaths waiting for her to continue with her fantastic tale.

"I fainted again as he drove, and I didn't come to until he stopped again." She faltered, putting her hands to her face to cover her tears. She continued after a moment. "Juba wasn't there anymore. I don't know what happened to her." After she calmed herself, Stella went on. "We were in a small cove with a panga anchored to a stake. He untied the woman in the front seat and dragged her to the panga, where he dumped her body in the prow. Then he turned back to the RZR to get me. That's the first time he realized I was still alive. He looked as terrified as I felt. I don't know much Spanish, so I just said 'está bien,' it's okay, over and over and over." The two police officers in front of Stella remained silent. At his desk, Ricardo had stopped drinking his coffee and sat leaning forward staring at his monitor, waiting. Stella continued after more water and another bite of tortilla.

"I was sure he would kill me and dump me in the boat with the other woman. I could see he was considering it. He was holding the rope he'd used to tie up the other woman like a garrote. I was so scared. But he decided not to. He used the rope to secure me more tightly into my seat and shoved a filthy kerchief he'd been using against the dusty desert air into my mouth. He took the panga out into the sea and must have dumped the woman's body there. She was gone when he returned. I realized it was supposed to be *my* body going into the sea, and I lost it. I started crying and screaming. No one would have heard me, though. Not with the gag. That's when he first punched me, in the stomach and the face. I don't remember anything else until I woke up in a tiny room in a house. There was a filthy mattress on the floor, a plastic bucket, my water bottle, and a pair of ragged woman's slacks in the room. Nothing else. I figured it must have been where the woman who died had slept. I suspect the man must have been her pimp. He had likely kept her locked in this room, much as I was being kept. She was as much a hostage as I was, though I'm pretty sure she was forced to have sex. The mattress was covered with stains. The thought of it made me sick.

"I was still tied at the ankles, with my hands behind my back. The putrid kerchief was still in my mouth. I had no idea what the man had in mind for me. It became clear he didn't plan to kill me, but I couldn't guess what he did intend to do. Then I got the idea he was waiting for someone else to come, and that person would kill me. I was so afraid. I was there for days like that.

"He brought me a tortilla or a few beans once in a while and always stood and watched while I ate and drank and used the bucket. The one time I tried to scream for help when the kerchief was out of my mouth, he punched me again. That one dislodged a tooth, just here," she said, as she pulled her cheek back to show the gap.

"He checked the ropes binding me every time he came in my cell, and he retied them every time I was allowed to eat or use the bucket. I thought it was unlikely that I might be able to get free, but I started working the ropes on my wrists, anyway. I never did get them loose.

"Then I got my chance.

"There was a knock on the outside door, and I heard the man knocking yell something that included 'policía.' I heard my captor throw open the door and take off running. Then in a bit, I heard the officer putting him into the police car. That's when I broke out of the room I'd been kept in. I just kept smashing my body into the door until the lock broke. It was only a hook and eye, but it must have taken me a few hours to break it. I'm so weak. I found a kitchen paring knife and got free of my ropes, then staggered from the house. There was an American couple walking up the street, and I begged them to bring me here." The last few words opened the floodgates. Stella began to weep. Her pent-up terror had found release through the telling of her ordeal. She cried until she had no more tears. Julia held her until she was spent.

Julia had been taking notes during Stella's amazing monologue and, once they'd been typed and run through translation software, Stella signed her statement. While they were awaiting the completion of that process, Stella got cleaned up, and then Julia explained what had happened earlier in the day. Stella learned that Rob, Simon, and Chuey, her captor, were all in jail on various charges. The following morning they would be transferred to the state jail in Mexicali to await their trials. Chuey's charges would be amended to include Stella's kidnapping and sex trafficking. Julia also told Stella that Juba was most likely living with a farming family between the mountains and the cove where she'd realized Juba was gone.

When faced with the information that Stella had escaped from his home and was now safe, and that the police knew about his disposing of the remains of another woman at sea, Chuey finally provided the name of the woman who had helped him. Selina Morales had been his accomplice and his employee, he'd said. She was known to the San Amaro Police and had been arrested twice for solicitation and prostitution several years before. She was also a known meth user. No doubt Chuey kept her captive by exploiting her addiction.

Ricardo and Julia modified the arrest warrants of Rob and Simon based on this new information and with the input of the state attorney general. Murder and attempted murder were still the charges, respectively, but the name of Selina Morales replaced that of Stella Monroe Wakefield as the murder victim. Even if they were all given the least amount of time for the crimes with which they'd been charged, each of the three men would be in Mexican prison for a very long time.

Dr. Juáraz, a local, bilingual doctor, had come to the station and given Stella a checkup. She had not suffered any lasting injuries that he could diagnose, though he advised her to have a cardiologist check that her two weeks without her heart medicine had not done any long-term harm. Julia had called Molly and Jaime so that Stella wouldn't be alone.

When her friends arrived to pick her up, all three wept together. Then Molly gently loaded Stella into the car and climbed into the back seat with her. They would stay with her that night and stay close until Stella started to feel able to face her new future.

It was after midnight when Ricardo and Julia joined Hector in his office. He had lined up three small glasses. As the two sergeants entered, he poured two fingers of tequila into each. "I think we've earned this. Tomorrow we will have to update all the reports and other paperwork on this case, but tonight let's drink to the life of Stella Monroe and the loss of Selina Morales."

In the following weeks, Stella regained her strength and most of her confidence. Her physical injuries healed, but her heart would remain wary for many years. She regularly visited the dog-rescue facility, and one day adopted a medium-sized dog that looked like a cross between a collie and a shepherd. The next day, Julia drove Stella and the dog to the farm where Julia suspected Chuey had left Juba.

With Julia translating, Stella spoke to the farmer's son and offered to exchange the rescued dog for Juba on the understanding the boy would take good care of it. Stella gave him a large bag of dog food, and the boy accepted. Julia mentioned she'd stop by occasionally to check on the dog's health. A warning, it was clear. The boy nodded. He understood.

Juba was beyond excited when she saw Stella. She howled and danced and licked her owner's face over and over. Stella and Juba sat in the back seat of the truck while Julia drove them back to town. In watching the pair in the rearview mirror, she was hard-pressed to tell which of them was happier at the reunion.

Once her facial bruises were gone and her cuts were mended, Stella drove to Pleasant Valley, Arizona, to The Villas. There, after almost seventy-five years of separation, she met her mother. It was a cathartic experience for both women.

Stella presented her mother with an idea that had been forming in her mind since her ordeal in captivity had begun. Althea was thrilled. When Stella inherited her birthright, she would use the majority of her inheritance to create the Selina Morales Fund to provide social and financial support to Mexican women trying to escape lives of sexual imprisonment. Althea gave her a large check to get things started.

Her next stop was Madison, Wisconsin. Gerald Drummond had died on April 27 of complications related to his muscular dystrophy. Pippa had planned his memorial service to coincide with Stella's visit. Together the lifelong friends mourned his passing. Afterward, Stella helped Pippa pack up her home.

Pippa had decided she'd had enough of snow. She wanted to help her friend start her new charity. She would return with Stella to San Amaro. It would become her new home with her old friend. They would continue to heal, together.

If you enjoyed Death in the Baja, don't miss the next book in the San Amaro series. Death in the Kitchen, a Pickleball mystery, is scheduled for release in 2024.

Go to MarnieJRoss.com and subscribe to follow the writing process.

Acknowledgments

I owe huge thanks to Liz Faletti for her editorial help as this book took shape, and Tricia Sikes, my wonderful wife, who helped me in more ways than I can possibly list. I might not have survived the publishing process without the input, encouragement, and calming presence of many friends, most notably Linda Wiggins and Cal Whedbee.

About the Author

Marnie Ross is an expatriated dual citizen of Canada and the United States now living permanently in San Felipe, Baja, Mexico with her wife and three small, rescued dogs.

Her passion for her adopted home and murder mysteries is the impetus behind the San Amaro Mystery series. If you want to learn more about Baja living and being an expat in Mexico while enjoying a gripping murder mystery, please sign up at, ***marniejross.com****,* and experience the adventure.

Printed in Great Britain
by Amazon

DEATH IN THE BAJA

A SAN AMARO MYSTERY

Julia Garcia is the first woman seargeant in the San Amaro State Police. She is also the most educated officer on the force, with aspirations of someday becoming the station comandante. But solving petty robberies and domestic disputes isn't getting her closer to her goal. And her male superior officers don't have much time for females in their ranks.

When an ex-pat American resident of Julia's small Baja town on the shores of the Sea of Cortez goes missing on a desert hike with her friends, Julia's fluency in English brings her into the high-profile case. As the search for the missing woman goes on, Julia suspects something more sinister has happened. She must use her wits and her training to separate truth from lies. Is she strong enough to follow her instincts and intuition to discover what really happened that day?

Ross's characters are well-rounded and engaging. Readers will enjoy—and learn from—this page-turning thriller and will undoubtedly look forward to Ross's future San Amaro mysteries.

Sarah Poulette, *The US Review of Books*

...captivating, fast-paced, suspense-filled, and enlightening. This book would appeal to lovers of crime, suspense, detective, and mystery stories. I loved the storyline and impressive character development...a riveting story!

Jennifer Ibiam, *Readers' Favorite*

ISBN 979-8-9860071-1-
51399
9 798986 007113